THE TOWER BETWEEN

Printed in Australia
Cover design by Shawline Publishing Group Pty Ltd
Images in this book are copyright approved for Shawline Publishing Group Pty Ltd
Illustrations within this book are copyright approved for Shawline Publishing Group Pty Ltd

First Printing: February 2023
Shawline Publishing Group Pty Ltd
www.shawlinepublishing.com.au

Paperback ISBN 978-1-9228-5061-4
eBook ISBN 978-1-9228-5068-3

Distributed by Shawline Distribution and Lightningsource Global

A catalogue record for this work is available from the National Library of Australia

THE TOWER BETWEEN

MARK KRAMARZEWSKI

For Nicholas and Ava,
for you I would write the world.

CHAPTER 1

MOVIE NIGHT

"There's more incoming," Zack called out as another three zombies hobbled into view.

The hard-fought battle had depleted his reserves. He called forth a magical ice storm, hoping to slow the zombies' advance.

"What are you doing?" Art asked. "Cold magic is useless against zombies."

"Damn, sorry," Zack said. The undead figures ignored the barrage of ice and snow and lumbered forward.

"Hang back there and try not to die. I'm going to attack the front line before the others reach us."

Art charged forward, his sword glowing with mystic light. One of the zombies fell back from the strength of his blow, but two more closed the distance on him. He managed to deflect one attack with his shield and the zombie fell back. A second slipped past the shield, raking at him with its putrid claws. Off balance, he swung again. The blow went high, and the zombie grabbed him.

"A little help here would be nice, Zack. I can't take much more of this," Art grumbled.

Zack panicked and chose a spell almost at random. An eldritch bolt of green energy flew towards the nearest zombie and struck it in the chest. It dropped to the ground, lifeless.

But it was too late—the next wave had arrived. They walked over their fallen comrades to reach Art, overwhelming him and bearing him to the ground. Zack's hands shook as he threw a lightning bolt at the centre of their ranks, electrical energy arcing between their undead bodies, and yet more came for them. The zombies surrounded him, landing one attack and then another, before he was knocked unconscious.

Art dropped his controller onto Zack's desk. "Damn, that sucks. I thought we were going to finish the map that time."

"I just don't think we're high enough level." Zack exited the game and tossed his controller aside in frustration.

"We might have done better if you were using the right spells." Art gave Zack a soft jab in the ribs with his elbow.

Zack nudged him away. "Yeah, you're right. My mind was wandering."

"Thinking about what? Girls? Her?" Art grinned.

"What — 'her'? No, I wasn't thinking about anything in particular. School, maybe?"

Art scrunched up his face like he'd sipped spoilt milk. "School? Last day of the holidays and you want to think about school?"

"I didn't want to. Mum and Dad were on my case last night about putting in the effort this year. First term is already down and they kinda noticed I haven't been studying." Zack ran his hand through his short, brown hair.

Art tsked. "That's why you need to have at least three textbooks open at your desk while you're gaming."

"Yeah, that'll fool them." Zack rolled his eyes. "I don't have a choice. If my marks don't go up—a lot—then Mum's going to come down hard on me. Grounded, no gaming and whatever else she can think of to remove my distractions."

"But this was supposed to be our year! Girls, parties, popularity, girls…"

"You've been saying that for years, mate. That's not us."

"But it could be. We're seniors now." Art crossed his arms.

"Well, if I can't pull up my grades, there's no parties for me, even if we do get invited." Zack rolled his eyes.

"Ugh, that sucks. Well, it's still technically holidays for one last day, she can't expect you to study now. Want to come over to mine and hang? Then we can head into the movies together?"

"Nah," Zack said. "I have to swing by my grandparents' place first. Family Sunday dinner. I'll grab a bite and then meet you on the bus into the city."

"Cool, I better get home and get ready then." Art stood up.

"It's like two hours from now," Zack said.

"Yeah, but you never know who you're going to bump into. Might be my lucky night." Art half turned towards the wardrobe mirror and pinched at his deliberately messy blonde locks.

Zack looked at him with suspicion. "We're going into the city. What are the odds we're going to see anybody we know?"

"Nah, I'm just saying. You should put a bit of effort in too. You can't wait around for girls to do all the work. You have to put yourself out there."

Zack stood up and hunted through a pile of clothes, coming away with a reasonably clean hooded jacket.

Art grabbed it from his hands. "Dude, at least wear something clean."

Zack tried to snatch it back, but Art held it above his head, well out of Zack's reach. Zack jumped onto his bed, making them roughly level in height and wrenched the jacket from his friend's hands.

Art laughed as he let go. "You're not going to impress anybody if you don't put in the effort."

"I'm not trying to impress anybody."

"Yeah, alright. Well, I'm going to go get ready. At least one of us will look good."

Zack heard the rain plinking against his window and climbed off the bed to look outside; clouds had rolled over and it was much darker than he had expected.

"Want to borrow an umbrella or something?" he asked.

"Nah, mate. I'll be good. I'll see you on the bus."

Zack's mother came to the door as Art was leaving. "Did you want a lift home, Art? It's looking awful out there."

"All good, Mrs. M. Thanks for lunch."

Zack's mother lingered as Art walked past her. "We're leaving in five, Zack."

"Okay."

Zack started to put his arms into the jacket before he stopped and sighed. He dropped it back onto the floor and hunted through his closet for a clean one.

Zack snatched another ladle's worth of dumplings from the middle of the table and deposited them onto the remains of his goulash. Conversation hummed around him at the table as his uncles, aunts and older cousins chatted their way through the weekly meal. Zack devoured the rest of his food and pushed away from the table. He held up his hand in a general farewell, kissed his mother on the cheek and moved up to the head of the table to his grandfather. He gave him a hug goodbye, which his grandfather returned, swallowing Zack in his strong, broad shoulders.

When he was released from the embrace, Zack turned to his father. "Can I say goodbye to Babi?"

Zack's father shook his head. "I'm sorry, mate. She's on some new, stronger painkillers since she visited the oncologist. She's sleeping now."

"You're a good boy, Zacharias." His grandfather always used the Czech version of his name. "I'll tell her you said goodbye."

"Thanks, Deda. I'll see you next week. Sorry I can't stay longer." Zack missed the way the family gatherings used to be, with his grandmother at the end of the table, holding him close, before sneaking him some extra lollies she had in an old butter tub.

"No, you're young. Go have fun with your friends." His grandfather gave him a warm smile before turning back to the table to continue arguing about politics.

Zack let himself out the front door and hustled up the street towards the bus stop, his mind lingering on his grandmother's suffering. He couldn't help her—nobody seemed to be able to help her—and it made Zack's chest ache and filled his mind with dozens of 'what ifs.' He was so distracted; he almost missed the bus approaching. The driver screeched to a halt as Zack ran to flag it down.

The driver scowled at Zack as he swiped his card. Art waved to him from a seat near the back and Zack was halfway up the aisle before he noticed a second head of blonde hair sitting next to his friend—Art's little sister, Jackie. The blonde siblings shared enough features to mark them as related, but Art towered over Jackie even more than the four years that separated them should have allowed.

Zack also thought Art towered over him more than their one month of difference should have allowed, but he kept that to himself.

"Hi, Jackie," Zack said with a smile as he sat down on the seat in front of them. "I didn't know you were coming."

She smiled back without quite meeting his eyes. "Hi, Zack."

"Mum made me," Art said, "but I've made her promise not to embarrass us in front of the girls."

Zack's eyes narrowed. "What girls?"

Art avoided eye contact. "Tabitha, Charlie and some others, I think. I'm not sure."

"Oh, screw you. This is why you wanted me to dress up."

"Putting on a clean jacket should not count as dressing up, man. Besides, you like Charlie. The movies are a good place to make a move."

"Yeah, her boyfriend would love that."

"He's not even coming tonight," Art retorted.

"It doesn't matter if he's not there, he's still her boyfriend," Zack said back. His friend didn't get it. He leaned his head against the bus window.

"Nah, he's just a speedbump."

"That's disgusting, Art," Jackie said, screwing up her face.

Zack rolled his eyes. "I'm not hitting on a girl with a boyfriend."

"Fine. But you can be my wingman with Tabitha. Might be my lucky night." Art grinned widely.

Zack smiled at his friend's optimism. "Has she shown, like, any interest in you?"

"She's always nice to me."

"She's nice to everybody. She's probably going to be school captain next year."

"Don't know if you don't try." Art shrugged.

Zack glanced out the window as the bus took the bridge across the harbour and into the city. The rain and clouds had left the water a dark blue that deepened as afternoon turned into early evening. Small waves crested and crashed against each other in the wind.

Art tapped him on the shoulder and Zack tore himself away from the window. "We're here."

Zack blinked and looked around. "Sorry, yeah."

The three teens trundled off the bus and onto the footpath. The afternoon's rain, together with the clouds that were threatening more, had coaxed the already light Sunday foot traffic off the street.

Art gave an exaggerated stretch and then pointed down the street. "Hey, is that the girls over there?"

Zack looked in that direction. There was a small group of teens huddled together and while they were too far away to see their faces, Zack would have recognised the messy dark blonde curls, anyway. Charlie. His stomach twisted. "Um, might not be, I can't tell."

Art looked at him, his expression flat. "Nice try. C'mon, let's catch up." He strode down the street, forcing Zack and Jackie to jog to keep up.

Before they could close the distance, the other group turned left into a service street between a convenience store and a Vietnamese takeaway. Art moved to follow, but Jackie stopped walking.

"Can't we go around, Art? I don't think we should go through an alley."

"Alley?" Art stopped and turned around. "This isn't Gotham City,

Jack. It's fine, it's not even dark."

"Okay," Jackie said, not looking convinced.

"It's okay, Jackie," Zack said. "It's not far and if it starts raining again, we'll be drier in there."

Jackie nodded and the three turned the corner. The other group had stopped in the middle of the alley and were staring at one of the side walls. Closer now, Zack could see it was Charlie and Tabitha, as well as two others from their school—Bast and Kimmy. Zack didn't know either of them very well and regretted letting Art push him into this.

Art hurried towards them. "Hey everybody, Tabitha. What's up?"

The four other teens looked over at him. "Oh hey, Art," Tabitha said. "Come check this out. There's this weird light and I can't work out where it's coming from."

They walked closer and Zack saw what the others had been looking at. There was a strange oval of grey light on the wall, about one metre wide and one and a half tall. Tabitha, closest to it, seemed almost silver by the glow. Her jacket, jeans and brown ponytail were all cast with a steely sheen in front of the wall.

"It's deadly, right?" Bast asked.

"It doesn't look dangerous to me," Art said, stepping closer.

"Nah, mate. Deadly in Koori. It means cool."

"I don't like it." Jackie's voice was almost too soft to hear.

"I agree. Whatever it is, let's get away from it," Charlie said.

"Don't be silly," Tabitha said. "It's got to be one of those light projector things, like they have at the Vivid Festival. If I stand somewhere over here, you'll see my shadow."

She moved closer, sliding from side to side and contorting her body in an effort to create a shadow against the grey. Regardless of where she stood, the circle of grey light remained unbroken.

Zack also took a step closer. The strange grey light was almost fluid against the brick. Stranger still, it was dense enough that he couldn't see the brickwork underneath. "Actually, Tabitha, I think Charlie's right. You should get away from it."

Tabitha looked over her shoulder at him. "What are you talking about? It's just a…"

An inky green-black shape surged out from within the circle. It was long and thin and made Zack think of a root, or tendril, of some unseen nightmare of a plant. Before any of them could scream, it wrapped itself around Tabitha's thigh and pulled her towards the grey light.

CHAPTER 2
ATTACK

Tabitha was yanked from her feet and her back thudded hard onto the wet asphalt. Zack and Art leapt towards her, grabbing hold of the teenage girl's arms. The tendril jerked in response to their efforts and both boys fell to their knees. They scrambled to hold tight onto Tabitha as the three of them were dragged towards the circle of grey light.

The initial shock gave way and the momentary silence was shattered. They grunted, shouted, yelled and screamed, but all were drowned out by Tabitha's frantic pleas. "Don't let go of me! Don't let go!"

Charlie grasped a discarded glass bottle and threw it at the tendril. The bottle arced wide but, instead of shattering against the hard brick, it disappeared, sinking into the strange greyness of the wall.

Kimmy scrounged behind a dumpster and found a short metal fencing pole. Without hesitation, she attacked the tendril, but it seemed to have little effect, bouncing off its rubbery exterior. Jackie gave a quiet shriek and pressed her back against the opposite wall, watching on with wide eyes.

Bast joined Tabitha and the other boys on the ground and threw his arms around her waist. It was clear straight away that Bast was stronger and fitter than the other two boys and, planting his feet against the ground, they finally halted the tendril's progress. Tabitha cried in pain as her attacker's hold tightened around her leg. Zack and

Art scrambled to their feet, bracing against the unrelenting pull of whatever this thing was.

Charlie knelt down and grasped for another discarded bottle. This time, instead of throwing it, she smashed it against the ground, creating a jagged edged bottleneck, gripped tight in her hand. She screamed and charged forward, throwing herself the short distance between her and the creature and thrusting into it with the sharp glass. She stabbed at it again and again until it reacted, letting go of Tabitha. The boys and Tabitha fell down hard on the asphalt and the dark green appendage thrashed and flailed, slamming Charlie backwards.

Tabitha and the boys struggled to untangle themselves from each other as the tendril loomed overhead, threatening to crash down on them. Kimmy stepped in between them, brandishing a rolled up newspaper she had set fire to with the lighter in her other hand. The flame cast an orange glow over her scowl and dark, bobbed hair. She thrust it at their attacker and it recoiled. Zack cheered as he and the others clambered to their feet. Kimmy charged at the retreating tendril, forcing it back into the grey light. It disappeared and a terrible screech came from within the wall.

"Guys. Help me." Bast had both hands on the corner of the large dumpster and was attempting to force it towards the circle of grey light.

Zack hesitated a moment before joining Tabitha and Art in pushing at the bin. The wheels gave a protesting squeak as they conceded to the teenagers' demands and screeched across the alley. Kimmy leapt out of the way as the four youths slammed the bin against the wall, sealing the strange grey circle between it and the wall.

The dumpster shuddered as it was hit from the other side. Tabitha and the boys pushed hard against it to keep it in place.

Art shouted, "Somebody lock the wheels."

Kimmy stepped down on the lever, testing the lock on the wheel closest to Zack. "It's not working."

Zack pointed at the metal pole Kimmy had discarded for her flaming newspaper. "Kimmy, break them off!"

Kimmy didn't hesitate. With grim determination evident on her face, she snatched up the pole and jammed it down at the nearest wheel. The thudding from their attacker continued as Kimmy brought the pole down again and again until one of the fastenings snapped and the corner of the dumpster tilted violently down.

"The others. Quick." Art shouted at her, straining in the efforts of holding the dumpster against the wall.

She shot him the briefest of glares before moving to the next wheel and repeating her assault. Clanging sounded from the opposite side of the bin as Charlie joined the attack on the wheels. After a few short moments, the bin crashed hard to the ground. The thumping continued, but without the wheels, the dumpster held safe.

"C'mon, let's go. Now!" Kimmy shouted and the others pushed away from the bin.

Art lingered to throw a stunned and silent Jackie over his shoulder and they fled out of the alley and on to the main street.

They didn't stop running for four more blocks, finally pausing in an area well-lit by street and shop lights. Breathless, they knelt or leant against the wall of a store as they tried to regain their wind and wits. The streets around them seemed deserted.

Zack squeezed Tabitha on the shoulder. "Are you okay?"

She flinched at the touch. "What do you think? God knows what tried to do God knows what to me…" She sobbed a moment before turning to face him. "I'm sorry, Zack. Yeah, I'm okay I think." Her jeans were scratched, but not torn through and she was already clearly favouring her other leg against the pain from the attack.

Art put Jackie down, but didn't let her go. "What about you, Jackie? Are you okay?"

"Yeah, I'm fine. It didn't get anywhere near me." Her wide eyes reflected the shock of what she had seen, though. Hers and everybody else's.

"What was that?" Kimmy broke the momentary silence.

Nobody offered an answer, but Charlie asked, "Should we call the police?"

Tabitha snorted. “And say what, exactly? They wouldn’t believe us. Hell, I barely believe us and it had my freakin’ leg!”

Bast nodded. “I don’t think there’s anything we can do. I just want to get home.”

Zack’s heart slowed down and his body replaced his adrenaline with exhaustion. They headed for the bus terminal together and without any further discussion, shared their trip with each other as far as possible, despite it extending their travel. No words were spoken even when they parted, replaced by silent nods and a squeeze of the arm or hand. Zack, Art and Jackie exited their second bus and walked the two blocks to home. The normally shy Jackie gave Zack a fierce but wordless hug as they parted and Zack walked down his driveway and unlocked his front door.

“You’re back early.” Zack’s mother called out as soon as he closed the door behind him.

Zack couldn’t respond straight away. The normalcy of the situation threatened to overwhelm him in comparison to what happened earlier.

“Zack, is that you?” His mother raised her voice.

He forced himself to snap out of it. “Yeah, it’s me. We decided to give the movies a miss. We, um, just hung out instead.”

“Oh, okay. Have a good time?”

“Yeah, good. Listen, I’m not feeling great, so I’m going to head up to bed.”

He bit his lip at his own words, but it was too late and an instant later his mother appeared from the lounge room.

She held the back of her hand against his forehead. “Well, you don’t feel warm. But you do look a bit pale. Did you get caught in the rain?”

He latched onto that as an easy way to his room. “No, but the wind had a bit of a wet chill, so I really want to warm up and go to bed.”

“Okay, good boy,” she kissed him on the cheek. “You’re still going to school. Second term starts tomorrow and I meant what I said. You start putting in the effort or you’re going to lose some of your privileges.”

Sighing, he escaped to his room and closed the door behind him.

In the back of his mind, he knew he should shower, but then he caught sight of his reflection in his wardrobe's mirrored door. His skin appeared so pale with shock it made his brown hair look almost black in the dim light and purple rings were already visible around his dark brown eyes. He decided the shower would have to wait for tomorrow. He kicked off his shoes and dropped onto his bed, where he was asleep within seconds.

CHAPTER 3

AWAKENING

Zack's eyes jolted open. He laid staring at the glowing red numbers on his alarm clock; 4:52. His body, especially his limbs, protested against the shortened sleep, but not only was he wide awake, there was an energy inside him, an urge to do 'something' he couldn't quite place a finger on.

Cobwebs of an unremembered dream clung to his mind, but as he lay there, he forced himself to consider that the dream had begun long before he thought he'd collapsed on the bed. Perhaps he didn't go to the movies at all yesterday, or maybe the dream had been so intense it had muddled a normal night out at the movies. He knew, deep down, this wasn't the case, but he was determined to take a mature approach to it all. He was pondering his next course of action when his phone vibrated. He grabbed it and saw it was a text message from Art.

"*Z R U awake? Can I call?*"

"*Yep and yep,*" he replied.

Zack sat up as the phone vibrated from the incoming call. He answered as quietly as he could. "Hey mate."

Art's exaggerated whisper boomed in his ear. "How are you going?"

"I don't know, mate. Last night was full on. And I feel… a little weird, maybe."

"Like your bones are itchy and you want to go for a run?"

Zack exhaled. "Yeah, maybe something like that? So, you too, huh?"

"Not just me, the three of us. Jackie feels the same way. We all probably all do."

"I reckon you're right. I bet all of us are awake right now."

"What should we do? Jackie's freaked out. I'm trying to calm her down, but I kinda feel the same."

"I don't know, mate. Maybe… I think we all need to catch up before school."

"Yeah, agreed. Where and when?"

"How about Tatters Park?" Zack suggested. "That's pretty close to school. At seven?"

"Seven? Yeah, fair enough. Jackie and I'll be there."

"Okay, I'll tell the others."

After they hung up, Zack tapped out a message to send to the others. "*Hey guys. I assume you're awake. We need to talk about last night. Meet at Tatters at 7.*"

Within the space of a minute Bast, Kimmy and Tabitha all confirmed and agreed. But instead of texting like the others, Charlie called. When he saw her name flash on his screen, even amidst the bizarreness, his heart slid up into his throat.

He took a breath and answered, "Hello?"

"Hi, Zack. What's going on?"

"Hey, are you okay?"

"Yeah, thank God you messaged. I've been laying here in the dark, not knowing what to do."

"That's why I think we need to meet up, get everybody on the same page, work out what's happening."

"I agree. Except… I was going to meet up with Dave this morning."

"There should be time after, but I think this is important."

"I know, but what should I tell him?"

Zack paused to think. "I don't think you should tell him the truth, at least until we work out what the truth is."

"Yeah, okay. See you at seven." She took a long breath down the phone. “Zack, thanks for texting. I’m glad I’m not alone in this.”

And then she was gone. It was ridiculous that a phone call from Charlie could make his heart beat faster than being attacked by an otherworldly tendril, but that didn’t make it any less true.

He lay back in bed, hoping for another hour or so of sleep, but the frantic energy in his mind pushed away any chance of that as it chased after the mostly forgotten images from his dream. He gave up and, ignoring his body’s complaints, Zack clambered out of his bed and stretched. He grabbed the various components of his school uniform from his wardrobe and left his room to creep towards the bathroom. He showered, brushed his teeth and dressed. It was a little past six as he headed to the kitchen.

“You’re up early.” His mother was standing in the kitchen in her dressing gown and slippers, peering at him over her cup of coffee.

“I bumped into Bast last night. He bullied me into going for a run with him before school.” The lie he prepared in the shower flowed from his lips.

“Bast?” she thought for a moment. “Oh Sebastian? He’s one of the Walker boys? His father is lovely. And managing all those boys on his own.”

Zack smiled despite himself. The world could fall apart, but his mother would remain the same, making sure she knew something about everybody. “I’d better get going.”

“Don’t forget to eat.”

“Okay, see you.” he kissed her offered cheek and grabbed a banana on the way out the door.

As planned, the others met him at the park. Zack sat down off the side of the see-saw; his weight balanced by Kimmy on the other end. Tabitha leant against the slide’s ladder while Art and Jackie stood against the climbing frame. Bast and Charlie claimed the swings, their legs dangling as they drifted, waiting for somebody to speak. Since he had organised this, Zack decided it was his job to start the conversation, but he didn't quite know how.

"So, I suppose we should start by acknowledging that what happened last night in the alley did happen."

"You're damn right it happened. See?" Tabitha stood up from where she had been leaning on the ladder and lifted the skirt of her uniform. The group leaned towards her to see the dark, wide serpentine bruising wrapped around her thigh.

"Eyes back in your head, Art," Kimmy said and Tabitha dropped her skirt back into place.

"What? She asked us to look." Art replied.

Kimmy scrunched up her face.

"Are you okay, Tabitha?" Jackie asked, "Does it hurt?"

Tabitha nodded. "It does to sit on, but otherwise it's a bit of a soft ache."

"So," Zack said, "last night obviously happened, but what else? Art and I were talking and we've got this weird feeling inside. Like an urge to do something."

Everybody nodded.

"But what does it mean?" Charlie asked.

"I don't know," Zack said.

"I don't love the idea, but maybe we should go to the cops," Bast said.

Tabitha shook her head. "It would have been hard enough getting anybody to believe us last night, let alone now."

"Maybe there's a special unit, or something, that deals with this kind of thing," Art said.

"I don't think the Australian government has an X-Files department," Kimmy said, rolling her eyes.

"I didn't think Australia had monsters coming out of the walls before last night either, Kimmy. Maybe there's lots that we don't know."

"I'm sure there's lots you don't know," Kimmy muttered.

Tabitha stepped in between them. "I still think we shouldn't go to the police."

"But I want to do something!" Kimmy leapt up off the see-saw, crashing Zack to the ground. "Sorry."

Zack eased himself up. "It's okay. And I get wanting to do something, but I think we should just keep quiet about this. People will just think we're crazy, or that we're doing some weird prank. Let's just take it slow, see if this weird feeling goes away."

Everybody agreed, but Zack saw the hesitation in Charlie's face. He continued, "I really don't think we should tell anybody else anything. Not until we know more."

The look on Charlie's face said she knew that was aimed at her.

"Let's at least go find some breakfast. I'm starving," Bast said.

Charlie claimed her backpack. "You guys go on; I'm going to catch up with Dave."

Tabitha gently squeezed her on the forearm. "Remember Charlie, you can't tell him anything."

"I know. I won't."

Zack barely suppressed his groan as he checked the time on his phone to discover only two minutes had passed since the last time he had tapped it; he was now eleven minutes into his first class of the day. He tried to focus on his teacher, but he had been finding Biology to be a dry subject even before last night's events. Now, his mind filled with impossible things, he stood no chance of concentrating. He was beginning to think it was a mistake taking the subject, but it was too late to switch it now.

None of the others from last night's encounter took Biology and instead, he sat at a lab bench with Stephen and Craig. He wasn't particularly good friends with either of them, but they were decent enough guys. At least when they weren't trying hard not to be. At the moment they were discussing their unlikely weekends, each gratuitously describing their alleged 'conquests'. Zack was fairly certain Craig was describing Emma Watson, including the British accent, while Stephen simply described each attribute of his liaison as 'so hot.'

Zack checked the time again: another minute had passed. Stephen and Craig stopped their conversation at the sound of Zack banging his head against the desk.

Zack's friend Matt sat down next to him in English. "So, Art tells me last night didn't go as planned."

Zack almost choked on a combination of saliva and his sharp gasp at Matt's remark. Matt was one of his and Art's closest friends, having been together since kindergarten, but his mind was reeling at the idea of Art breaking with the agreement to stay silent.

"Wh… what did he tell you?"

"That the weather turned and you guys decided to head home rather than watch the movie? Why?"

Zack's eyes watered, as a combination of the initial confusion crashed against relief. There was also a surge of guilt at keeping something like the alley and the dream from somebody who, on any other night, would have been there. He couldn't say why it was important for him to lie to his friend, but it was something beyond what he voiced to the others in the park. "Yeah, sorry, choking on something."

"Oh well, serves you guys right for trying to see it while I was away. Anyway, want to do something this afternoon?"

"Sorry, I can't, I'm…" his mind raced for something to say. He was hoping to meet up with the others from last night. He reached for a subject Matt didn't take. "I'm going to study a bit for Biology. I'm struggling with it…"

"Pffft, nerd. I'll see you online later though. Maybe we can play something." Matt pulled his books out of his bag as the lesson started.

"Yeah, sure, sounds good." Guilt and relief churned against each other as he listened to his teacher read from their text. Focusing on Shakespeare's Antony and Cleopatra was all but impossible.

Tabitha slid in beside him in the corridor on their way to Maths. "Ugh! Could this morning be going any slower? I swear I counted every second in modern. I can't remember a single thing Purves said, either."

"I know the feeling," Zack said.

Art intruded from Zack's other side. "You guys need to keep your minds off it. Stop stressing."

"Keep our minds off it? Really? Like you?" Tabitha jabbed with her finger at the folder he was holding.

Zack added his own gentle disgust to Tabitha's; Art's folder was covered in badly drawn sketches of brick walls with shaded grey ovals over them.

They found their seats in the class and were relieved to find Ms Agarwal intended the lesson to be spent with the students working quietly on exercises from their texts.

Halfway into the period, Zack had done little more than stare at the summary sheets on his desk. The speaker in the hallway crackled into life. "Would the following students please come to the front office immediately? Sebastian Walker…"

Zack turned wide-eyed and found Art looking back at him with the same questioning expression.

"Could be a sport th…" Art started.

"… Rachel Kim…" the announcement continued.

"Kimmy doesn't do sport," Zack whispered back.

"…Charlotte Cooper…"

Zack looked across the room at Tabitha. Her skin was pale as she stared back at the boys.

"…Tabitha Stewart…"

She took a deep breath as she stood and collected her books.

"…Arthur Stevenson…"

Art stood.

"…Jacqueline Stevenson…"

Art winced as he slid his books into his backpack.

Zack sat still, waiting for the name that would complete the list.

"…Zachary Marek."

CHAPTER 4

OATH

Zack sat with his hands tucked under his thighs in an effort to stop himself fidgeting. Bast sat next to him, his leg bouncing hard enough to shake the chairs until Kimmy shot him a look that froze him in place. The principal's secretary sat at her desk a few metres away, so all that was available to them was alternating between sharing worried glances with each other and staring forward at the closed door to the principal's office. Zack felt sure he was going to be sick.

The door opened and the principal, Mr Nguyen, stepped out. Zack wasn't sure what he had expected, but the principal's ear to ear smile was not it.

"Good morning everybody, you have been busy, haven't you?" He ushered the seven of them into his office with a wave of his hand. "Come, come."

The teens shared a final, more confused glance before flowing single file in through the door. Two people were standing beside the desk, facing them as they entered. The first was a short, thin woman with blonde hair in a sharp bob. She was wearing a medium length light blue dress and stood with her hands pursed together at her waist. Zack guessed her to be in her thirties, but he was never good with ages.

The second was an average-sized man with slicked back dark hair and a wispy beard limited to his chin. He wore an expensive dark grey suit and stood, leaning back slightly on the desk. He seemed a little older than the woman, perhaps in his forties.

Mr Nguyen walked in behind the group of students, closing the door. "I have to say, it was a delightful surprise to hear seven students have been found successful in this scholarship program. What did you say it was called again?"

"The Endeavour Mentorship Program," the blonde woman answered, with a crisp, British accent.

"But we nev…" Kimmy began.

The woman turned her attention away from Mr Nguyen and faced the children. "I appreciate that you may be feeling some confusion at the moment, but I assure you that I can offer an explanation and that all will be well."

Kimmy nodded slightly and closed her mouth. The woman gave a slight nod to the man in the grey suit, who smiled in response.

"Mr Nguyen," he said, in a rich Russian accent. "Perhaps it is time for you and me to step outside for a small moment."

The principal blinked slowly before smiling again. "Yes, of course."

The two men left the room, closing the door behind them.

Art gasped. "Did he just Jedi mind trick our principal?"

The woman raised her hands in front of her. "Please. Don't be alarmed. My associate, Timur, and I mean you no harm. We are here to talk about what happened last night. Please hear me out, and at the end of it, I'll answer any questions you have and you will be free to go about your lives. Is that okay?"

Zack struggled to find his breath, let alone any words. He nodded and the others did the same.

The blonde woman smiled. "Thank you. My name is Junie. Timur and I belong to an organisation called the Tower. Last night you encountered something not of this world. Our wards informed us of that breach and we followed the trail to you."

The door opened again and Timur entered, alone. "Our principal has gone to walk his rounds; we will have as much time as we need."

Junie inclined her head and Timur reclaimed his position against the desk to her right.

Junie continued, "Our world is at the centre of many others. It is surrounded by realms of magic. These worlds seek to enter our own, to taint it with their chaotic corruption. You saw an example of this last night. The Tower seeks to protect our world from these intrusions. It is our calling and our purpose." The words flowed from her like a well-rehearsed speech.

"The Tower maintains a number of tenets with the purpose of keeping our world safe. Primary among them is the Silence. As was true for you until last night's breach, the world does not know of the existence of magic, of the realms, nor the Tower. If too many knew, it would invite the very chaos we work so hard to defeat. The Silence must hold. But how you will hold it is up to you."

The teens glanced at each other.

"You have a choice to make. You may join the Tower and serve its cause. To do so, you must swear an oath to hold the Silence, as well as the Watch - the duty to be vigilant against breaches and ungoverned magic. Service to the Tower can take many forms, depending on what you are willing and capable of doing, but the Silence and the Watch are the minimum. And even this comes with a cost. When you walk through those doors, back to your normal lives, you will lie to your friends and family. You will look uneasily into the shadows and you will always know the dangers that threaten our world. But your discretion and vigilance will save lives.

"Or you may choose to return to your innocence," she spoke directly to Art, "you are correct that Timur influenced your principal's thoughts. Using similar magic he can, harmlessly, remove your memory of last night's event. You may return to your lives in blissful ignorance of magic and perils."

The group was still and silent as Junie peered at each of them in turn.

"The choice is yours to make, with one caveat. You must decide as a group. The risk to the Silence is too great if some of you choose service and others do not. I will give you some time to decide. We will be just outside." Junie and Timur left the room.

"She's gotta be gammon, right?" Bast asked, eyes wide.

"Yeah, Bast. She made it all up and we imagined a demon-octopus attacking us last night," Kimmy replied.

"It's a no-brainer," Art bounced out of his chair to face the others. "Why would we want to forget this? There's magic in the world."

Kimmy followed. "All I know is, nobody is messing around with my memories."

"Guys, we need to decide as a group," Tabitha said, staying seated. "Let's slow down and talk about this."

"What's there to talk about, Tabitha?" Kimmy asked. "Why would you, of all people, choose ignorance? You don't want to be ready for the next time some magic squid tries to grab you?"

Tabitha's face paled and her hand drifted to her injured leg.

"Go easy, Kimmy," Charlie said, "Tabs is just trying to talk it out."

"And I'm saying there's nothing to talk out." Kimmy's arms crossed tight against her chest. "You think I'm going to let you, let them mindwipe me?"

"Well," Bast said, stretching his legs out in front of his chair, "technically, Kimmy, you wouldn't remember it happening, so I think we'd be okay."

"This is serious, Bast," Tabitha said.

"I know, I know," he said, "but Kimmy's right. I can't see any of us choosing to forget about this."

"What about Jackie?" Charlie said, gesturing toward the tiny blonde girl. "She's what, thirteen? And we're deciding this for her?"

Jackie spoke without looking up from her feet. "I, uh, I want to know. What if something happened to Mum and Dad, Art? I'd want to know enough to get help."

Zack thought about his own family. "How about a vote? If we're all agreed, easy. If not, we keep talking."

"All in favour of taking the oath?" Kimmy asked, her hand already up.

Bast and Art raised theirs, followed by Zack and Jackie. Tabitha looked towards Charlie, who shrugged.

"I think I'd rather know, Tabs," Charlie said, raising her hand.

Tabitha nodded and raised her own. "Yeah, alright."

Kimmy, with a pleased look on her face, opened the door.

"Excuse me? Junie? We've decided. We'll take your oath."

Junie and Timur re-entered the room.

"Excellent. Timur, if you would please?"

The bearded man bowed in reply and chanted. A soft, violet light bloomed from his hand.

"Timur has cast a small truth seeking enchantment. If you place your hand into the light, any mistruths you tell will become apparent. I am going to ask you to repeat an oath that will commit you to keeping the Silence, that is, the secret of magic, and the Watch, which is the promise you will contact us if you encounter magic. Now please, in turn, each state your full name, and 'swear that you will hold the Silence and the Watch until the end.'" The last of Junie's instruction had the flowing cadence of formality.

Kimmy rose and took a half step forward, holding her hand in the purple glow. "I, Rachel Kim, swear that I will hold the Silence and the Watch until the end."

Bast, Art and Charlie followed behind Kimmy. As they each spoke, Zack watched as Tabitha continued to think it over. Her eyes darted around the room as if trying to soak it all in while she processed what was happening. Finally, she stepped forward and gave the oath. Zack went next and then Jackie stepped forward to complete the line.

"I, Jackie Stevenson, swear that I will hold the Silence and the Watch until the end."

When they had all reclaimed their seats, the light from Timur's hand dimmed and Junie rewarded them with a smile.

"Well done, the Tower has heard your oaths, and will remember.

Before we continue, I must ask. Have any of you spoken to anybody not present about your experience last night, or about coming here today? Do not fear if you have, no harm will come to you or those you have told, but we must know."

Zack couldn't help casting a glance towards Charlie. She returned his glance with a hurt look and he snapped his head forward again.

Junie continued. "Good. Now, with that settled, we may begin to discuss the nature of your service to the Tower. The majority of those who take the oath choose to do no more than that. They return to their lives, uphold the Silence and the Watch, and barely think of the Tower again. There are those of us, however, who do more."

Junie paused for a moment, facing Zack and his friends. "Please understand, magic is not what you have read about in books or seen in movies. It is chaos manifest, almost alive in its drive to corrupt. Without the Tower, the order our world relies on to survive would be destroyed and many lives along with it. We guard this world from magic, closing breaches and expelling any magical entities that try to enter.

"To achieve this, we manipulate these forces and turn them back against themselves. More than simply fighting fire with fire, by bringing order to the chaos of magic we are able to harness it as a tool for good. In essence, we have learnt to wield the magic ourselves. And we teach it in service to the Tower."

Zack struggled to believe what he was hearing. It was one thing to understand there were strange forces in the world and beyond; it was quite another thing to hear one of his childhood fantasies being offered to him.

Art, eloquent as always, voiced his friend's thoughts. "Do you mean you're going to teach us magical spells and stuff?"

"In a way of speaking. Yes. I am offering to teach you how to control the chaos of magic and use it to protect this world and those within it that you love. And further, to reward you in this undertaking, you may use magic to improve your own lives, so long as you do not risk the

Silence, jeopardise the work of the Tower or harm another member of the Tower."

Art couldn't contain himself. "We're allowed to go around doing magic?"

Her patient smile strained. "Within reason, yes. Although you can see that most abuses would constitute a breaking of the Silence. Whether it's flying alongside an airliner, turning an enemy into a frog or simply growing an eight foot high pumpkin. But if you can do it subtly, then yes, that is the reward for services to the Tower.

"I understand it is hard to believe. It wasn't too long ago I was sitting in your place listening to the impossible offer I was being given. Even if you do not quite believe what is happening, leave yourself open to the possibility of this being real. But you do not need to decide immediately." Junie reached into her pocket and removed a small card, handing it to Tabitha. "If you would like to know more, come to that address after school today. If not, so long as you hold the Silence and the Watch, you are free to go about your lives. Return to your day now as if it had been uninterrupted. Your principal and his assistant will not recall this meeting."

The teens trundled from the room and down the corridor before stopping around the corner.

"I mean, what the hell?" Bast let out a long breath. "What do we do?"

"I need time to think," Tabitha said, "let's get back to class, get through the day and meet up after school to work out what we do next."

The others nodded, except for Kimmy.

"Kimmy?" Tabitha asked.

"Fine. I mean, I've already decided, but yeah."

"Okay, see you all then," Tabitha said, before turning and heading back to class. Zack moved to follow and Art, giving Jackie a comforting squeeze on the shoulder, did the same.

Zack sat down next to Tabitha and Bast at a bench during lunch, picking a spot in the shade of the tree that grew at the edge of the schoolyard. Bast tore apart an orange and offered some to Zack, who declined.

"How do you guys feel about this morning?" Zack asked.

"Well, it's definitely full on," Bast said through a mouthful of citrus.

"Do you… do you think we should consider not going?" asked Zack. He had asked the same question of Art during the morning break and received a look of confused horror as his reply.

"I know what you mean, Zack," Tabitha said, munching on her rice crackers. "It's like, I want to jump right into this Tower thing, and what they're offering is incredible, but what are we signing up for?"

"Exactly." Zack was relieved somebody else was thinking the same way.

Bast shook his head. "I don't think we're signing up for anything, or at least, nothing other than what we gave an oath for already. If we don't like it, she said we can walk away at any time. But I don't want to walk away now, just because it might be a bit dodgy, and regret it years later. I mean, c'mon, we're being offered magic!"

"We need to keep our eyes open, Bast," Tabitha said, "I'm not in a hurry to turn down being a wizard, or witch, or whatever it is we're being offered, but I'm trying to think about this rationally too. If it turns out to be some kind of weird cult, or some elaborate hoax, we need to be ready. Still, I've tried to run through every possible way it could be fake and nothing stacks up. The best I've come up with is that we all suffered some form of mental shock in the alleyway on Sunday and we're now in a shared delusion."

Bast took another bite. "So we're either crazy, or there's magic in the world."

"I think those are our options," said Tabitha.

"Well then, my mob have always believed there's magic in the world. Or at least that there's more going on than you white-fellas believe, anyway. So I vote that over the loony bin." Bast said.

Zack smiled. “Fair enough, I suppose.”

“Like I said, Zack,” Tabitha added. “We’ll all keep our eyes open. But Junie seems like good people.”

Zack nodded. “I’m not saying I don’t want to go there. Honestly, I can’t wait to. I considered skipping the rest of the day and going straight there, but I’m trying to look at this logically.”

“I think logic went out the window yesterday,” Bast said. “Or at the very least, we’ve got a new kind of logic that includes tentacles, hidden towers and magic.”

“Okay, good.” Zack felt better for the discussion and rummaged through his bag for his sandwich.

CHAPTER 5
TEACHER

There was nothing remarkable about the single story office building across the road from Zack and his friends. Nothing, except that it matched the address on the business card given to them by two wizards claiming to belong to a secret society. Zack shuffled his feet at the edge of the gutter, along with the others.

"Well, screw this," Kimmy declared and strode across the road towards the building. The others pursued her, seeking the small amount of safety in maintaining the group. Zack spotted a small plaque by the door and read it out softly as they walked towards the door. "'Managerial and Financial Actuarial Services.' Guys, I think this is an accountant..."

Zack followed behind Kimmy and the rest of his friends through the open automatic doors. His eyes adjusted to the change in light.

"... or something." His comment fell flat as the group of seven found themselves standing in a dark room, surrounded by a slightly curved stone wall. There had been no sensation of movement or displacement, only slight disorientation.

Zack spun around. Where the automatic door leading back onto Milton Street should have been was an open stone doorway, dark with shadow. The room was lit by sconces, spaced around the curved walls of the room. In the shadows, in between the flamelight, were hints of stairs leading up and down and other doorways.

Charlie ran her hands over the coarse stone bricks of the wall. "This isn't possible… This can't be the same place as the office building. It's too big."

"And the wrong shape," Bast said.

"It's a trick or something," said Tabitha, "we've gone down a slight ramp and all this is underground."

Zack shook his head. "We've barely taken three steps from the door."

"Well then, it's mirrors, or lighting," Tabitha said.

Jackie's quiet voice intruded. "Guys, over there."

Zack's eyes were drawn to a well-lit section of the room where Junie was standing in front of a mezzanine that loomed over a quarter of the room.

"Welcome to the Tower." She beckoned them towards her.

The teens moved across the stone tiles to join her in the centre of the room.

"I take it from your arrival that you have decided to see what more the Tower has to offer?"

The teens nodded.

"Excellent. Let's continue."

Tabitha raised her hand before gesturing around the large room. "Can I ask a question? Why is this place, this 'Tower' in Australia?"

"In short," Junie answered, "it is not. The Tower exists at the edge of our realm. The doors behind you open to and from many places across the globe. Australia currently has five entrances, including the one in Sydney."

Tabitha nodded, her eyes narrowing in thought.

"Any other questions?" Junie asked. "We are in no hurry."

"I have one," Charlie said. "What are we committing to by coming here tonight? Or by taking the next step?"

"Nothing," Junie said. "You have made the only true commitments we require earlier today. The Silence and the Watch. At any point from here, you can leave through those doors and cease your engagement with us. The Tower rewards those who assist in the protection of our world, but only seeks those who are willing."

When no more questions were asked, Junie clasped her hands in front of her. "Let us begin your journey with the Tower."

She stepped back from the edge of the balcony for a moment and returned holding a large jar. Inside the jar were several floating coloured balls, and as she removed the lid, the balls escaped to waft towards the group. The balls shone in a range of colours, no two the same. While Zack's eyes were drawn to the approaching spheres, Junie spoke again.

"There are thirteen different schools of magic. Air, Earth, Fire and Water. Body and Mind. Animal and Plant. Movement and Protection. Knowledge, Life and Creation. Each of you will find yourself naturally attuned to one of these schools. Open your mind to possibility. Walk amongst these orbs, gaze upon them and you will find yourself drawn to one of them. Do not overthink it. Instead, allow yourself to be led."

They stood, seemingly mesmerised by the strange lights wafting around them. To Zack, they reminded him of the lazy fairies or will-o-the-wisps from the old Disney cartoons he used to watch at his grandparents' house. Lost for a moment in those memories, Zack found his eyes tracking one orb in particular. Turquoise in colour, it was beautiful and as Zack approached it, he felt as if the light was somehow both cooling and warming him, filling him with a sense of comfort. He glanced around, expecting his friends to be standing close beside him. How could any of them be interested in any of the other orbs? Not when this one stood out so starkly from all the others. To his surprise, he found each of them entranced by a different colour.

Tabitha's was not too different; she was looking up at a light blue sphere. But Art was grinning at a bright purple orb and Charlie's was a rich rust colour.

Junie's voice intruded on their bemusement. "Now that you have each found your orb, follow it. It will lead you through these halls to one who will become your mentor. Take the opportunity to connect with your school. Return here in an hour and I will speak to you again before you leave."

The turquoise captor of Zack's attention floated towards a set of stairs to the left of Junie's balcony and he climbed them in pursuit. He was joined by Bast following an orange orb and Jackie following a steely grey one.

After one flight of stairs, the orange ball raced ahead of the others and Bast was forced to jog to keep up with it. "Good luck, guys," Bast called out as he followed his guide.

For several more flights of stairs, Jackie and Zack climbed together.

"It's strange," she whispered to him, her smile illuminated more by the light of their orbs than by the sconces' flickering flames. "I should be scared by everything that's happening, but this feels right."

Zack nodded. "I know, it makes more sense than maybe it should. Still, if you need me, shout out, I'll come find you."

"Thank you, Zack," she said softly and soon they and their orbs parted ways.

His turquoise guide led him up one more flight of stairs alone, before stopping in front of a closed wooden door. It hovered there, almost expectantly and he hesitated a moment before he tapped on the door.

"Enter," came the reply and he did so.

The owner of the voice was a diminutive, grey-haired woman with bronze coloured skin. The rows of deep wrinkles on her face and arms gave testament to her age. She smiled as he stepped into the room, gesturing to a comfortable looking wooden seat opposite the one in which she rested.

"Oh, I'm so pleased one of you ended up here. With so many in one go, we were all hopeful."

Zack glanced around as he entered the small room, roughly the size of his bedroom at home. There was a large rectangular table holding dozens of boxes in one corner. The remaining walls were lined with bookshelves, which were themselves filled with a well-ordered clutter of books, some with faded old cloth and leather spines, but others with the shiny gloss of modern dust jackets.

Zack sat down, holding himself straight-backed in the chair in reflection of the woman's posture.

"Welcome." She extended her hand. "My name is Sara."

"Zack." He took her hand and she gently squeezed his, rather than shaking it. Her skin was warm and soft, like old paper left out in the sun, but her grip was strong and steady.

"As I said, it's a pleasure that you were chosen. The school of magic to which you and I are both attuned is Life." She paused. "Does this surprise you?"

"To be honest, the last twenty-four hours has been pretty overwhelming. I don't know how I feel. What is the school of Life?"

"Life, in a way, is what fuels living beings. Other schools of magic may alter living beings in some way: making them bigger or faster, making them confused or scared, or even harming them outright. Life does not do these things. Instead, it interacts with the essence of what being alive is, the energy of being. I will teach you how to harness it, to encourage it to flourish at times of need. Indeed, one reason I love this school so dearly, is that it is the greatest irony in magic: we take this chaotic and destructive force, one that does such harm and we bend it back upon itself, using it to heal the damage it does."

"I… I will be able to heal people?" Zack's jaw loosened.

"Indeed, in time. But we must work slowly and surely together because Life is not something that can be manipulated without care. Your patient has life, that is true. But so does the bacteria in her blood, the tumour in her lung. Life magic can look like a miracle, but it can also become an abomination. Learning Medicine and Biology is as important as learning the magic itself." She gestured around at her bookcases.

Now that he was closer, Zack could see the vast majority of books appeared to be textbooks on Chemistry, Biology, Surgery, and Anatomy. A flicker of disappointment must have shown on his face.

"My boy, magic is never the quick answer. It is not the easy answer. It is only the answer to a rare question. Never forget that." She eased her sternness with a smile. "Still, we must begin your training and I'll not send you away with nothing."

Sara stood up and slid a wooden stool in between the two chairs. She then placed five porcelain cups and saucers on the table and then retrieved something tiny Zack could not see and sat back down. She opened her hand to reveal a red ladybird and rolled her hand from side to side to prevent the little creature from escaping. She placed it down on one of the saucers and trapped it with an upturned cup. Next, she upturned the other cups onto the empty saucers and instructed Zack to close his eyes. He obliged and listened to the gentle clink of the porcelain being moved.

"Now," Sara said, "keep your eyes closed. Empty your mind of all thought, except for the memory of the turquoise orb. Remember how it felt, how it smelt or sounded. Then reach out your hand and find the ladybird."

He held out his hands over the cups. He relaxed his brow in an attempt to open his mind, and in his personal darkness, ever so tentatively, he felt it; the same cold/warm sensation the orb had given him. He opened his eyes and removed the cup on his left, revealing the ladybird.

She smiled at him again. "Very well done. First try, in fact. Now, close your eyes and repeat."

For half an hour, Zack practiced. More often than not, he was successful. Sometimes his mind wandered, as he wondered how his friends were doing and what schools of magic they had chosen. Or as he fantasised about healing injuries and sickness, on one occasion impressing a distressed Charlie with his miraculous gifts. These distracted thoughts brought an empty cup, failure and the disapproving 'tut' of Sara. His mentor also made the task more difficult on a few occasions: removing the ladybird, adding a second, or hiding it under the table. But Zack discovered as long as he was focused, he could find it.

"Enough," she said as she pulled the ladybird from her pocket at Zack's instruction, "you've done very well."

The newest apprentice in the school of Life sat back in his chair, now noticing the perspiration on his arms, face and neck.

Sara nodded at his observation. "And here is your next important lesson. Magic, even as simple as that which we have done here, is tiring. Regardless of the school, the practitioner uses Life to channel it. Manipulating magic will exhaust you and, if you are careless and attempt more than you should, it can harm or even kill you. As your skill increases, so too will your ability to wield more of it and for longer, but there are still always risks. Now, do you have any questions?"

"About the lesson?"

"About anything. You've had a lot to think about today. My mentorship is about more than just the magic, it is about you. Let me help you process your thoughts."

Zack paused for a moment. "How did you come to the Tower? If that's okay to ask."

"It is. An old woman is always happy to talk about her life." She closed her eyes and settled back into her chair. "I was older than you when I was Awakened."

"I was born in Honduras, in a fishing village not too far outside the capital, Tegucigalpa. Honduras was not a safe place when I was growing up. There was political unrest, workers unifying, but mostly it was normal people trying to live their normal lives. One day, some of the fishermen were out on the river and I was sitting on the shore, tending to a cooking fire in preparation for their lunch. All of a sudden, they were shouting and I looked out at them. The water was churning and a strange dark purple light illuminated the area underneath the boat. The boat capsized and I watched as the men, one by one, each of them strong swimmers, were pulled under and the water turned red against the purple. I didn't know what it was. No crocodile could do that.

"But then I saw them, swimming towards the shore where I was standing. They were humanoid, but dark red, with long reptilian tails. They crept up the riverbank at me, but I grabbed a burning branch from the cooking fire and thrust it at the closest one. All three of them shrieked and dived back into the river. I ran.

"I told my family what I saw and they thought I'd succumbed to madness. They kept me inside, telling the other villagers seeing the fishermen killed by crocodiles had shocked me, and that I was recovering. After a week, they let me out again and I was free to go about my duties. One day, not long after, two from the Tower came to me. They were terrifying. No fault of theirs really, but they were outsiders and they waited until I was alone before they approached me. They spoke to me, explained to me what I had seen, and offered me their choices. First I swore to uphold the Silence and the Watch and then I left my home and travelled with them to the Tower."

She finished her story and opened her eyes.

Zack sat, trying in vain to imagine the ordeal. "Do you still live in Honduras?"

"No. I never returned, not home at any rate. I travelled the world, learning what I could of medical sciences and now I mostly live here."

"You live in the Tower?"

"Yes, my boy. Many of us do, at least those who serve long enough. You would not be permitted to yet."

He shook his head, to indicate he wouldn't have wanted to, but her words drew another question from him. "Who runs the Tower, who is in charge?"

"The Tower is ultimately led by the Thirteen. The Thirteen consist of one member from each school. Who they are is a secret, at least to most, but the Tower itself knows and responds to them and they each speak through one or more representatives. I do not currently know the member for Life, but I have my suspicions."

Even amongst all he had been through, Zack found this strange. "Why the secrecy?"

Sara shrugged. "It has ever been so. I imagine it is a combination of safety and politics, with a healthy dose of tradition. But now it is time for you to go. You may return to me at the same time each day this week." She stood and he followed her lead.

"It was good to meet you, Zack. I believe you have potential. Keep your patience, find your focus and you will do well."

He beamed at the praise. "Thank you, Sara."

On his way, he found Jackie waiting at the point where they had parted. She was lost in thought, although she smiled when she saw him. They set off down the stairs together.

"How was your mentor?" he asked.

Jackie looked over her shoulder, as if to be assured they were alone. "Was yours strange? Mine was really strange," she said in a whisper.

"No, mine was fairly normal. At least for an old woman living in a magical tower," he said, matching her volume. "What do you mean 'strange'?"

"Well, he introduced himself as 'Mr Smith,' but giggled a little when he said it as if it was a joke that we both knew it wasn't his name. And he had about twenty locks on his door. I guess it probably goes with the territory, though," she said.

"What territory?"

"Oh, Protection. That's my school! It's all about sensing danger and preventing it, so I guess that could make you pretty paranoid. What did you get?" she asked.

"Life. Which means I'll be able to heal people, at least I think so."

"I wonder what everybody else got."

They paused at the next landing, unsure of which way to go. After a moment of doubt, they heard footsteps in one of the directions and followed them to find Bast approaching from the direction he'd left them.

"Hey mate, how'd you go?" Zack asked.

"Yeah, good, I guess," Bast said.

Jackie whispered, "Was your mentor weird too?"

"No, maybe a bit of a dickhead, though. Still, he's going to teach me magic, so that's pretty great. What about you two?"

"I got Life magic, and Jackie got Protection."

Bast beamed. "I got Movement. Once I get good at this, I am going to kick serious butt on the field."

Jackie's jaw dropped. "You're going to cheat?"

"I prefer to think of it as using my training and innate talents," Bast responded, sticking his tongue out at his would-be conscience.

Jackie laughed.

As they descended further, Zack pressed him. "What was dickish about him?"

"Oh, pretty much everything. Everything in his room looks seriously expensive and not in a subtle way either. And he gave me a pretty hard time, even when I thought I was doing what he was asking."

"That sucks," Zack said.

"Yeah. But I've had coaches like that before. It's all good."

They found their way to the ground floor and were greeted by Tabitha and Junie. Junie motioned for Tabitha to go and join her friends and they were soon joined by Art, Charlie and Kimmy. Before they could share any more of their experiences, Junie addressed them.

"Congratulations to each of you for finding your School. You have been through much this past day. So I suggest you go home, take some time to remember you are still part of the normal world. You are welcome here at any time, but you are also welcome to never return, should you wish not to. As long as you remember the Silence and the Watch, which you have sworn to uphold. Until we meet again." Junie nodded to them, turned and left the room up a staircase.

They all started to speak at once before Charlie interrupted. "Let's go and talk about it on the way. It's going to be late by the time we get home."

The streets were darkening as they all boarded a bus to travel north together over the bridge. The sun had yet to set, but the long shadows cast by the skyscrapers of the city made it seem later than it was.

Art couldn't contain himself. "I'm going to be a Mind mage," he whispered at a volume that almost made his whispering irrelevant. "My mentor is that Timur guy from this morning. He's awesome. I'm going to be able to manipulate people's thoughts and memories. This is all so cool; I always knew there was more to this world. More than the boring day to day."

Kimmy didn't wait for Art to finish. "I picked Fire!" She fixed Art with a steely gaze. "And I'm going to be able to set my enemies alight."

Before Zack could question exactly how practical that would be, or how many enemies Kimmy had that were destined for these righteous flames, Tabitha pointed at the bandage wrapped around Kimmy's right hand. "What happened to your hand?"

Kimmy looked down at the floor. "My first lesson."

"Which was?" Tabitha asked.

"That fire is hot."

"Your mentor burned you?" Tabitha shouted, drawing the attention of commuters further down the bus.

"No! No, nothing like that."

"Then what happened?"

Kimmy murmured something in the direction of her feet.

"Please, Kimmy, tell us."

She looked up, her cheeks burning. "I grabbed hold of my orb, okay? Freakin' thing was hot."

Art and Bast burst into laughter, followed by Zack and Tabitha, and finally Kimmy herself. As the laughter subsided, Bast, Jackie and Zack shared their Schools with the group.

"I got the Animal School," Charlie said. "So, I guess I'm going to be able to talk to and control animals."

Jackie's eyes lit up. "Oh wow! Could you talk to my cat? I'd love to know what he's thinking."

Art groaned. "I don't! I don't want confirmation that furry little psychopath sees us as nothing more than food providers and potential victims."

"Shut up, Art. He loves us."

Zack cut off the well-trodden sibling argument. "That leaves you, Tabs."

"I got the Air School. I'm not quite sure what I'll be able to do with it. Junie says it's quite versatile. I might even be able to fly one day." She trailed off in blissful thought.

Zack latched on to something. "Junie?"

"Oh, yeah. She's my mentor. She was really pleased one of us was chosen for Air, since she's our liaison with the Tower, anyway."

Her brief embarrassment over, Kimmy was beaming with excitement again. "I can't wait to go back tomorrow."

As the others nodded in agreement, Zack said, "Me neither, but I think we're going to need a plan on how to manage this. We'll need excuses for parents, probably different ones for friends and… others." He looked at Charlie.

"Well, studying should work well enough as an excuse for parents," Bast said, "as for friends, I'm sure we can think of something."

"That's all I'm saying," Zack said, "we need to think about it sooner rather than later, we have to tell them something if we're going to keep disappearing."

"You mean lie to them," Charlie said.

"Yeah, I do. We all promised to… to maintain the Silence."

"He's right, Charlie," Tabitha squeezed her friend's shoulder. "We gave our word."

"Fine." Charlie turned to face out of the window, shrugging off Tabitha's hand in the process.

The rest of the group lapsed into silence, their eyes burning bright with their thoughts. Zack's eyes lingered over Charlie. He longed to comfort her, to place his arm around her and tell her it was going to be okay, but he knew it wouldn't be welcome. He closed his eyes and tried to think over his lesson with Sara, but he couldn't help but daydream about using magic to cure the sick and injured.

CHAPTER 6
TRAINING

"No. No. No." Sara's reprimand was stern rather than angry. "Where are your thoughts, Zack? They are certainly not here. They are certainly not where they should be."

Zack blushed. "I'm sorry. I don't think I've ever noticed how much my mind wanders."

Sara softened. Slightly. "This is okay. You are a young man, little more than a boy, really. What is that poem… 'A boy's will is the wind's will?' It is natural. And that is key to the problem. What we do here is not natural. It is wrong. Aberrant. I am teaching you to control magic, to master it, but never forget it is a contest against a chaotic force almost alive in its capacity to destroy. We are starting here with small things, so the danger is also small, but one day you may try and access greater magic and with it, greater risk."

Zack listened. He didn't doubt Sara's words, but the events of this past week did not lend themselves to steady thoughts. Each day he had gone to school and attempted to both learn his subjects and maintain the impression nothing out of the ordinary was happening in his life. Between the mental exhaustion and emotional exhilaration, he wasn't certain which was more difficult. Then each day after school, telling his parents he was studying, he had travelled into the city and attended the Tower for lessons, before returning home in the early evening.

He steadied his breath to calm his mind. "I will do better."

She smiled at him. "I know you will, and you are making good progress, so we shall cease for today. Your sense of Life is growing. Faster than mine did at this stage of the training, I have to admit. But then, I didn't have as good a teacher as you do." Her dark eyes twinkled at him from between her deep wrinkles.

Zack was so intent on the lesson; he missed the humour. "What was your mentor like?"

"He was a good man. Much more caught up in the theatrics and mysteries of the Tower than I'm sympathetic to, to be honest. And I think that made it harder for me at first than it may have been.

"It was challenging for me. I don't mean to be one of those elders who says children today have it easy, but in this case, it is true. My village was one scarcely connected with the rest of Honduras, let alone with the world. And I came almost delirious from my difficult journey to that abandoned temple. But, most difficult of all, I came alone. I had no one to share my Awakening with, no trusted friend to look me in the face and assure me I had not succumbed to madness. It is not rare for an Awakening to be a solitary experience. Seven together is practically unheard of, but pairs or trios are not uncommon and I have always thought it is easier for them.

"The Tower was a strange and alien place as I stood there, with only the light of the torches in the dark of the antechamber. My liaison was an older Englishman by the name of Coleman. He was brisk, dismissive and frightening as spoke to me of the realms and presented the thirteen orbs to me. I was filled with confusion and fear. And then I saw that turquoise ball drifting towards me and I towards it. You have mentioned the way it felt to you, but to me, it was its smell that stood out. It was like a strong antiseptic. It reminded me of the bottle my mother had stored away in case of emergencies. It was a sharp smell and it brought me out of my stupor. I wasn't alone any more but it wasn't Coleman who saved me from my solitude.

"Nor was it La'Lune, my mentor. In the weeks that came, he taught me words and gestures of arcane power. Words and gestures I'll soon begin to teach you, albeit with less melodrama than La'Lune. I studied, I practiced and I trained hard. And all through it, my potential loneliness was abated; not by any person in the Tower, nor by the Tower itself, but by Life. Life, and the connection it provided to magic, was like a companion and a friend I could rely on. As I learned more and began to form connections with other novices within the Tower, Life stayed as something I could rely on, something I could depend on in the darkness of fear and doubt.

"And it was a lie."

Zack was startled by the abruptness of her statement. "What do you mean?"

"I mean exactly what I have been trying to teach you from the moment you knocked on my door: Magic cannot be trusted. It is beautiful and intoxicating and it wants only to wreak havoc on our world."

"But the way you spoke about Life, you still seem to love it. All the good it can do, undoing the damage magic does?" questioned Zack.

"I do. Believe me, I do. I have given my days and years to Life and I love it exactly because of all the good it can do. But the lie I discovered, far too late, is that it could love me back." She spoke the last words in hushed tones, all but a whisper.

Zack lowered his own voice in response. "Too late?"

Sara paused and with forced levity, she answered, "I was not always this bastion of wisdom I have been imparting upon you. Put simply, in the early days of my magical training, I depended on magic for too many things and questioned its limits too little. I will have succeeded as your mentor if I taught you nothing but that. That is not to say I will not teach you more. Magic is a valuable tool, one that should be used at times of need. That need, however, must always be interrogated.

"I want you to keep practicing over the weekend, for next week we will begin to manipulate it." As his face grew excited, she qualified, "slightly."

"Next week? You're not giving me a lesson tomorrow?"

“No. Tomorrow, Junie has said you and your friends should gather in the entry chamber,” she smiled in a way Zack could only describe as mischievous. “You will have a different kind of lesson tomorrow.”

On his way down the stairs towards the entry chamber, he heard Tabitha and Kimmy speaking. The girls broke off their conversation and beamed a pair of smiles at him as he entered the room.

“Come look at this, Zack.” Tabitha waved him over.

He stood beside them. “Look at what?”

She nodded her head towards Kimmy. “This!”

Kimmy reached out her palms facing each other, almost as if grasping a ball between them. Her face furrowed in intense concentration and she was fiercely whispering something he couldn’t quite hear, over and over. A drop of perspiration rolled from her forehead down her cheek, but still nothing happened. Zack was about to turn to Tabitha with a questioning look when a spark flared in the space between Kimmy’s hands. It was like the first flash of a sparkler, but it lasted only an instant. Kimmy dropped her arms to her sides, panting.

The significance of this wasn’t lost on Zack; this was the first overt thing any of them had been able to achieve. “That’s amazing, Kimmy!”

Her grin was almost as bright as the spark had been. “I know it’s only a little thing, but…”

“But it’s a beginning!” Tabitha said. “And it’s far more than I’ve been able to do.”

As they walked out through the shadows of the unnaturally darkened exit, Zack tried to notice the exact moment when he left the Tower and entered Sydney. Not for the first time this week, he failed. There was something disorienting about the experience. At first he had blamed the change in lighting, but after a week of persisting, he was sure it was something else.

He gave up for the moment and rejoined the girls’ conversation. “Did either of you get specific instructions about tomorrow?”

“Junie said it would be good for all of us to come around noon. At least noon our time anyway,” Tabitha said.

"Did she say what for?" Zack's curiosity rose.

"No," she shook her head, "but she said it was for a different component of our training."

"I hope the others bother to come," Kimmy said, "I can't believe they've been skipping lessons."

"Most of them have only missed one and nobody said we had to come every day," Zack said.

"But who wouldn't want to?" she persisted.

"Well, some of them have commitments. Art and Jackie had a family thing tonight, and Bast had training. And Charlie is..." his voice trailed.

Tabitha finished his point. "Charlie is maintaining the Silence. It's hard for her, keeping Dave in the dark like this. And if she cancelled too many plans, he might get curious and that could lead to trouble."

"She should dump him," Kimmy said.

Zack tried to look disinterested while Tabitha shook her head.

"She'll have to eventually," Kimmy said, "might as well save them both weeks or months of pain."

"Not everybody chews up guys and spits them out, Kimmy," Tabitha said, "let Charlie figure her own way around this."

"Fine. Whatever. So, what do you think tomorrow will be about?"

The three of them shared their thoughts as they travelled home.

Zack swirled a piece of lamb backwards and forwards through the remains of his mashed potato, his thoughts adrift in the patterns of thought Sara had been teaching him only an hour earlier. His mind relaxed, with dinner warming his insides, and his awareness expanded out. He could feel, without looking up, the three other strong sources of Life sitting around the table. Further out, all but obscured by the healthy auras of his family, fainter hints of Life crept into his perception; the fish tank, a pot plant or two, a few things in the walls. He could almost reach out and…

"…ences at school?"

His mother's voice snapped his focus away and the cool-warm feeling of Life evaporated from his mind.

"Sorry, what?" he stuck the lamb in his mouth and raised his head to face her across the table.

Zack's elder sister, Ellen, snickered. "You are such an airhead."

"I said," began his mother with a sharp look at Ellen, "have they talked anymore about university course preferences at school?"

"A little," he said through a mouthful, "but it's about a year away, so not much, except we should keep thinking about it."

"And have you?"

"Have I what?"

"Been thinking about it?"

"Yeah, a bit." The last week had spurred a great deal of thought about the future, what he could accomplish in life with the healing power of Life in his hands. "I've been thinking of going for medicine, actually."

Ellen melodramatically choked on half a sip of mineral water. "Um, don't you have to be smart and hardworking for medicine?"

"He's both of those things," his mother said.

"Well, he's one of those things," his father said before sipping his drink.

"Jonathan!" His mother slapped his father on the upper arm.

"What?"

"You could try being a little supportive."

His father sighed and turned to face him. "Zack, I'll support any goal you set for yourself. You've got potential, buckets of potential. But you need to actually put the work in. I don't think I've seen you crack a book all year."

"Well, I've been staying back after school and studying there," Zack lied.

"That's right, he has," his mother said, locking eyes with his father.

"Great. That's great. Keep it up a bit longer than a week and you might squeeze your way into medicine. It's incredibly competitive."

"I will."

"Great. But, maybe, have a back-up plan, too."

"Oh yes, dear, definitely a back-up plan. Just in case," his mother added.

"Yeah, I know."

When the meal was over, Zack cleared the table before heading upstairs to his room. He didn't love that he had to lie to his parents about his after-school activities, but worse was the rise in expectations he was setting up for himself. He lugged his school bag over to his desk and pulled out his History text. Ordinarily, reading about the warriors of Sparta might be interesting, at least enough to hold his attention, but after his lesson with Sara, his mind felt like it had been through a clothes-dryer. He resolved to at least highlight sections that looked relevant in the hopes he could fake his way through Monday's lesson. A few minutes and three entirely highlighted pages later, he threw down his pen and turned on his computer. A message from Matt popped up.

"Up for a game? I'm not doing anything tomorrow."

Zack's hand hovered over the keyboard. He hadn't gamed all week and saying no on a Friday night as well was certain to make Matt suspicious. And worse, it might make him think he was avoiding him.

Zack messaged back. *"I'm pretty tired, but screw it, I can do a quick hour or so before bed."*

"Awesome."

Zack took one last glance at his text book before slipping his headset on and starting up a game.

Zack's mother pushed the door of his room open with a half empty laundry basket. He smiled at her obvious attempt to excuse an unannounced visit into his room and looked up at her from his textbook. She couldn't seem to hide how pleased she was to find him studying on a Saturday morning. The fact he was studying his Biology textbook to help him further his more 'extracurricular' lessons was beside the point.

"Do you have any plans today?" she asked.

"Probably another half an hour or so of this, then I was going to go hang out with Art."

"Good, good. I've been proud of you this week, Zack. You're finally putting in the work. Keep this up and I'm sure your results will improve. I'm sorry your father and I had to threaten you with the loss of your privileges, but at least it seems to have made a difference."

She left the room, notably not taking any of his dirty clothes with her and he was hit with a small twinge of guilt over his deception. He knew it was for good reasons and in some ways it was little more than stretching the truth. He did need to start studying his school work soon, otherwise when exam time came it would be all too clear he hadn't been putting in the work. Deciding that it was a problem for later, he finished reviewing the rest of the chapter and prepared to go out.

He was walking out the door when his phone announced an incoming message with the humming sound of a lightsabre. It was from Matt.

"*Hey, mate. Wanna do something today?*"

Zack grimaced as he read it. Between his trips to the Tower after school and his exhaustion afterwards, he hadn't seen much of Matt except in class and an hour of gaming the previous night. He was a good friend and he felt bad about neglecting him. Worse still, it didn't look like this was going to improve any time soon.

He decided to wait until he had spoken to Art before replying and stuffed the phone back into his pocket. He called out a goodbye in the rough direction of where he thought his mother was and made the brief trip to the Stevenson house.

A few minutes later, in response to his knocking, Art and Jackie's mother let him in. "Hi Zacky, they're upstairs."

"Hi, Mrs Stevenson. Thanks."

She stopped him before he could walk past her and, in a dramatically hushed tone, she added, "And thank you for letting Jackie tag along, it's been good for her."

"No problem, she's great. And the girls love her."

"Good, that's good. She's... Thank you."

Up the stairs, Zack walked into Art's room and was confronted with a strange scene. Art and Jackie were sitting cross-legged on his bed, facing each other with their eyes closed. Each had their hands up in front of their chests, palms facing inward. As Zack was about to speak, Jackie lashed out in an attempt to slap Art across the face. In the last instant, Art brought his opposite hand up and blocked the strike. She laughed.

Art responded with a smile. "That was so close. My turn."

Zack watched on as they returned their hands to the starting position. After a few seconds, Art struck out in a similar fashion, but this time, Jackie easily raised her arm up to block the slap. Art grunted.

"What the hell are you two doing?" Zack asked.

Both jumped in alarm before opening their eyes and turning to him.

"Whoa, mate. Don't sneak up on people like that!" Art said.

"In my defence, I don't think surprising you is my fault. And I repeat: what the hell are you two doing?"

The siblings shifted to sit with their legs off the bed, facing Zack properly.

Art took the lead in answering. "A game we've invented to help us practice. It turns out we've both been doing really similar exercises."

Jackie interrupted. "My mentor has been teaching me to sense danger. He says, 'The second step to protecting against danger is knowing the danger is there.'"

"Second step?" Zack asked.

Jackie screwed up her face. "I told you he was weird. But yes, the second step. The first step is the awareness danger might be there. Which he says is true all the time. It's hard to understand him all the time, so I do what he says."

Zack nodded, thinking of Sara's straightforward manner with renewed gratitude. "But why can you do it, Art? What does that have to do with Mind magic?"

"I can't do what Jackie does, but what I can do ends up being pretty close to it. Jackie can sense danger. I can sense hostility. It's supposed to be one of the loudest of thought patterns which is why Timur started me on it. She's picking up that she's about to get slapped, I'm picking up that she's about to hit me."

"That's really cool. I haven't worked out how to do anything with my thing yet." Zack checked the time on his phone. "Ready to go?"

They both nodded.

"Tabs' message said we had to wear clothes we could run around in?" Art asked.

Zack nodded. "I didn't realise our new school had P.E. too. My mentor didn't say anything about it when she told me, but Tabitha has been spending more time with Junie so she'd know."

Jackie sat down at the bus stop and Zack showed Art the message from Matt.

"Yeah, I got one too," Art said, "I guess we've been a bit absent this week. It sucks, you know, if he'd come back home a day earlier he'd have been there that night and be on the way in with us right now."

"But that's true of a lot of people," Zack furrowed his brow. "We're not the only ones being asked to lie to people who could have been with us that night."

Art snorted. "No points for guessing who you're talking about."

"I'm talking about all of us, Art," Zack said. "There's easily a dozen people that could have been there. But only seven of us were and that's what we have to deal with."

Art threw up his hands. "Fine, fine. Still, I want to do something with Matt."

"We could hang out tonight, play some games."

"Sounds good. Let's invite ourselves over to his place; he has the better TV, anyway."

Zack agreed and sent a message to Matt. The reply came almost instantly. "He says to come over at sevenish and we'll order some pizza."

"Awesome!" Art said. "Apart from getting yelled at by Mr Pitt in Chemistry, this is the most normal I've felt all week."

The three of them shared a laugh as they waited for the bus.

The seven stood in silence, taking in the large room to which Junie had escorted them. Rows and rows of weapon racks, side by side with armour stands, encircled the room. The stone floor was divided into various squares, rectangles and circles by coloured tiles and markings. At one end of the room was a row of over a dozen statues, each unique in design. One looked like a terracotta soldier from China's Forbidden City, while another had the appearance of a classical Greek Olympian. In front of the row, a single statue towered over the others. Its broad shoulders and thick limbs gave the impression of strength.

Junie was silent as they soaked in the scene before beginning her instruction. "Welcome to the Tower's combat hall. Serving the Tower can be a dangerous thing, and your magic cannot always be relied upon to protect you. For some of you, it cannot be relied upon at all, at least not against direct threats." At the last, she lingered over Zack and Art. She continued, "And so, the Tower also provides martial training. This is optional, as your magical training is, but if you intend to actively serve the Tower against our threats, it is recommended."

Kimmy eyed the rows of weapons. "Junie, swords and crossbows are impressive and all, but why wouldn't we want guns or something?"

"It's a fair question and like much in the Tower, it has a bit of a mixed reason. The first is that of tradition. We have always used weapons like this, so we continue to do so. But it is also true that we are often required to travel to the magical realms in defence of our own. The rules of nature in these realms often differ from our own, sometimes dramatically. "It is often safer to depend on the sharpness of a blade than whether the chemical reaction of gunpowder will work the same way."

Art needed no convincing. "To hell with guns. I want a sword!" He walked along the racks looking for one that interested him.

Bast was quick to follow him, eyeing them with a shared eagerness.

Junie smiled at their reactions. "Swords are a good place to start. Each of you, if you please, select a sword."

Zack walked with the girls over to the sword racks. Art and Bast stepped away, testing their blades against each other with the maturity of ten-year-olds with cardboard tubes from finished wrapping paper. While many were of similar design, each of the swords appeared unique and Zack's hand lingered over a few different choices before pulling one from its rest. He was surprised at how heavy it was, but once he adjusted to its weight, he couldn't help but feel strong with it in his hand. Charlie, Kimmy and Tabitha had each drawn a similarly sized sword, although Charlie seemed to be struggling with the weight of hers a little. Jackie instead chose a smaller sword, only three feet long and she held it with visible apprehension.

"You will have an opportunity to train yourselves in any and all of these weapons, so if these swords are not to your taste, do not worry. Today, you will learn and practice the basics of a few different weapons to both begin the fundamentals and to encourage you to find weapons best suited to you."

"What do we do first?" Tabitha asked.

"Oh no," Junie smiled, "I will not be teaching you. The Tower's weapon master has that privilege. Commander, if you please."

At this, the largest statue came to life, stone grinding on stone as it strode forward towards the startled group of teenagers. If Zack was surprised by the statue's sudden movement, he was almost dumbstruck by the rich sound of a Spanish tenor that addressed the Tower's liaison.

"Of course, Mistress Junie, it is indeed my pleasure."

CHAPTER 7

THE COMMANDER

With a grace that belied its bulk, the stone entity strode along the stunned line of new recruits. It paused in front of each teenager, taking a moment to look them up and down. All seemed to meet whatever standards it was applying until, at last, it reached Jackie. Its voice rose as if aghast.

"What is this thing?" It pointed at Jackie.

She bit her lip as her eyes went wide with distress.

"What do you mean, Commander?" Junie asked. "She is called Jackie and she is one of the new members of the Tower."

The Commander pivoted to face Junie. "But it is incorrectly constructed. It is too small!"

Junie's eyes narrowed and she spoke as if trying to tease apart this unexpected concern. "That is because she is a child."

"A child?"

"Yes, a young human."

"So it will become a complete human later?"

"Yes."

"Why not make it complete to begin with? What am I supposed to do with it until it is finished?"

"Train her, like the others."

"But it is so small."

Junie sighed. "Ordinarily, we would not train a child this young, but in this case, we are making an exception. Simply put, the Tower wishes her trained."

The giant statue nodded. "Very well, Mistress."

It strode away to stand facing the centre of their line and Jackie blinked the tears from her eyes, barely kept in check during the barrage of negative attention.

"We will begin today with the early basics of swordplay. I will pair you up and we will get started."

Zack dared an interruption, worried their stone trainer may be excluding Jackie. "But there are seven of us. We can't be paired up."

"No, no, no. You will not be paired together. That metal is sharp, your flesh is soft." The Commander's Spanish accent was thick with derision. It clapped its hands twice, stone on stone echoing sharply through the room. "Here are your partners."

From the rank of statues across the room, seven sprang to life. Snapping their feet free of their pedestals, they strode forward and stood so one was facing each of the youths. As the terracotta soldier stood facing Jackie, towering over her, the Commander stepped towards her and bowed down so its face was level with hers.

"I am sorry 'child', but I do not have a trainer of your size."

"This… this one is fine, thank you." She met its stone eyes with an attempt at a determined stare.

Zack was glued to his own statue. From the light green tinge, it appeared to be made out of either copper or bronze and was cast in the image of a Japanese samurai. Like the other six statues, it was unarmed. Even so, Zack couldn't help but tense, his hands grasping his sword's hilt, ready for an attack at any moment. However, the statue waited patiently until the Commander directed each pair to a separate area of the room. Once safely isolated, the statues left their partners and retrieved their own weapons before returning. Zack was relieved to see his partner's weapon was a wooden training sword rather than the real thing, like his own.

The samurai moved to stand alongside Zack, extending its sword-arm forward. With its other hand, it gestured at the hilt of its sword and then again at Zack's. Confused momentarily at this wordless communication, his instructor had to repeat the gesture before Zack understood and held up his own sword in reply. The statue shook its head and pointed more specifically at its fingers and Zack altered his grip to match.

This silent instruction continued for the next half an hour, with the metal samurai demonstrating hand grips, stances and basic movements. The only sounds in the room were the shuffle of footsteps and the occasional swear word from Kimmy as she argued against her own silent corrector. The Commander strode around the training room, observing each pair for a moment before moving to the next.

The Commander clapped again and, as one, each of the statues ceased their instruction and pivoted to face their student.

"It is time, my new recruits, to see what you have learned so far," the Commander declared, with an uncomfortable hint of glee in its voice. "Begin."

The statue opposite Zack shifted into the same fighting stance it had been teaching him and Zack hurried to do the same. He had not yet planted his unsure feet when the statue advanced, swinging its wooden sword in attack. Zack stepped backwards in a hurry, almost tripping over his feet and the statue pressed forward, attacking again with a backswing. His brief training abandoned him and he raised his blade, managing a clumsy parry with his sword. His triumph was short-lived as the samurai swung a third time, slamming him in the ribs. Zack's metal blade clattered to the ground as he doubled over, breath rushing out of his lungs. He was grateful when his voiceless attacker stepped back to its starting position, allowing Zack an opportunity to settle himself and look around at his friends.

None of them were doing particularly well. Tabitha and Bast seemed to be at least defending themselves with a grain of competence, while Art and Kimmy had each tried a more aggressive approach and were receiving hard wooden responses to their attempts. Charlie and Jackie had, similar to Zack, been disarmed by their foes.

The samurai tapped its training sword against its helmet, drawing Zack's attention back to it. He took a deep breath and he picked up his sword before assuming the starting stance again. The samurai responded and the lesson continued.

Again and again the statue's attacks came. Again and again, Zack failed to defend, let alone offer any threat, and again and again, the wooden sword struck his body. The assault that was his training continued for another half an hour or so before the Commander clapped and the statues stopped and returned to their place on the far wall. But not before Art took advantage of the pause to strike his own opponent across the head with his blade. Art leapt back, nervously holding his sword, ready to defend himself, but the statue returned to the far wall with the others.

"You may rest a few moments," the Commander gestured over to the wall near the entrance. "Water is available over there should you require it."

Zack winced as he walked over to join the others at the metal cistern. On his way over, he noticed Junie was no longer observing them and must have left some time after the training began. His friends looked like he felt.

Art dumped half his cup of water through his hair, cooling himself. "This is full on!"

"I like it," Kimmy said.

Tabitha pointed at the beginnings of a deep bruise Kimmy was sporting on her left cheek. "But how are you going to explain that?"

Kimmy winced as she touched it. "I'll think of something."

"A bit more of this and you'll be able to say a bus hit you," Zack said.

His friends laughed with the little energy they could muster.

"Maybe we're done?" Jackie said.

Kimmy was about to say something in response, but the Commander called them back to the middle of the room.

"Replace your swords back on their racks," it directed, gesturing over to the wall, "and return with a spear each."

The group groaned almost as one, their hopes of a finish to their training now dashed. Zack once again found himself being instructed in stance and grip by his silent samurai instructor. Over the next few hours, the teenagers were alternately instructed and tested by the statues in the use of spear, axe and mace.

By the time the Commander finally called for the maces to be returned to their racks, Zack could hardly stand through exhaustion and pain. Dozens of welts and bruises covered his body and blood welled from under his earlobe. He looked at his companions. They were a mass of scratches, bruises and lumps. And while they each had smiles on their faces from the exhilaration of the training session, the smiles quickly faded as they looked at their injuries.

Jackie struggled to hold back a sob as she limped over to Art. "Mum and Dad are going to kill us!"

Soft laughing came from the doorway where a man stood watching; he was middle-aged with a ruddy brown beard. "Dinnae worry yourself, girly. That's what I'm here for."

Zack realised he recognised the man, having once passed him during the week on the way to his lesson.

The man continued, "My name is Tom. And, like your man Zack here, I'm from the school of Life."

He stepped forward to Jackie and gently reached down to touch her forehead. He closed his eyes and chanted quietly; the words difficult to decipher. Zack felt a flare of Life from Tom before the man lowered his hand. The older teenagers gasped in astonishment. Her skin was free of the marks of her training and as she exhaled in a shudder, she was clearly standing more comfortably than moments before.

Her eyes were wide with shock and she shook out her arms. "It's all gone. All the pain, the aches, all gone."

Tom smiled. "Of course, wee one, all part of the service."

Bast, who was standing next to Jackie, stepped forward, but Tom gave him a harsh look.

"Ladies first, you unchivalrous fiend!" And, with a flourish, he stepped past Bast to Charlie. His hand against her forehead, he repeated his ritual and the Life took away her injuries. From there, he moved on to Tabitha and Kimmy before tending to the boys.

When it was Art's turn, Zack moved closer to watch Tom work.

"Steady on, pal. Dinnae look too closely at this. We wouldn't want you trying anything you're not ready for. Close your eyes and get a feel for the energy that's sloshing around between us."

Zack complied and sure enough, he could feel the cool-warm sensation he associated with Life flowing from Tom into Art.

When at last it was his own turn, Tom gave him an apologetic smile. "I'm sorry about this, but I'm under orders to only repair the surface damage, particularly around your pretty face."

Zack was confused into silence, trying to frame the right question.

"But that's not fair. Zack's as hurt as any of us!" Charlie said.

"True enough, lass. But Sara says it's part of his training and I'll nae act against her." Quieter, speaking more directly to Zack, he explained, "She's nae doing this to be cruel, boyo. Trust her. Use what she's taught you to feel your body repair itself. Feel *how* it repairs itself."

With this, Tom reached out and Zack could feel the flow of Life wash over him. But as the flow subsided, the aches deep in his body remained and while he could walk without wincing, it took a little effort. His friends smiled at him in sympathy, although Charlie still looked a bit outraged. Ridiculously, that made him feel better than the healing magic had.

"Well, that's it, my young friends. Nae… wait," Tom paused for a moment, scratching his beard in exaggerated thought, "aye, one more thing. Mistress Junie asked me to let you know you are free to return here for training any time. It is as optional and available as your magical training. You should do it though, if you're hoping to help the Tower out in its work. And if you need a wee help after your lessons, come and look for one of us. Zack knows where to find us. Good morning to you all."

"Good morning?" Kimmy asked. "It's almost evening."

"Not in Glasgow, m'dear. Beginning of a brand new day and I'm off to find a bacon bridie." And with that, he left.

Looking around the room, Bast's eyes lingered over the large statue who returned to rest with the others across the room. "Our lives have gotten stranger."

His understatement drew a laugh from his friends and they dawdled from the room. More than ever, Zack was looking forward to pizza, video games with a pair of good friends and collapsing into a soft beanbag.

Zack bundled himself into the car next to his elder sister, Ellen. He had spent the morning lying in bed, partly out of pain and exhaustion, but partly to follow Tom's suggestion. He had lost himself for over an hour, feeling the flow of Life around his body as it struggled to repair the previous day's damage. No, 'struggled' was the wrong word; 'endeavoured'. As he lay there, Life flowed tirelessly throughout his body, moving to his injuries and acting. There was no feeling of difficulty, simply of effort and the need for time to do the job. He had even managed to narrow his focus down, feeling the way Life approached a bruise as compared to a graze or a sprain. He had been mesmerised.

So mesmerised, in fact, he was holding his family up.

"Sorry, sorry," he said to the car in general, as he repressed a grunt of pain. Ignoring his weary muscles, he shifted his heavy backpack to the spot in between Ellen and himself.

"What's in the bag?" she asked as she opened it to look for herself. "Oh, books. Why are you such a nerd all of a sudden?"

"You be nice to him," their mother said from the front passenger seat, "it's good to see him start to take his schoolwork so seriously. We're very proud of him, aren't we?"

When there was no response from their father, she repeated herself. "Aren't we?"

He looked up from his phone. "Yeah, of course, good work, Zack."

Ellen responded by miming herself gagging.

A short drive later and they arrived at Zack and Ellen's grandparents' house for the weekly gathering of the extended family. His uncles and aunties were sitting around the table speaking with his grandfather, while Ellen joined their cousins on the back veranda. Zack did a quick round of 'hellos', including the necessary kissing of the aunties, before speaking quietly with his father.

"Can I sit in with Babi for a bit?"

His father gave him a smile with more than a hint of sadness. "Go ahead, mate. She's asleep, so try to be quiet, okay?"

"Yeah, of course."

Zack crept into his grandparents' bedroom. He was greeted by the soft sounds of his grandmother's unsteady breaths and took a moment to look at her. A woman once so tall and strong, he had felt like a bear cub in her arms. Before the cancer had reduced her to frailty and pain, he had spent many hours in those arms as she insisted on teaching him to dance. A dozen different medicines were piled on her bedside and the scent of fresh flowers clashed against the sterile smell of sanitiser.

He sat in the armchair next to her and slid out his copy of Antony and Cleopatra. If he was claiming to study as often as he was, he should at least do some. Otherwise, come exam time, he'd be proven a fraud. After fifteen minutes, however, realising he'd turned the page twice without reading any of the words, he accepted he didn't have the focus for it right now. Instead, he closed his eyes and turned his attention inward to feel the flow of Life healing his body.

He opened his eyes and glanced at the bedroom door; it was closed to keep out the noise from the other rooms. Reaching out his hand towards his sleeping grandmother, Zack shut his eyes again and sought out the Life in her. Finding it with ease, he trained his attention on what the Life was doing. He found it far more difficult than he had when observing his own body, because at least then he was able to focus on where his pain was.

Zack persevered, clearing his mind of everything but his grandmother's Life and he started to gain awareness. Her Life was everywhere, industrially working against a 'something' he couldn't quite understand. He turned his mind to that something. It had its own kind of Life, a strange one that crashed against his grandmother's without mixing, like oil and water. The cancer, he concluded.

When his mother opened the door, he had his Shakespeare text open in front of him again, reading the words he'd been staring at for ten minutes.

"Dinner's ready," she whispered.

He nodded, picked up his bag, and crept from the room.

The school bell boomed over the loudspeakers and Zack slid his English working book and text into his bag. Bast lingered by the door so they could walk out together.

"Kimmy's in a foul mood," he whispered,

"I think even Mr Hancock was too scared to say anything today."

Bast laughed. "Well, he's a smart man, then. I'm going to kick a ball around with the boys on the oval. Want to come?"

"No thanks, mate. I'm still way too sore."

His friend looked at him in sympathy. "That's what you get for picking a fight with a magically animated samurai."

Zack scanned the hallway to make sure they weren't overhead, but Bast shook his head.

"Relax, nobody's listening. And even if they did, they'd assume I was talking crap," he started to head off. "I'll catch you after school."

"Well, are you coming or not?" a voice hissed in his ear. Zack turned to find Kimmy glaring at him.

"Sure…"

They walked across the schoolyard towards their usual lunch time spot on the benches under a large tree.

"Are you okay, Kimmy?"

"Obviously not. My cow of a mother came into my room last night and accused me of smoking."

"But you do smoke."

"I know, but I'm not stupid enough to get caught. I was practicing…" she looked around and dropped her voice, "I was practicing that thing I showed you on Friday night. And I accidentally set fire to a box of tissues. That was the smoke she smelled. She came bursting into more room and started going through my things. Eventually, she found one of my packets of cigarettes. She was screaming, so I started screaming."

"So, what? Are you grounded or something?"

Her laugh was like acid in his ears. "It wouldn't matter. I don't let her tell me what to do anymore and as long as my grades stay high, she can't really do anything about it. But she's going to be a pain to be around for a while."

Zack nodded along, even though he didn't have a strong understanding of Kimmy's family dynamic. Up until a few years ago, Kimmy had been one of the quiet, studious girls. Then at the start of Year Nine she arrived back at school looking like a different person, and two years later she had thrown off all resemblance to that other girl, with the exception that she was still top of most classes.

By the time Zack and Kimmy reached their usual bench, Matt, Tabitha, Charlie and Dave were already there. Zack claimed the spot next to Matt, as much to sit with his friend as to avoid the hand-holding couple. Matt gave him a goofy-looking grin and pointed across the yard with a nod of his head. Zack followed the line of sight and found Art speaking to a girl named Stacey. He was leaning against the brick wall in an attempted pose of confidence, but Zack could see from the way he was fidgeting with his tie that he was nervous. The conversation continued for a little longer before Stacey shook her head and fled towards a group of her friends having lunch.

Art paused for a moment and then turned to walk towards Zack and the others. In doing so, he met a wall of eye contact from his friends and he blushed and looked down.

"Swing and a miss, Casanova." Kimmy laughed at him as he approached.

"Don't be mean," Tabitha said. "Good on you for having a crack."

Avoiding any further eye contact, Art hurried to sit down next to Zack, who gave him a silent look of sympathy.

Matt tried to help by changing the subject. "Want to come hang at my place after school today?" he asked the boys.

"Sorry. Can't today, we're staying back to do catch up on some Chemistry study," Zack said, picking the one subject he and Art didn't share with Matt.

Matt's face changed to a look like he'd inhaled something particularly foul. "When did you two become such a pair of nerds?"

Kimmy had clearly been listening in. "They've always been nerds."

"No," Matt said, "you used to be a nerd. We're geeks!"

"Same difference."

"No. Nerds study. Geeks play computer games and argue about superheroes. And these two," he said, "have betrayed the brotherhood and become nerds."

"I'd be up for some gaming later tonight if you're online?" offered Zack.

Matt smiled. "Sure, sounds good."

Zack felt a little guilty, but mostly, he was excited about Sara's promise of teaching him something new after school.

CHAPTER 8

THE WILL

Zack entered the Tower with his six friends, eager to begin a new week of lessons. He followed Bast and Jackie up the stairwell to their mentors' rooms and was soon sitting down opposite Sara.

She smiled at him and after a brief greeting said, "I hope you forgive me for instructing Thomas to not heal you fully."

"No, I understand. And I've done as he suggested. I think I've learned a lot from it."

She beamed at him. "Good. Good. You've made excellent progress in only a week. Let us see if that can continue."

Zack and Sara claimed their usual armchairs in the alcove between her bookshelves.

"Today, I'm going to teach you how to manipulate the flow of Life. In essence, that is the entirety of what we do and we will begin with the simplest form of that manipulation. But first, we need to discuss the *how* of this manipulation. Many here at the Tower call these 'spells'. That terminology is unimportant, but what I will teach you now *is*. Regardless of the School, whether it is Life, Fire, Movement or any of the others, it begins with the Will.

"Magic is a chaotic, corrupting and violent force and to bend it to your purpose, you must first apply your Will. You have already begun training yourself in this. The relatively simple task of observing Life is still an exercise in Will. Concentrating on the outcome you want and restricting yourself from distraction: that is Will.

"To do more than observe, however, you must apply that Will to the world. I will teach you some phrases and gestures that will aid you. These are not truly magic and there is nothing particularly special about them, although they are likely where the idea of magic spells comes from in many cultures. But they enable you to channel your Will, allowing you to manipulate Life for a specific purpose. In time, you may be able to do it without these gestures or phrases."

Sara stopped and looked at Zack, who was staring at her wide-eyed, attempting to understand everything she'd said.

She smiled. "Other mentors do not necessarily tell you these truths straight away. They tell you the words and hand movements have power of their own. Only when you've mastered them do they tell you the truth. That is how it was for me. I can see the wisdom in it, but I also found it jarring. I prefer to be honest with you."

Zack nodded, still not quite sure.

Sara brushed her hands together. "I have spoken enough. Let us learn in the doing. The first manipulation is a simple one, but not without danger. It is the sharing of Life from yourself to another person."

"And in doing so, I'll use my Life to heal someone?" Zack said, attempting to understand.

"No, not in this," Sara said. "To begin, the flow of Life will be too generalised to heal. But it will provide your target with energy, as if they have rested, or perhaps even slept."

"At the cost of my own energy?"

Sara gave a sharp nod. "Excellent. You understand. Now observe."

Sara placed her hand on his shoulder. He watched as, with her free hand, she traced a delicate pattern repeatedly with her index finger. Her lips mouthed strange syllables in a soft refrain. And then he felt it, the flow of Life, from her body directly into his.

It was incredible, as if he had simultaneously finished some exercise, but was rested enough to undertake it again. "That is amazing!"

"And now it is your turn. First, you must hold what you intend to do in your mind and turn your Will to achieving it. Did you feel how the Life left me and, importantly, how it entered you?"

Zack struggled to find the words. "It was like a mist. Or maybe more like a shower on a mist setting. It seemed to come from you in a more concentrated way, but then it spread out. Is that right?"

"That is good. That is a helpful way to think about it. When we do magic, at least in our School, we must consider three elements. The Source, the Target and the Intent. In this case, the Source was my Life, the Target was all of you and the Intent was to share the life. Changing any of these elements alters the effect. But for now, let us focus on this."

Over the next two hours, Sara taught Zack the strange, arcane words and gestures with which to channel his Will. They were simple enough to master, but complex enough to hold his attention, with a strange counter-rhythm between the syllables and the signs that pushed out other thoughts. By the end of the lesson he was drenched with sweat but, due both to the flow of Life between teacher and student, as well as his excitement from the magic, he was energised.

Sara too, looked enthused. "You have done remarkably, Zack. You truly have. I think you will be ready soon for the next thing, but we must both exercise our caution and patience in this."

"Thank you, Sara."

"I mean it, Zack. This is not empty praise. Your progress is excellent."

There was a timid knocking at the door. Sara called out, without standing, "Yes? Come in."

The door creaked open, revealing Jackie. "Miss… Sara? Mr Smith sent me to ask for…"

Only then did Zack notice the bruises and welts around her cheeks and neck, as well as a slight split lip. He launched himself to his feet. "What happened?"

Sara put a restraining hand on his shoulder. "Gentle now, Zack. Come here, child." She motioned for Jackie to sit down in the seat Zack had vacated.

"What is your name, my dear?"

"Jac… Jacqueline. My friends call me Jackie."

"Jacqueline," Sara repeated it, as if savouring the feel of it in her mouth, "that is a beautiful name. I assume Mr Smith is teaching you some shielding spells?"

"Yes. It's okay, Zack. That statue gave me more trouble than this on Saturday. It doesn't even hurt that much, but I can't go home looking like this."

"Of course not, Jacqueline," Sara said. "Zack, I want you to close your eyes and feel the flow of Life. Concentrate on my Source, for unlike before, now I shall draw Life from all around us. A little here and there, so nothing misses it. Do not pay too close attention to my Intent, for you are not ready and in unready hands, magic is deadly."

Sara began her work and Zack, his eyes closed, turned his mind to the flow of Life around him. At first he was drawn to the concentrated flow of Life into Jackie but, as instructed, he followed it back and opened himself to where Sara was drawing the Life from. Like eyes adjusting to a dark room, he could feel faint Life all around him, like a fine mist, being drawn in by Sara's will.

He opened his eyes to find Jackie's welts gone and her unblemished face beaming. "Thank you, Miss Sara."

"Just Sara, Jacqueline. That absurd mentor of yours may insist on a title to go along with his ridiculous pseudonym, but I am satisfied with the name my mother gave to me."

She walked them both to the door. "Zack, you may come to me as often as you like from this point on. If you wish to skip some lessons and focus on your martial training downstairs or heavens offend, your school work, that is okay. I will make myself available at this time, but it is your choice."

"Thank you, Sara," Zack said as Jackie nodded her thanks again and the two left Sara's room.

"You are so lucky, Zack," Jackie said once they were a few flights down. "She's amazing. Nothing like mine."

"Exactly what happened?"

"Well, after about five minutes of a discussion about my psycho-magical need to protect myself that barely made any sense, he started to 'encourage' me to protect myself."

"And how did he..."

"He threw rocks at me. For an hour."

Zack gasped, but before he could say anything, she continued.

"It's okay, really. I mean, I'm definitely jealous of you having a mentor like Sara, but Smith gets results. By the end of the lesson, I was able to block a few."

"How?"

"By psycho-magically protecting myself, I guess. No, seriously. Like I said, Smith gets results. Last week he taught me to sense danger and now I can do that pretty well. It's like the danger itself is a thing."

"Well, it was a thing, wasn't it? It was a rock."

"No, I'm not explaining it well. There's the rock, sure. But the danger was something apart from it. The danger is the rock hitting my body and causing me harm. And that... point. That'll have to do. That point, that's the danger and I can feel it like it's a thing that exists separate from the rock. And once I could feel it, I was able to react to it. I could protect myself from the danger. I made a shield in the air and could deflect the rocks. Kind of."

She rubbed her chin, almost wincing even though the bruise had been healed. "I'm not very good at it. Yet. I'm not very good at it, yet."

On the ground floor, they found Art and Tabitha waiting for them.

"Finally," Art said. "Let's go."

Zack looked around. "Where are the others?"

"Bast and Kimmy are down in the training room and Charlie's gone home already," Tabitha said.

"Already?" Zack asked.

"Yeah. I don't think she's enjoying this as much as the rest of us."

Art snorted. "Some people are impossible to please. We've been given the opportunity to learn magic. Frickin' magic! What's not to enjoy?"

"It's her choice, Art," Tabitha said, "none of us have to be here if we don't want to be, as long as we keep the Silence and the Watch."

Art shook his head in response, but didn't say anything more as they left the Tower. Walking along the Sydney streets, towards the bus stop, Art spoke under his breath to Zack, "Apparently, she didn't even spend much time with her mentor. She spent nearly all of it down in the training room. When Bast got there, she left to go home."

Zack forced his feelings down. "I think Tab is right, Art. It's her choice."

Art threw up his hands. "Whatever. She made the wrong choice, though."

CHAPTER 9

ROUTINE

Zack glanced in the direction of the school librarian as he surreptitiously manoeuvred another piece of muesli bar from his backpack into his mouth. Returning his attention to his English assignment, he rubbed his eyes with his palms in frustration. He had barely drafted the introduction, but rather than being able to focus on an essay due the next day, his mind was swimming with the latest spell Sara had started teaching him.

It was similar to the first spell she had taught him a few weeks ago, involving the transfer of Life energies between people. In this instance, however, it included maintaining a channel that allowed the energies to flow back and forth, to be drawn on by either person. The last time he had tried it, he had almost succeeded, except for the minor issue of instantly exhausting both he and Sara as the channel collapsed and the energies poured out into the room. And Sara claimed it would be possible one day for him to branch the channels and include more people.

Forget swimming. His mind was drowning in it. And in the face of this, his essay had the audacity to not write itself.

Resisting the urge to slam his laptop closed, he instead folded it with care and slipped it into his bag. He stood up to leave and noticed a familiar set of blonde curls at a table near the window. Charlie had her laptop open, but she was staring out through the glass with her shoulders slumped. Zack paused in a moment of indecision.

Taking a deep, steadying breath, he chided himself for being so ridiculous and walked over to her table. Leaning over the chair opposite her, he asked in a hushed voice, “Are you alright, Charlie?”

She turned to face him, taking a moment to focus. She smiled, but the smile didn’t quite reach her deep blue eyes. “Oh, hi Zack,” the smile faded, “to be honest, no. I don’t think I am.”

She pulled her bag off the seat next to her and he took it as an invitation to sit down.

“I’m struggling… with everything,” Charlie said. “I’m slipping behind in my school work. My friends wonder where I am these days. And I’m not even sure what I’m working so hard for.”

She glanced around and lowered her voice further. “I haven’t done anything like the others. I’ve seen Kimmy literally make fire dance and I’ve seen Bast move a coin without touching it. I’m sure you and the others are doing amazing things as well, but I can’t do anything. Maybe it was a mistake, maybe I’m not cut out for all this and I’m paying the price for nothing.” She caught her breath and met his eyes. “I don’t know what to do.”

Zack nervously reached out to squeeze her arm. “So, what’s the deal with your lessons? Not going well?”

“They aren’t going at all.”

“At all?”

“At all, Zack. Sadie, my mentor, hasn’t even tried teaching me any spells. Beyond teaching me how to sense and understand Animal energy, we sit there discussing vague philosophical concepts of what Animal is. How feline energy differs from avian, which differs from insect, which differs from fish. I’ve asked when I’ll start learning spells like the rest of you and she smiles and says we’re making progress and when I’m ready, we will. Honestly, I’ve spent more time in the weapons room lately than I have with her.”

“Does she think you’re struggling with it in some way?”

"I don't know. Maybe? I seem to be able to do everything she's asked me to do. I can close my eyes and sense Animal energy with ease. I can even tell it apart. Do you want to know how many spiders are within ten metres of you? Because I know. I don't want to know, but I do."

Zack shivered. "No, I don't think I want to know that."

"Because it's a lot, Zack. A lot!"

"Okay, I believe you."

"But that's where it's stopped. Am I wasting my time? It's been over a month now. Maybe Sadie has some sense that I'm not suited to the Animal school. I mean, I've never even had a pet. What if I'm not even suited for magic at all? Maybe she doesn't have the heart to tell me? I'm thinking about giving up."

Zack pictured Charlie leaving their strange, secret little group. No evening bus rides through the city. No late nights training in the Tower. No special moment where he used his healing magic in front of her and earned her love. He felt the urge to make any argument he could to convince her to stay, to persist. But instead he said, "You should do what's right for you, Charlie."

Her eyes widened in surprise and perhaps with a little bit of hurt.

He then realised his fingertips had been brushing her arm through the whole conversation and jerked his hand back, holding it up in a gentle defence. "I'm not saying I think you're not cut out for it. You're smart, you're focused, you know terrifying statistics about local arachnids," he was rewarded with a smile, "but this has to work for you. Nobody is making you stay. As long as you maintain the Silence and the Watch, Junie says there's nothing else required. You don't have to do anything you don't want to do."

"And that would be okay with you, I mean all of you? If I walked away?"

"Doesn't matter what the others say, it's not our call. It's yours. And if you walk away, I don't think you'll be burning any bridges or anything. You can come back as easily."

Realising how physically close they had become due to their

whispering, he was hit by a wave of awkwardness and tried to relieve his tension. "Of course, by then I might be a master of the healing arts, performing miracles around the world."

Charlie cracked a brief smile and tucked her messy hair behind her ear.

The bell rang, marking the end of lunch and they moved to gather their bags. Before picking hers up, she threw her arms around him in a hug. Caught unprepared, he froze and she pulled away before he could return the embrace.

"Thank you, Zack. I think you're right. I've been trying to work out what I should do, rather than what I want to do."

As they were leaving the library, Zack thought of something. "Also, Kimmy and Bast may be making it look easy and Jackie is doing well, but I think you're closer to the rest of us than you think."

"Really?"

"Yeah. I haven't been taught much and I can't do any of it well. Tabitha's the same. And then there's what happened with Art this morning."

"What happened?"

"Well, the first spell Art's been taught is about implanting fear in another person's mind and he's not really getting it."

"That's a bit creepy. No wonder he's struggling."

Zack shook his head. "Oh, no. He thinks it's awesome. But he's struggling with pulling it off. Specifically, or so he says, with getting it into somebody else's head."

"What do you mean?"

"As he explains it, he can create the 'fear' but then he's got to push it out. This morning in Maths, without really thinking about it, he must have tried. He's been pushing himself a bit hard on it. Anyway, he created the fear, but didn't do anything with it and dropped it into his own mind by accident."

Charlie's eyes grew wide. "What happened?"

"He had a massive panic attack and ran from the room."

Charlie burst into laughter. "That's so mean of me. Poor Art."

"Honestly, I think he's happy he didn't piss himself."

She laughed again as they walked off to class together.

Zack flinched in sympathy as Bast lunged at Jackie with a thrust designed to skewer her kidneys. Art tilted his packet of corn chips in an offering gesture to Zack as they watched from the wall. Bast wasn't holding back, and while the blunted tip of the long training rapier would have prevented any serious damage, it still would have hurt. His aggression showed a certain level of respect for his tiny opponent.

Jackie responded with a sharp muttering and a wave of her hand. The blunted point of the blade struck against an invisible force in the air, deflecting it to her left. She had made four similar magical parries now and Bast had yet to land a strike against her.

"She's getting good at that," Zack said to her brother between chews.

"Yeah. I don't think I want to play the slap game with her anymore. It might break my hand. And it's not the only thing she can do."

"No?"

"No. Two nights ago, she locked me in my room."

"Wait. Your door doesn't have a lock, does it?"

"No, it doesn't! But right before I went to bed, she appeared at my door grinning like the evil goblin she is. She shut the door and I could hear her chanting her dark magic. So I go over and try to open the door to see what she's doing, but I can't. The door won't open. I could hear her laughing her arse off."

"How long did she leave you in there?"

"Until she opened it the next morning."

Zack looked over at Jackie, his mouth dropping open, before he erupted into laughter, spitting corn chips into the air.

"It's not funny, man. I had to piss in a glass! Like a prisoner in solitary."

"Yeah, I'm pretty sure prisoners don't have a computer with internet access and a queen sized bed in their cells. Anyway, what did you do to Jackie to bring it on?"

"Who said I did anything to her?" Art asked.

Zack responded with a single, silent eyebrow lift.

"Fine. I may have snuck into her room last night and given her nightmares."

"Dude!"

"I know, I know. But there's a limited number of people I can practice a fear spell on. Nobody is exactly lining up to be a guinea pig."

"Well, I'm on her side, mate. So get used to pissing in jars for a while."

"I promised I wouldn't do it again and she let me out last night."

Two more deflected lunges and Jackie put her hand up, asking for a rest.

Bast theatrically saluted her with his blade before reversing it and walking over to join her. "That was deadly, little sis. I didn't stand a chance."

Between breaths, she grinned. "Thanks, but I think you would have if we continued. It may be effective, but it's so tiring."

Zack walked over to them. "Do you want to keep going?"

She nodded. "I can't though. I'm done."

"Maybe not," he said. "Can I try something?"

She hesitated for a moment. "Sure. If you're sure."

"As sure as I can be. I've been practicing this and I think I've got it down." Concentrating and rolling his mouth around the words he had been taught, Zack reached, holding his hand over Jackie's chest, less than an inch away. Drawing the Life from inside him, he visualised it flowing from his body, down his arm and out towards her, feeding her Life's hunger. A deep ache spread through his body, as if he'd been up late, perhaps after a day of standing on his feet and after a few more moments, he stopped.

Jackie's eyes lit up. As if testing herself, she bounced on the balls of her feet, from side to side. "That's incredible! Sword up, Bast. Let's go."

Zack slumped back down next to Art as the sparring continued.

"How do you feel?" Art asked.

Zack sighed. "Exactly how I should be after doing that, exhausted. And hungry." He stole a few more chips.

"I was hoping you'd want to go a few rounds."

"Thanks to that spell I basically did, but give me 20 minutes or so, I might be up for a light round."

Art stood up, handing the almost empty packet to his drained friend. "Suit yourself. I guess I'll have to go get humiliated by one of the statues then."

He walked over to the sword rack and chose a large broadsword. He swung it a few times to test the feel of the grip. "Commander, if you would be so kind, I would like a sparring partner."

"Certainly," came the response, and a suit of European plate armour sprang to attention, retrieving a wooden training sword before approaching its young combatant. Art was acquitting himself respectably against his metallic opponent and Zack conceded the hours his friend had been putting in over the past few weeks were paying off. And he further conceded he would have to do more of the same if he were to keep up. Feeling too tired to stand up, let alone train, he concluded: tomorrow.

Zack reached the bottom of the staircase and spotted Kimmy standing by the door, speaking with a tall, thin, dark-skinned man in a loose, casual suit. Zack hesitated, not wanting to intrude, but Kimmy saw him and waved him over without interrupting the flow of conversation.

"The important step is to learn to combine them both together. It really is key. If you throw some magic as instinctively in combat as striking with your weapon, then you will be truly formidable."

Kimmy nodded. "Zack, this is Ramesh. Ramesh, Zack is one of us newbies."

"Hello, Zack. Pleasure to meet you. To which school have you been called?"

"Uh, Life. And nice to meet you too," Zack looked closer at the man. Indian, he guessed, by the name and the accent, with features that hid his age. He guessed late thirties, perhaps early forties. "And you are in the Fire school, with Kimmy?"

"Oh, no, no. It is the Earth school for me, but the elemental schools tend to interact a fair bit. I've also seen Tabitha around the Tower quite a lot, but I've yet to meet the rest of you."

Zack nodded, but then thought for a moment. "How many are in the Tower?"

Ramesh looked a little confused. "Right now?"

"No," Zack said. "I mean, how many people are connected to the Tower?"

"Oh. Well, that would be hard to say. There are those who simply know of the Tower, but have never really interacted with it, beyond the Silence and the Watch. They could number in the thousands, perhaps? Otherwise, of those who engage more, probably around four hundred, maybe five? It is hard to say."

"We haven't seen many people beyond the mentors and a few others."

"Ah, and you wouldn't. You are at an intense stage of training, I would expect. I remember my early days with the Tower. I was so thirsty for knowledge. But you progress to the stage where you will need less and less time with your mentor. You'll find you return to the Tower infrequently, coming back only to undertake missions for it, or to collaborate with others. Anyway, you look like you were getting ready to go and I will not keep you. A pleasure to speak with you both," he smiled at Kimmy and then strode off up a nearby stairwell.

Kimmy made a sour face once he was gone. "Perv."

Zack's eyes widened. "Sorry?"

"Not you, dope. Him. Ramesh. He's been trying to lure me down into the training room with him for like a week now. I think he's angling to see me in my shorts."

"Are you okay?"

"Yeah, yeah. But thanks for interrupting," she smiled at him, "anyway, you're still up for tomorrow, right?"

Zack nodded. "Absolutely. I think we're all coming."

Kimmy rolled her eyes. "At least she comes to weapon training with us on Saturdays. It's pathetic."

There was no mystery as to who 'she' was and Zack couldn't help but defend her. He spoke with a low voice. "She's trying. I think her mentor's a bit rubbish. She hasn't even been trying to teach her spells, apparently."

Kimmy snorted. "I know, she's told me. My money is that it's a test. And Charlie is failing. If she was truly dedicated, she'd push through."

"Either way," said Zack, "at least she's coming tomorrow."

"Actually, I'm afraid none of you will," a voice interrupted. Zack and Kimmy turned to find Junie approaching with Tabitha. "I was about to inform Tabitha, but I can tell the three of you. Tomorrow, the Tower will be engaging in a powerful ritual. When we do this, it weakens the barriers between the Tower and the other realms, increasing the potential for breaches. During this time, only those who are deemed able are permitted in the Tower. I have spoken with your mentors, as well as the Commander and none of you are quite ready yet."

Kimmy looked ready to offer rebuttal, but Junie pushed on. "Some of you are close, very close. But you are not there yet. Before the next ritual, I'll speak to you all. Some of you will likely be ready by then and your service to the Tower can truly begin. But enough, it is Friday night in Australia, isn't it? Go and enjoy yourselves."

Kimmy scuffed her feet as the three left the Tower and entered the Sydney evening. "That sucks. I'm totally ready!"

Tabitha laughed and Kimmy looked at her harshly.

Tabitha held up her hands in defence. "I'm sorry Kims, but ready for what? You don't even know what it involves."

"Whatever. I'm sure I'd be ready for it," but then she smiled, "so, I guess we've got tomorrow free all of a sudden."

"How about everybody comes to my place?" Tabitha said. "I think it would be good to spend some time together away from the Tower. My parents are away and Victor's moved out. We'd have the place to ourselves."

Kimmy's face lit up. "Party?"

Tabitha shook her head. "Well, I was thinking just the seven of us. We could order some lunch. Vent a little about the Tower and school and stuff and spend the afternoon chilling out."

Kimmy nodded. "And then after that, party?"

Tabitha looked a bit hesitant. "Well, I'm not…"

Kimmy squealed. "Party!"

"A small one," Tabitha said.

"Sure, sure." Kimmy furiously tapped at her phone with a big smile on her face.

"Are you sure, Tabs?" Zack asked.

Tabitha smiled a look of resignation. "Yeah, I'm sure. But you're all helping clean up."

CHAPTER 10
HOUSE PARTY

Art pushed in between Zack and Bast as the teenagers crowded into Tabitha's kitchen to watch Kimmy perform. She had expressed her disappointment at finding both the stove top and the oven itself were electric rather than gas, but she had persuaded Tabitha to let her light a small fire with some paper towel on the stovetop, under the exhaust fans. The kindling flames grew as Kimmy chanted, gesturing with an outstretched hand.

Zack couldn't tell if anything was happening, but Jackie clapped.

"She's beautiful, Kimmy," Jackie said.

Zack didn't know what Jackie meant, and peered closer. He realised the shape of the flame had formed into a rough silhouette of a woman, and that she was swaying from side to side, as if dancing. More murmurs of appreciation joined Jackie's, until the paper towel rose into the air and floated into the kitchen. Kimmy's chanting ceased and so did the fire's feminine form. The friends pushed against each other in an attempt to flee the moving fire.

Bast burst into laughter and ceased his own quiet chanting as the ashy remains of the paper towel fell to the floor.

"Jerk," Kimmy and Tabitha shouted, almost in unison.

"I'm sorry, but I couldn't help it," Bast said with a smile, "as if I'm going to let Kimmy be the only one to show off."

Out of the range of the exhaust fan, the last of the burning paper had produced smoke that, while far from filling the kitchen, was also far from pleasant.

"Well, if nothing else, you've given me a chance to show the one thing I've learnt to do, so far," Tabitha said.

She too, started chanting, moving her fingers in a rapid pattern. The smoke dissipated until even the smell of it was gone.

"That's pretty cool," Zack said.

"Yeah, I know it's not much," Tabitha said, "Junie's teaching me a few more things at the moment, but this is really the only thing I can do. Anyway, who's next?"

Zack hesitated. Charlie stood in silence at the edge of the group, trying not to make eye contact with anybody.

"I've learnt a new one," Jackie said.

She closed her eyes and muttered some words, flexing her fingers almost as if she was typing on something. When she opened her eyes moments later, nothing noticeable had happened.

"It's okay, Jackie. I still fail at mine a lot," Bast said.

"Oh, I didn't fail." She rested one hand on the countertop and in one smooth motion, pulled a knife from the nearby block and plunged it down into her hand.

The six older teens shouted and Art lunged towards her, trying too late to stop her.

Jackie looked up laughing and Zack stopped his shouting. Where her bleeding, wounded hand should be, there was nothing, not even a scratch.

Art's face was tight and red. "Don't ever do that again!"

Jackie's eyes narrowed and the timid girl disappeared, replaced by an angry young woman. "Don't do what, Art? Practice my magic? While you're going around scaring people, I'm learning how to protect myself. And others. And one day it's going to be my job to protect you. So get over it!"

The kitchen was silent, until after a long moment, Art exhaled. "Fine. Fine. But Jeebus, Jack, give me some warning next time."

She smiled and stuck her tongue out at him. "Your turn. Who are you going to scare?"

"Well, I'll have you know I've recently perfected a new one, but I do need a volunteer." Art looked around and found no willing participants. He turned towards Zack and raised his eyebrows in question.

"Oh no. I still need to do mine. I don't want to be shaking off whatever you do to me," Zack said.

"Fine. Do it to me," Bast said with a sigh.

"Awesome, Bast. Thanks," Art held out his hand towards Bast's head, moving his arm in a slow circular movement while he chanted. Not unlike with his sister, the effects of his magic weren't immediately evident, until Bast spoke.

"Uh… whuh… whuh do to me?" he slurred.

"I reduced the rapidity of firing between your synapses," Art said with a smirk.

Bast's face furrowed in concentration. "Whuh you say?"

"I lowered your brain's speed."

Bast's face furrowed further.

"I made you stupid."

"Oh! Me no like," grunted Bast.

"Awww, I think it's sweet," said Kimmy, caressing the bespelled boy's cheek. "How long is he going to be like this?"

"It shouldn't be long," Art said, "I'm still not great at it. But while we wait, I think Zack's next."

"Zack's last," Charlie said, "I don't have anything to show. Unless you want to know how many spiders are under us right now."

Her friends stared at her in wide-eyed horror.

When nobody spoke, she gestured to Zack to have his turn.

"Actually, I'll try something that'll affect all of us. It… it probably won't work, but I'll try."

"What do you mean, 'won't work'?" Tabitha asked. "What'll happen?"

"Probably nothing. Nothing bad anyway. Trust me. Everybody stand still."

Zack concentrated on Art, opening a channel between the two of them. He could feel, more than see or hear, the sharp intake of breath from Art as the connection was established. He branched the channel out to include Bast. He had never achieved a split channel and as he connected with Bast, he was surprised to find he could feel the difference between his two friends; their Life had different qualities, almost like a frequency at the edge of his range of hearing. He returned his attention to the channel itself and branched it out again to Kimmy. The feeling of her distinct Life filled the channel, mingling with the others'. Sweat gathered on his forehead and arms as he split the channel even further, visualising a branching magical plumbing system connecting them to both Tabitha and Jackie. He added Charlie to the flow of webbing across the suburban kitchen and, feeling the connection click into place, he couldn't help but look at her. Her eyes widened at the sensation and Zack marvelled at how beautiful she looked. How beautiful she always looked.

Even though it was for just an instant, he had let his concentration stray too far. "Uh oh."

The channel shattered. Life energy poured out in a misty spray and everybody in the room groaned.

"What the hell was that?" Kimmy yelled.

"Sorry," Zack said, leaning against a kitchen stool, exhausted, "I screwed it up."

Tabitha lowered herself to the tiles. "It feels like I ran a marathon. What were you trying to do?"

"I was trying to connect us all, which means we could draw from each other when we're casting spells," Zack said, "but I botched it and it broke and, well, this."

"No like," Bast shouted.

Art levered himself to his feet. "Well, I know what I'm doing for the rest of the afternoon," he said as he collapsed against an ottoman in front of the television. The rest of the group followed suit, with Kimmy coaxing a distressed Bast along by waving a bag of nacho flavoured corn chips in his direction. Zack was the last to follow. With exhaustion and embarrassment battling inside him, he claimed his own small spot on the carpet, resting against the side of the couch.

He felt a comforting pat on the top of his head and he looked up to see Bast giving him a tired smile. Then Bast looked at him seriously and whispered loudly, "No again. No ever."

Zack agreed. "No again. No ever."

Bast grunted in satisfaction before turning back to the pretty lights coming from the machine in the corner.

"What are you doing in here?" Tabitha's voice dripped with suspicion.

Zack jumped and slammed shut the kitchen drawer. He hadn't heard her approach over the music booming and the growing number of party goers outside. "I'm searching for a bottle opener."

She appeared to be discerning whether the reason was acceptable and Zack couldn't tell whether she was drunk, exaggerating, or both.

"That's fine then. There's a magnetic one on the fridge," she pointed a finger at him, "but no sex in my room."

"What?" Zack fumbled for the bottle opener and it fell to the ground.

"I caught Kimmy trying to sneak in there with some random. Not okay. No sex in my room. Or my parents' room."

Zack looked over her shoulder. "Where is she?"

"Oh, I pushed them into Victor's room. Sex all day in Victor's room, I don't care."

He followed Tabitha out into the backyard where, despite the chilly June air, most of the party-goers were sitting. Tabitha moved off towards a small group of friends who were dancing around a set of portable speakers, effortlessly joining in despite the open bottle of beer in her hand.

Zack elected to return to where he'd been sitting with Art, Matt and

Bast. Tossing Matt the bottle opener, he plonked down in between him and Bast.

Matt used the opener on a bottle of boutique beer he'd nabbed from his father's stash. "Thanks, mate."

"No problem. Where's Art?"

Bast pointed across the backyard to where the tall blonde boy was talking with a girl Zack didn't recognise. She was fairly short, pretty, with neat, auburn hair. "How's he doing?"

Matt shook his head, while Bast said, "No good. He's come on too strong."

"Twenty says he gets slapped," Matt said.

Bast laughed, but shook his head. "No, he's not that bad. She'll give him one word answers until he gives up."

Zack leant back against his chair; his eyes fixed on Art's attempt at flirting. "He might surprise us."

Matt's snort made his opinion clear.

"He could," Bast said, "but he won't. He tries too hard. Girls like him fine — well, except Kimmy. But plenty of the other girls think he's a nice guy. Funny. Cute. Even I'd admit he's a good-looking dude, if it wouldn't weird him out. But the moment he turns his attention on one girl in particular, he freaks them out. He's too eager."

"He's super keen on Tabitha. He should ask her out instead," Matt said.

Bast took a long sip. "No, he shouldn't, trust me."

Zack decided to change the subject. "So, if you're such a love guru, why are you sitting here with us? Nobody else on your team here?"

"No, there's a couple. I'm not really keen for anything right now?"

"Why? What's wrong with them?" Zack asked.

Bast turned from watching Art and gave him a hard look. "Who says there has to be anything wrong? I'm supposed to be up to doori any other queer dude within reach, am I? The guy who's hung up on the one girl he can't have thinks I should be open to fooling around with anybody?"

"Doori?" Matt asked.

"Doori. Hook up. Sex." Bast rolled his eyes. "Seriously fellas, if I'm going to let you live on my people's land, the least you could do is pick up some Koori lingo."

"That's not what I meant," Zack said, "I thought that…"

"You thought gay dudes go around screwing each other at the drop of a hat? Yeah, sometimes. When I feel like it, but I don't like the stereotype. And anyway, I don't feel like it now. So, Zack, if you think one of us should be chasing some action, I suggest you get on with it. I'm drinking."

"Me?" Zack asked.

"Yes, Zack. Like Art, the girls like you. You're not bad looking, particularly with all the training…" He glanced at Matt for a moment. "…the athletics training we've been doing. You're smart and nice. But you're the opposite of Art, you don't put yourself out there at all. Stop waiting for something to happen with Charlie and go make a connection with somebody else."

"Who?" Zack asked.

"Dude, anybody. Anything would be better than you sitting here wishing for a 'one day' filled with ifs and maybes." Bast softened his voice. "I'm sorry for going off at you, mate. You pushed a button of mine and I didn't mean to hit back so hard. But I mean what I said. What about her?"

Zack looked to where his friend gestured. Another girl he didn't recognise was sitting on a seat with her back against the outside table. She had long brown hair, tied up in a ponytail and even from this distance he could see she had large, dark eyes. She was wearing jeans and a dark grey hooded jacket, with one hand wrapped around a bottle of mixed vodka. She appeared to be half listening to the conversation happening at the table, half lost in thought.

"She's pretty," Zack said.

"And she's moping around with a drink in her hand on the edge of people who are actually enjoying themselves. You're perfect for each other," Bast added, causing Matt to laugh.

Zack stood up, but found himself unable to take the first step.

"What do I say?"

"Start with your name, then ask her if she wants another drink. Work out the rest after that." Bast slapped him hard on his behind. "Now go get her, tiger!"

Matt saluted him with his bottle of beer.

Zack took a long, steadying swig from his own bottle and gathered himself. He hoped he looked as casual and confident as he was trying to be crossing the backyard. Without thinking about it, his mind moved through the mental control exercises Sara had taught him and was surprised at how effective they were at calming him. He unconsciously made eye contact with the girl and she gave him a shy smile. He smiled back.

Before he reached the table, however, he was distracted by some movement over by the gate that divided the front and back yards of Tabitha's house. Charlie was slipping out of the party with a bottle in her hand. The back porch light caught her face and he could see that she looked upset.

He hesitated for a short moment, but made up his mind. He gave the girl a nod in a passing greeting and he hurried after Charlie to see if she was okay. He wasn't sure if he imagined or could hear a groan from where Matt and Bast were sitting.

Zack closed the gate behind him. Charlie was already on the footpath outside the front yard. "Hey, Charlie. Wait up," he called out.

"Oh, hey Zack," she said as he approached. "I felt like going for a walk."

"Are you okay?"

"Yeah," she said, "I don't know. I needed to get out of there for a bit."

"Want some company?"

"Sure."

They walked along in silence for a few minutes, each sipping from their bottles. Zack found himself, as he often did around Charlie, intensely aware of her presence and of where his awkward body was in relation to hers.

Zack found himself wondering if this would be easier if he had had more to drink. He was overthinking, as usual. "Did you want to talk about it?"

She was silent for a moment. "I don't know, maybe." She took a long swig from her drink. "It was hard this afternoon, you know. Watching you all master your magic while I can't do anything."

"Well, I didn…"

"No, even you Zack. Your spell may have gone wrong, but at least you were able to do something. Before it broke, that connection you made felt awesome. And I have my suspicions about whether it really was an accident, or whether you were trying to make me feel better," she said, narrowing her eyes at him.

"No, it wasn't on purpose, I promise."

"So you didn't want me to feel better?"

"No… I…"

"I'm just being a jerk, Zack. But anyway, I thought tonight would be easier, being around a whole bunch of other people who can't do magic either."

"And?" Zack asked as they turned up a side street.

"It wasn't. Like it or not, I'm not one of them anymore. They don't know about magic. So I'm not with them and I'm not with you guys. I'm in between. It feels pretty lonely."

"You're not alone though, Charlie."

"No, I know. I've got Dave. If he wasn't at work tonight, I probably wouldn't feel that bad. But even with him… I don't know. It's hard to have this big secret from him."

Zack hated that it still hit him like a fist to the stomach when she mentioned Dave. Her boyfriend was not who he'd meant when he said she wasn't alone. Zack had thought that spending so much time around her would make it easier to accept just being her friend, but it hadn't.

"Anyway, hearing about my boy problems is probably really boring. Let's talk about something else. Do you know what you want to do at uni?" Her voice held the effort of a forced cheeriness.

He decided to play along. "Still not sure. Lately, I've been thinking I might like to try for medicine. But I probably won't get the marks."

"I'm sure you will, if you want to. You've always been one of the smart ones."

Zack was glad the shadows hid his blush. They had made their way up to a collection of local suburban shops; all closed, with the exception of a Thai restaurant across the road. They turned another corner and sat down in a bus stop shelter.

"What about you? Do they run courses on Travel Journalism?"

Her face lit up. "How'd you know that's what I wanted to do?"

Zack blushed again. "Oh, I've heard you mention it once or twice, I think."

"Yeah, there are some subjects, probably under an Arts or Liberal Arts degree or something. Stuff that would make me employable as a travel agent or a writer if I get lucky. But I think I'll take a gap year first, actually do some of the travelling. That's probably the one thing that hasn't made me give up on the Tower."

"What's that?" Zack asked.

"Those doors that can apparently drop you off wherever you want to go. It would make my gap year a lot cheaper."

Zack thought about it. "It would. But you'd have to be careful what you posted online. Hard to explain how you were in Peru in the morning and Mongolia in the afternoon."

Charlie rolled her eyes at him, her voice dripping with attitude. "Duh, Zack. I'd be careful. I'd still make it look like I was travelling on a round the world ticket." When she spoke again, her voice was softer. "Actually, the real problem with travelling through the Tower is that I'd have to do it alone." She paused again. "But maybe that's for the best."

"What do you mean?" Zack asked.

"I mean I'm probably going to have to break up with Dave sooner or later. Kimmy says sooner."

Zack's heart slipped up into his throat. He took a slow breath. "It doesn't matter what Kimmy says. I mean really, she's one of the smartest people I know, but I wouldn't take her advice on relationships."

Charlie's soft laugh didn't match the tears glistening in her eyes. "Well, that's true."

"Like your choice about the Tower, you need to do what's right for you, Charlotte. Nobody else gets to choose who you love."

She smiled and crinkled her nose at him and he was struck by how close their faces were.

"Nobody calls me Charlotte."

He could see himself kissing her and, somehow, he convinced himself she might kiss him back. No, she was with Dave. Then again, she was here right now with him. But she'd been drinking. A list of opposing ideas flooded his mind, preventing him from acting, while begging him to act.

"What's that?" Charlie said, pointing over his shoulder. The moment was gone.

He was still arguing with himself when he turned his head to look through the perspex back of the bus shelter. He caught a glimpse of something slinking through the late night gloom. Zack would have called the dark form a wolf if he was not presently in suburban Sydney. But, while not a wolf, as it stepped out into the illumination of a streetlight, it revealed itself to be the largest dog he had ever seen. He had always been uncomfortable around dogs, particularly large, lupine ones like this.

He spoke under his breath to Charlie, "Slowly, let's move out the way we came."

"No," she said.

Remembering she'd mentioned she had never had a pet, he thought she might also be a little bit scared. "It's okay, if we walk away slowly and don't make eye contact…"

"No," she interrupted, "there's something about her."

"Her?" he asked.

"Yeah, her." Her eyes widened. "Why do I know that she's a 'her'?"

She stood up and walked towards the approaching canine. Zack followed, still unsure but willing to trust Charlie's instincts. They came closer and it showed how large this dog was. Charlie wasn't tall, but this dog, perhaps a Husky or a Malamute, was easily past her waist while on all fours. Both Charlie and the dog stopped, less than a metre away from each other. Charlie stood as if unsure of what to do next and the dog likewise appeared unsteady, sniffing the air. The dog leapt forward.

Zack hesitated, and by the time he had reached for Charlie to try and pull her back to safety, she had stepped forward. He stared in horror as the dog lunged with her mouth towards Charlie's face. Charlie laughed, falling to her knees, as this strange dog, tail wagging happily, licked at her face. Charlie, in turn, affectionately rubbed at the dog's head and ears.

Charlie broke the embrace for a moment, turning to Zack with tears in her eyes. "She's mine, Zack!"

Zack still couldn't make sense of what was happening. "But you said you didn't have…"

"No, I don't. But somehow she is. I know she is."

The dog looked questioningly at Zack, assessing him with a pair of too intelligent eyes. "He's a friend," Charlie said, "Zack."

The dog's body language changed and she nuzzled up to the legs of the still intimidated Zack. "Uh, good girl. What do you think this means?"

Charlie was smiling so hard Zack thought she might hurt her cheeks. "I don't know, but I know she's mine. And I know I'm hers. I think I need to go speak to Sadie tomorrow."

"Well, good luck getting that thing on the bus," Zack said.

The dog growled at him.

"I don't think she likes being called a thing, Zack."

"Sorry! Does she have a name?"

Charlie thought for a moment. "Hmmm… how about Max? How's that?"

"Short for Maxine?"

"Yeah," Charlie grinned, "Max and Charlie. What do you think, girl?"

The newly named Max barked happily in response.

"Well, it's settled then," Charlie said.

Zack sat back down at the bus stop and watched as Charlie and Max played together in the shadows between the streetlights. The two chased each other through the trees of a small suburban park, stopping regularly for Charlie to throw her arms around Max's chest, or for Max to lick Charlie's cheeks with saliva and enthusiasm. Zack was left babysitting Charlie's drink while finishing his own. He couldn't help but smile. It was like Charlie and Max had known each other all their lives, but had been apart and were now catching up for lost time.

CHAPTER 11
GAIN

Zack rubbed his right temple in a futile effort to relieve his headache. He was grateful a bit of pain and nausea were all that remained of the hangover he had earned the night before. Half an hour of meditation, using some techniques Sara had taught him and life had almost been worth living again. No amount of meditation, however, could protect his delicate stomach from the rich smells of meatloaf and baked capsicum his aunty had prepared, so he had retreated to sit beside his grandmother as she slept.

He stared at the text in his lap, the reading guide to Antony and Cleopatra, before closing it and tossing it aside. He wished it was as simple to toss aside his worry about his upcoming end-of-year exams. The lure of his magical study and the weapons training regularly overpowered any efforts to focus on his more mundane academics. Worse still, the more time he spent practicing magic, the more time he pretended to be studying his school work. Come exam time, the gap between the amount of work he had been doing and the amount of work his parents thought he was doing would be stark. And if he didn't do well in his exams, his parents were going to ground him. How would he be able to keep going to the Tower when he wasn't allowed anywhere but school and home? This week, he promised himself. Starting tomorrow, he'd set aside time each day for school work. He remembered making that promise a few weeks ago, too.

He turned his attention to his grandmother. Like in the weeks before, he extended his awareness over her, seeking her Life and then the Life of her slow assassin. He could make little sense of the interaction between the two, but they were there, locked in a glacial war. She stirred in her sleep, a soft groan of pain escaping from her lips. He pulled back from the sites of the conflict and observed her Life more generally. With his growing sensitivity, he could sense her fatigue, caused by the medicines that held her symptoms at bay.

Zack knew what he had to attempt. What would be the point of being able to do what he could do, however limited it may be, without using it to help her? He closed his eyes in concentration and sought out the Life within himself. He whispered the strangely rhythmic syllables Sara had taught him and reached out to his grandmother with both his right hand and his thoughts. The Life began to flow and the nagging throb of his headache increased. The pain pulled him from his task and reminded him of the previous night; the image of Charlie and him playing with Max in a moonlit playground, began to form. Aware of the danger, he forced his mind away from the thoughts, focusing on the words and the patterned movements of his fingers. He could feel the Life flow down his arm and into his grandmother.

He had not drawn too much, but his body ached from the exertion and the pain in his head tightened. He relaxed back in his chair. It was so easy, he reflected, for his thoughts to stray, even if for a split second. He had always been distractible; a dreamer, his mother would say. Magic required such dedicated focus and he struggled often to keep his mind clear of multiple thoughts. His mind went to Charlie; it was particularly challenging when the thoughts were so pleasant.

"I know that smile," said a soft, amused voice from the bed.

Zack half jumped and turned to see his grandmother looking at him with a smile of her own. "Hello, Babi," he said.

"Who is she?" she asked.

"Who do you mean?" he asked.

"The one who put that smile on your face, Zacharias. It looks just like your father's did." She winced as she attempted to sit up in her bed. Zack stood to help her, but she waved him off. "I can do this."

"Are you okay?"

"I am sore, and I am dying, but I am okay. I'm afraid there will be no dancing today, though. Never get old, Zack. It's not fun. Stay young, stay smiling about pretty girls."

"Can I bring you anything?"

"A cup of tea?"

"Sure."

Zack left the room, almost floating with the thrill of his success. He found his mother talking to one of his older cousins in the doorway to the living room. "Mum, Babicka would like a cup of tea."

"Oh Zack, you didn't wake her, did you? She needs her rest."

"The boy didn't wake me, Vanessa!" his grandmother called out from her bedroom.

His mother shook her head as she entered the kitchen. "That woman's hearing is ridiculous."

Zack's grandfather, a look of slight worry on his face, moved past Zack into the bedroom. Zack waited outside while they conversed in Czech. He didn't speak any Czech beyond some food names, but occasionally his grandparents would use some English words and it seemed they were discussing whether his grandmother needed more painkillers. The discussion ended with his grandmother shouting at his grandfather, who left the room with his hands up in surrender. His grandparents had always argued like this and Zack noticed a smile on his face as he walked past.

Throughout the rest of the afternoon, Zack's family members sat with his grandmother, taking advantage of the rare reprieve from her near constant fatigue, but as the sun started to set, her fatigue returned and they left her to rest. Zack was the last one out of the room, with the excuse of collecting his school bag. He took a moment to listen to her drift to sleep and kissed her on the forehead.

"I'm not done yet, Babi. I'll find some way to beat this."

Zack and Sara were discussing the nature of poison and its effect both on the body and on Life for half an hour. Beyond a small amount of supervised practice of the magic she had already taught him, most of their lessons lately had become theoretical. Despite her assurances these lessons were a necessary step towards new and more complex magic, he thought of what he'd seen some of the others accomplish and he couldn't help but be frustrated by his lack of progress. He was dwelling on this and realised Sara had said something to him that he hadn't heard.

"I'm sorry, Sara. I was thinking of something else."

She tutted. "You were distracted, as usual. But despite this, what I said still stands. I said I have indicated to Junie you are ready."

"Ready?" he asked, although he was hopeful he had understood.

"Ready to serve the Tower. Sometime later this week, or maybe next, you'll meet with Junie alone. She'll test you on your magic, your weapons and on your readiness in general. If she is satisfied, you will be able to begin your service."

"What does service involve?" Zack closed the text he had opened on his lap and tried not to fidget.

"Nothing overly exciting at first, but it's a start. Your earliest duties will likely be to join in guarding the Tower during one of its rituals. The Tower occasionally engages in activities that require powerful magic. This could be to enchant an object, interact with another realm, or a number of other things. As I've said more than once, the more powerful the magic, the higher the risk. Magic that powerful weakens the barriers between the Tower and the other realms, and in doing so, increases the risk that magical entities from those realms breach their way into the Tower. Against that possibility, those who are not involved in the rituals directly are engaged to stand guard."

"What was your first service like?" asked Zack, his mind swimming with fantastical images.

"Terribly boring, I'll be honest. Breaches are incredibly rare and even when they do occur, they keep the novices on the furthest edges. I stood guard three times and saw nothing. Still, I was paid regardless."

"We get paid?"

"Absolutely. Which was just as well, really. La'Lune had found me lodgings and some employment in Lyon, in France, but between my studies with the Tower, my difficulties with French and my low level of education, it was always a struggle to make ends meet."

Zack averted his eyes. His family wasn't rich, but they'd always had more than enough and he struggled to imagine what it would be like to always be wondering whether you could afford to get through the week. He changed the subject. "So when did you first actually do something in service?"

"It was on a different kind of duty; an excursion. I was accompanying a number of other novices in pursuit of a breach. The breach was deemed minor enough to send us rather than a more experienced group. A more powerful response could always be dispatched if we failed, but the Tower does not believe in coddling. We are all that defends our world from chaos and that defence must be tested and tried.

"The breach occurred in rural China. Five of us were given the responsibility of tracking down whatever had invaded our world and destroying it. We exited the Tower in Beijing, bluffed our way into the countryside and spent two days hunting down the creatures. A pair of harpies; half woman, half bird flying monstrosities. We destroyed them, burying their remains as deeply as we could, before returning to the Tower."

Zack was dissatisfied with the lack of details. "What was the fight like?"

She laughed at the question. "Mostly fought by the others. I did manage to cut one of them along her leg as she attempted to pick me off. But the true fighting was done by the others. Your role will be similar to mine. Stay back, stay calm and support the others as they need it. You'll have to leave the glory for those with more violent magic than Life.

"In truth, I can't remember much from the fight. We didn't find the harpies; they found us. It was frantic and brutal and in the end they were dead and I was doing my best to bandage up my allies."

"Were they okay?" Zack asked.

"Eventually, but injured enough that it took us a lot more time to sneak back to the Tower than it might have. Service is dangerous. It is why we learn the magic we do, especially Life magic. But it is also necessary. Think of the damage those monsters could have done had they found prey less suited to destroying them."

Zack nodded, his eyes wide.

"Do not worry. Your first service will be like mine and everybody else's: uneventful. And you will complain with your friends about how boring it was, while I will be glad. But go now. Prepare yourself as best you can. Junie will let you know when and where to be for your assessment. Good luck, Zack. I'm sure you'll be proven ready, as long as you keep your focus."

Zack was seated on a school bench eating his lunch with Art, Bast, Kimmy and Tabitha. He looked around to make sure none of the others were nearby and caught himself in the thought.

'Others'? Is that how he thought about Matt, Dave and the rest of their circle of friends who weren't involved in the Tower? The answer was clear and immediate: it was. He could easily rationalise the thought, but that didn't alter how guilty it made him feel. Surely friendship was more important than what he was doing with the Tower. But his lessons and training consumed every spare moment and, since Sara had recommended him for assessment, almost every thought. That was what he was hoping to talk about with his friends. At least those that weren't 'others', he brooded to himself.

"So, um, have any of your mentors said anything about your progress lately?" Zack asked, still unsure about where he was in relation to their magical development.

Thankfully, he could depend on Kimmy to have less tact.

"You mean Junie testing us to see if we're ready? Yeah. My mentor told me last Wednesday he'd recommended me. I'm still waiting for the actual test, though."

Bast's face relaxed in relief as he joined the conversation. "Patrick only cleared me last night. Prick said he'd thought I was ready for a while, but he didn't want me to embarrass him in front of Junie."

"Timur gave me the go-ahead last week as well, but I haven't had my test either," Art said.

"Maybe they're waiting to test us all at the same time?" Kimmy said.

"Nah," Art said through a mouthful of ham and cheese sandwich. "Jack's weirdo mentor gave her the green light on Thursday and he said she was ready earlier, but he'd been waiting for someone else to pass Junie's test first. Safety in mediocrity or something, I don't know."

"Well, who's passed then?" Kimmy said, her voice trailing off as she looked at the obvious candidate.

Tabitha had been sitting quietly and turned a shade of red. "Yeah, okay, I passed a couple of weeks ago."

"Why didn't you say anything?" Kimmy asked.

"None of you did," Tabitha said, "except for Zack, the rest of you were keeping it quiet. Then after I passed, Junie told me not to. And before you ask, no, I can't tell you anything about it. She made me promise."

Kimmy and Art opened their mouths to protest, but Tabitha cut them off. "It wouldn't do you much good, anyway. It's different for each school."

Bast was about to say something, but shut his mouth at the sight of Matt approaching. He was doing his best to run while juggling a sausage roll and a can of lemonade and he looked worried. "Art… Jackie's…" He paused for a breath.

Art shot to his feet. "What?"

Matt sucked in some more air. "Jackie's been cornered by those girls. Outside the science block."

"Right." Art's face clouded over and he set off at a sprint, tossing the rest of his lunch to the ground.

"I'd better tag along," Zack said to the rest of them and chased after his friend.

They ran together until they found Jackie. A group of half a dozen girls were standing in a semicircle around her, while she stood back from them, staring down at her feet. They hadn't made it close enough to hear what the girls were saying to her before Art roared at them.

"Hey skanks! Why don't you piss off?"

Despite being a few years younger than Art and Zack, the girls barely paid him any notice.

"Oh look, your pov brother is here to rescue you. Or is it his turn to use your shared backpack?" the ringleader of the girls said.

Zack decided to name her Britney.

Art moved closer to them. "I'm warning you, back off!"

Zack noticed Art's wrist twitch and he grabbed onto it. "Don't, mate."

Britney laughed. "You going to hit me? At least if you get expelled, you can find a job cleaning floors and double your family's income!"

Zack looked down at Art's fingertips. Faint purple light, almost invisible in the sunlight, gathered.

"Art!" Zack squeezed his friend's hand.

"What are you all doing out of bounds?" The teacher on duty, Mrs White, had likely been attracted by Art's shouting and was taking short shrift of a group of children in an out-of-bounds area. "All of you, out of here or I'll be holding you all back after school."

"Sorry, Miss," Britney said, "we got caught up talking after class."

Mrs White responded by crossing her arms and raising her eyebrows.

Britney smiled sweetly to everybody and led her companions away.

Art guided Jackie in the other direction. As Zack let them pass so he could follow a few steps behind, he noticed the tear stains down her cheeks.

After they had turned the corner, Art asked her, "Why do you let them get to you?"

Jackie's voice was part sadness, part anger and all distress. "'Let them', Art? They used to be my friends. I told them everything. For years. Now they use it all against me!"

Art tried to pull her into a hug. "It's okay. It's okay. I understand."

She pushed away from him. "How could you understand? When dad lost his job, you had him," she said, pointing at Zack. "You had him and I had them. I don't seem to remember Zack laughing, throwing bread crusts and apple cores at you 'in case you were hungry'. Leave me alone."

Art let her storm away and he and Zack walked back to their bench.

After a few moments of silence, Art said, "I thought it would get better, you know? Dad got another job. I think we're actually better off than before. But those girls, they've decided to make Jackie their victim. And she's perfect for it. She's smaller than the rest of them. She doesn't fight back or speak out. She just takes it. I almost wish you didn't stop me."

"You were going to use magic on them?"

"I was going to give a few of them enough of a scare to wet themselves."

"And how would we explain that?"

"It's not like teachers would believe I'd cast a spell on them."

"I don't mean to them; I mean to Junie."

Art looked deflated. "Well, there is that. One day though."

CHAPTER 12

TESTING

Zack rounded the corner onto Milton Street and paused for a moment to catch up with his thoughts. He stared across at the unassuming office building that was the Sydney entrance to the Tower. His heart rattled against his chest as the anxiety of the test he was about to undertake threatened to overtake him. He forced himself to cross the street and enter.

The antechamber was empty and, as he stood waiting for Junie, he distracted himself by looking around the room. His eyes were drawn to the stone walls and the sconced torches, and he remembered back to that day, almost four months ago, when they'd all walked into the Tower for the first time. Had it only been four months? It felt like a lot longer.

"Welcome, Zack."

He jumped, spinning around at the sound of Junie's voice. "H- Hi, Miss Junie."

"It's just Junie, Zack. Nervous?"

"Y- yes." His mouth was drier than he could remember it ever being before.

She smiled at him as she approached. "Zack, relax. I'm sure you'll do well. Sara is an astute judge and she wouldn't have put you forward if you weren't ready. And even if you're not quite ready, there's no real consequence to failing; simply train a little harder and we'll look at you again next month."

Zack appreciated Junie's attempt, but the idea of being the only one of his friends to fail spun his stomach like it was in a washing machine. He imagined facing them as a failure and being on the receiving end of an awkward mix of pity and sympathy. He took a deep breath and wrested control of his thoughts.

Junie smiled again and nodded. "Follow me."

She led him down to the training room. The room was empty except for the two of them, and the Commander and his warriors, standing silently at attention at the opposite end of the training floor. Junie moved to sit on one of the benches and, at her direction, he took his place beside her.

"As Sara has told you, the Tower offers its members an opportunity to serve. Regardless of the specifics of the task, the purpose of the service remains the same: protecting our world from the destructive effects of magic. Service is not compulsory. Like training, like any involvement with the Tower at all, it is truly voluntary. But service is rewarded."

Zack nodded. "Sara mentioned you pay us."

"That's true. But that is only the beginning of the reward. Service offers you an opportunity to prove yourself. Without service, your mentors will soon limit what they are teaching you. And service is also a way to rise within the Tower, gaining positions of importance. But before any of that, I need to determine whether you're ready.

"And understand this: if you succeed, you will be judged an active member of the Tower. You will receive no special treatment. Regardless of your age or your junior standing, you will be expected to complete the tasks you have been assigned, whatever the risk and whatever the cost. There are no safety nets or training wheels; the world cannot afford a coddled Tower. That is why this test is so important. After this, you're all in."

Zack's eyes widened at the gravity of Junie's words.

"We don't assign anything to you we don't think you can handle and your training will continue. In many ways, it never stops. But the risks of service are real. They are real, because the risk to our world is real. This life is an exciting adventure filled with great reward, but it is first and foremost a responsibility to the seven billion people with which we share our world."

"I understand."

"Excellent. Let's begin. First, we will test your understanding of magic. What is magic?"

Zack sat quietly, thinking about his answer. Junie showed no sign of impatience at his silence and he took that as a sign a considered answer was desirable. He framed his answer a few different ways in his mind before settling on what he hoped was the right one. "Magic is a force, a kind of almost intelligent energy, that exists outside our world and seeks to enter it."

"And if it succeeded?"

"Then it would result in chaos, distorting the way our world works and destroying our way of life."

"Can magic ever be harmless?"

Again, Zack paused, biting back the answer he immediately knew was wrong. "No. While we can learn to use it for positive ends, the magic itself is always dangerous."

"Good, Zack, very good. You are right, magic is always dangerous, and where it cannot be controlled, it must be destroyed. Now, we will test your ability with magic. Take a moment to compose yourself. You may sit, stand, whatever you like, but your task is to show me the most complex magic you are capable of."

Despite having expected and prepared for this aspect of the assessment, Zack's heart raced. While most of his practice with Sara was conducted sitting down, he found sitting on the bench sideways from Junie a bit awkward so instead he stood, directly facing her. He closed his eyes and began to focus when Junie interrupted him.

"Sorry, Zack. What are you about to attempt?"

He looked at her in confused panic. "I thought you wanted me to show you what I had learned?"

"Yes, but before you cast it, I'd like to know what to expect, please."

"Of course. Sorry. I'm going to draw Life from all around us and pour it into you. It should feel refreshing."

She nodded. "Proceed."

He closed his eyes again, using Sara's techniques to calm his rapidly beating heart and push away his distractions. They were all still there; the fears of failing the test, the worries about school, the excitement of serving the Tower. But for the moment, they were to the side, and all his focus was on his Will, drawing Life from the air around him. Opening his eyes, he gathered it together into a single source. He then reached out with his awareness to find the edge of her own Life and connected the two. He could feel it click into place and the gathered Life surged forward into his assessor.

Junie's smile reached her eyes. "Okay, then. That leaves one last element: combat." Raising her voice, she called down the room. "Commander, could you please provide a partner for our candidate?"

"At once, mistress."

Zack sighed in resigned horror as the familiar bronze samurai collected a wooden sword and strode across the room towards him.

"Can I have a moment to rest, Junie? The magic took a bit out of me."

"I'm afraid not, Zack. You will rarely step into battle fully rested and I'd like to assess you in the same form. Please go and select your preferred weapon and then join your opponent in the centre of the room."

Zack moved towards the weapon racks. He had suspected some kind of combat would be part of the assessment and he had given hours upon hours of thought to what weapon he would choose. He had practiced with a variety, and often used swords as he sparred against Art and Bastian, both of whom preferred them. However, when he was being honest with himself, he wasn't sure he could stab anything when it counted. He worried this might make him seem unready or unable to serve the Tower, but he moved down the line of racks and pulled down his chosen weapon, a quarterstaff.

Junie said nothing as he approached his metal adversary. He stopped a few paces from the samurai and they exchanged bows.

"Begin," Junie said.

Zack stepped back into a fighting stance. The wood of the staff was slippery in his sweaty hands and his feet were clumsy as they moved into position. The statue leapt forward, swinging its wooden sword towards Zack's ribs. He gave an awkward push with the centre of his staff, blocking the blade half an inch from his body. The statue followed up with a high counter swing and Zack managed to duck underneath it.

Focused on the battle, Zack managed to find his balance and parried the samurai's attacks again and again. His own attacks were also deflected by the statue's blade and, as his arms grew heavy from both fatigue and the constant impact of the training sword, Zack decided to take a chance. When the statue next attacked, he faked a parry and, instead, stepped inside the arc of the statue's swing. He shifted his grip lower on his staff and swung hard. The end of his staff thumped solidly against his opponent's back and he had a brief moment of elation.

Then the wooden training sword struck him in the side of the head and he fell to the ground.

He lay there for a moment, his head ringing in pain and disorientation. When his vision cleared, he forced himself to his feet and found the statue returning to its place among the others. He moved back to where Junie was waiting for him, leaning heavily on his quarterstaff to make the short distance. She gestured for him to sit.

"Are you in a well enough condition to discuss your assessment?" she asked. "That was quite the hit to the head."

Zack nodded and then immediately wished he hadn't and grunted in pain. "I'm fine, really."

"Okay. You expressed a strong understanding of the threat that magic poses and your ability with Life magic shows good promise."

Zack could hear the 'but' beginning to form and his heart sank.

"But your skill in combat needs work. Your footwork is a bit clumsy and you need to spend more time practicing different grips with your staff. Not to mention that you should have been ready to block that hit to the head you took at the end there."

Zack was so lost in his disappointment; he almost didn't hear Junie continue.

"I expect you to keep practicing until your first service."

"Sorry?" Zack asked.

"You passed, Zack. Welcome to the Tower."

"Sorry, what?" Zack had been staring at his potatoes, lost in thought and hadn't heard what his father said. It had been two days and he still didn't think he'd properly come down from the relief and elation of passing the test.

"Can you pass the sweet chilli sauce?" his father repeated. "What's with the goofy grin?"

Ellen snorted. "He's had it on his face for days. My guess is some girl has let him touch her…"

"Ellen!" their mother half shrieked. "I don't even think Zack has a girlfriend."

Ellen rolled her eyes. "I didn't say he did, I'm saying…"

Zack interrupted. "No, it's nothing like that. I, um, did really well in a test this week."

The big smile on his mother's face made him regret his impulsive answer and he silently berated himself. Again and again, using school as a cover, he kept building his parents' expectations. And his mother quickly confirmed this.

"Well done, Zacky. I can't wait to see your end-of-year results. All this work you're putting in is going to pay off. If only somebody else would follow your lead," she finished, pointedly glaring back at Ellen.

"It's first year, I'm doing fine," Ellen said. "I'm managing to actually have a life. Not staying back every night studying. And I've got myself a job, not like this moocher."

"Well, I kind of picked up a job, too." Zack grabbed at the opportunity to explain away any income service to the Tower would grant him. "It's not really constant or anything, tutoring some of the juniors here and there. Cash in hand."

His father nodded at him in quiet congratulations, far too wise to jump into the latest argument brewing between the two women in his life.

His mother opened her mouth to continue the argument, but seemed to think better of it. "Okay, okay. Your father and I are proud of you both. It's Friday night. What do you say we crack open a board game or something?"

"Can I have a glass of wine?" Ellen asked.

Their mother stared back at her. "Fine."

"Then, yes. I'm in. As long as it's not some boring Euro game trash."

"Okay, you can pick it," their father said, holding up his hands in surrender.

Zack honestly didn't care what game it was. It had been a good week.

CHAPTER 13

GUARD DUTY

Bast's leg was bouncing so hard it was shaking the whole bus seat. Zack didn't bother saying anything; he was nervous too. He'd been so caught up with his own worry that, for the last ten minutes, he'd thought it was the regular vibration of the bus. He glanced around the aisle and, unsurprisingly, found all of his friends lost in their own thoughts; they all had more than enough reason to be anxious.

Zack had been the last to pass Junie's test and they were all ready and willing to be called. But over a month had passed with no word, until two days ago, when Junie had given them notice they were to be called into service.

Across the aisle from Zack, Art and Jackie sat with visible tension between them. They had been in a constant argument as to whether she could participate. It had only ended when Jackie had threatened to lock Art in his room and leave him behind.

The group was so lost in thought, they nearly missed their stop and it was only prevented by another passenger also needing to disembark. After they shuffled down the steps of the bus, the teenagers were pulled from their introspection by the sight of Max bounding out from behind some fencing to greet Charlie. Zack wasn't sure how, but Max never failed to meet Charlie here, despite the distance the dog would need to travel.

The group of friends milled for a moment before Kimmy took charge. "C'mon guys, we can't be late for this."

They followed Kimmy, without further discussion, over the threshold and into the Tower. Junie was standing in the centre of the antechamber, appearing to give instructions to a group of three people Zack hadn't seen in the Tower before. She acknowledged the youths with a brief nod of her head and directed the trio up a stairwell.

Junie approached them, spreading her arms wide in a calming gesture. "It's okay to be nervous, but you will be fine; we wouldn't have allowed you to be part of this if we thought you were not ready. You'll be guarding one of our storage rooms, down three floors using those stairs. It's quite a distance away from the ritual's epicentre, so it's unlikely anything will happen. But we leave nothing unguarded."

"Guarding it from what, exactly?" Bast asked, sounding more unsure than Zack had ever heard before.

"Any unwelcome visitors. Which means *any* visitors at all. When the Tower engages in powerful rituals, it weakens the barrier that protects our world. Think back to that evening so many months ago, in the alley. There is a small chance a breach like that could open up. Your job is to defend against anything that breaches the Tower. Retreat if you must, send for help if you must, but anything that enters the Tower must be destroyed."

"You mean killed?" Charlie asked.

"Potentially. But remember, magical beings aren't alive, not really. It's magical energy that mimics life and that mimicry is seeking to enter our world and infect it with chaos and destruction. If you don't think you can do this, tell me now. I'll have to rearrange things a little, but it can be done."

"No, we're all in," Kimmy said.

"Kimmy," Tabitha said, "you can't speak for all of us."

"But we are all in. We said we'd do this and we're here. We're in."

Everybody murmured in agreement with Kimmy.

"Good," Junie said. She gave them directions to the storage room.

"On your way, stop by the training room and arm yourselves."

The Commander was supervising another group of Tower members when the teens entered the room. Each of them left with a short blade.

One, a young man with his hair pulled back in a ponytail, paused by Jackie on his way out. "You'll be fine, little Jackie. You must remember what teacher Smith has taught you. Endure." He bowed slightly to her.

Jackie bowed back with a little awkwardness and he left to catch up with his companions.

The Commander's voice boomed in greeting as they approached. "Welcome, recruits. You have all been found passingly adequate. Congratulations. I am confident you are unlikely to stab yourselves or one another with these weapons so, please, choose from among the racks."

Despite the words, the golem's voice sounded genuine and enthusiastic as it gestured towards the weapons.

Art and Bast strode straight to the sword racks, as Zack had suspected they would. Slightly self-consciously, he moved towards the staves and pulled one down. Art approached him, broadsword in hand, and looked with amusement at the weapon Zack had chosen.

"A staff? Really?"

"I'm a traditionalist. If I'm going to be a wizard, I've got to have a staff, right?"

Art laughed. "Fair enough."

As they were joined by Bast and his rapier, the three boys turned their attention to the girls. As always, Zack's eyes were drawn to Charlie. Her hair today was pulled back in a messy ponytail and she was shouldering a quiver of arrows to go with the curved bow she had selected. Tabitha and Kimmy were comparing a light chained flail and a light, wicked-looking axe they had each, respectively, chosen. And that left Jackie.

"I am sure I have a shorter one for you," the Commander said, its voice a mixture of genuine support and undisguised disdain.

The young girl gripped the spear that was only a little taller than herself. "This one is fine, thank you. I've been training with it."

"Yes, of course. It would, however, reflect poorly on me if it fell on you."

Jackie rejoined the group rather than continue the conversation and Kimmy once again took charge.

"Okay, let's go."

Halfway down the stairs, Bast broke the silence. "Who was that guy that spoke to you before, Jackie?"

"His name is Shige," she said. "All I know is that he's from Osaka. My mentor discourages us from sharing personal info."

Zack thought for a moment. "His English is pretty good."

Art laughed. "He wasn't speaking English, Zack."

"What do you mean?"

They reached the bottom of the stairs and Kimmy led them down a corridor.

"Don't you think it's strange how everybody here speaks English, and is really fluent? Despite everybody coming from all over the place?"

Zack realised he'd taken it for granted. "Yeah, I guess."

"It's Mind magic. None of them speak English. Well, a lot of them probably do, I guess. But in here, whatever language someone is speaking, you hear it in your native language." Art looked pretty pleased with himself. "I thought it was obvious."

"Maybe if you've been studying Mind magic. I kind of assumed everybody knew English," Tabitha said.

"I guess. Even Junie isn't speaking English, I don't think. I can sometimes feel it around the edges when somebody is being translated. Timur, my mentor, says one day I can learn to hear both at the same time."

"Sounds lame," Kimmy's voice was flat, "I've been learning to light things on fire with my mind. Anyway, we're here."

The door opened easily into a large, dark room. Despite the gloom, it was clear there were hundreds of boxes and crates in the room.

"It's a bit dark." Charlie peered deeper into the room.

Kimmy pulled a lit torch from the sconce in the corridor. "There should be more torches along the walls inside. We can light them with this."

Art couldn't resist. "Why don't you light them all with magic, oh mighty pyromancer?"

"I could," Kimmy said, "but then I might be too tired to blast whatever monster shows up. What are you going to do? Read them some Dutch poetry and give them bad dreams?"

Bast had already begun lighting some of the torches inside the room, and the gloom was fading fast. "Will you two quit it? We need to focus."

"Fine."

"Whatever."

Everybody joined in lighting the torches and soon the large room was illuminated.

"What do we do now?" Charlie asked.

"I guess we wait," Tabitha said, lifting herself up to sit on one of the large wooden crates.

"This one's got clothes in it too," Art said.

"What kind?" Zack asked.

The teens had been waiting around for what might have been half an hour and a mixture of nerves and boredom had driven them to explore the room. So far, they had found several boxes of clothes, a few with camping equipment and one large box filled to the brim with different kinds of blank paper.

"I don't know. But it's kind of fancy." Art pulled some coloured silk garments out of the crate.

"Stop it." Jackie's voice rose with a sense of urgency.

"Relax, Jackie, I'll put it back."

"No, not that. Something's coming... something dangerous." She had one hand on her right temple. The other six teens stopped in immediate silence. Even Max seemed to sit more attentively.

When nothing happened, Art asked, "Are you sure?"

Jackie's closed eyelids were crinkled from the strain. "No? Yes. There." She snatched up her spear and pointed with it to the far wall opposite the door. They all looked in response. Nothing was evident, at first, but then a familiar grey light flowed from what may have been a thin crack in the wall. Like a gravity defying liquid, or perhaps more like a stain, it flowed out unevenly from the crack until it was roughly a metre in diameter.

They all followed Jackie's example and readied their weapons. Kimmy, Art and Bast crept towards the breach. A creature emerged, stumbling out of the grey. It was roughly the size and shape of a toddler or a large monkey and its face was similarly in proportion. However, there the similarities ended, as its skin was covered in coin-sized earthy red scales with tufts of coarse black hair sticking out randomly. On its head were two stubby horns and it had a matching pair of stunted wings sprouting from its back. It peered around the room, squinting its beady yellow and black eyes against the light.

"It's kind of cute," Tabitha said. "Ugly. But that cute kind of ugly. Like a sphinx cat."

"Junie said to destroy anything that came through." Kimmy hefted her axe.

"Yeah, but we were expecting a monster or something, weren't we?" Bast argued.

"Hang on a sec." Art inched forward, reaching out with his arm and probing with his Mind magic. "I'm not sure it's hostile. The strongest feeling I'm getting from it is that it's frigh..."

His sentence was cut off as the creature leaped at him, the jagged claws on its hands gripping onto his left arm, cutting into his skin.

"Ahhh!" Art screamed. "It's hostile! It's hostile!"

Kimmy and Bast ran towards him to help, but when Art caught sight of Kimmy raising her axe to swing in his direction, he screamed louder and spun away from her.

"Guys, there's more," Charlie shouted, as several similar creatures spilled through the breach into the storage room.

"What do we do?" Jackie asked.

Tabitha whirled her flail. "What Junie said: Destroy them!"

"Okay then." Charlie released an arrow into the small pile of creatures that had tripped over each other on their way out of the breach. The arrow pierced one in the side and it fell limp to the ground.

Bast still attempted to help an uncooperative Art. "Stand still, dude."

Holding his arm out still and closing his eyes tight, Art obeyed and Bast thrust his rapier through his friend's attacker. The creature ceased clawing at Art's arm and he was able to shake it free. Blood dripped from numerous cuts, but Art took a breath and turned his attention to the growing number of horned invaders.

Bast closed his eyes for a moment, tracing and chanting rapidly. As two of the creatures approached, his attention faltered and his right arm spasmed outward, his rapier clattering to the floor. He took a deep breath and another step backwards and tried again. This time, his attention held and as his gestures flowed, his body sped up. Moving with supernatural speed, he snatched up his fallen rapier and faced off against the approaching creatures.

Kimmy screamed a wordless battle cry and charged at the growing group of creatures regaining their senses in front of the breach. She swung her axe with both hands, cleaving down through the shoulder and into the torso of one of the diminutive attackers, felling it instantly.

"Fall back, Kimmy," Charlie shouted, "you're in my shot."

Kimmy ignored her and raised her axe for another blow. Rather than retreating from the deadly blade, the creatures surged forward to attack, leaping at her with claw and fang. They screeched as, instead of finding soft flesh, they crashed against an invisible wall.

Art shot his sister a glare. "Oh, you'll protect Kimmy, but not your own brother."

"Shut up and help her," Jackie's voice was strained, "I can't keep this up forever."

Art and Tabitha ran forward to help Kimmy, but they were forced back against the growing number of creatures. There were at least ten in the room now, and one more was in the process of coming through the breach. Zack stood, unsure of what to do. Fear of getting in the way, as well as of leaving Jackie alone, kept him where he was.

Kimmy and the others had stepped back far enough that Charlie was able to start firing arrows again, and the creatures spread out to engage the defenders. Art and Bast fought against two creatures, both focussing on defending themselves against two pairs of razor-sharp claws. A few metres away, Tabitha and Kimmy had each defeated their own single opponents and traced and spoke the words that would call magic to their aid. Kimmy finished first and a column of flame flowed from one of the sconces and became a swarm-like ball of fire, moving towards the invaders. However, as Tabitha finished her own incantation, a narrow but strong gust of wind picked up and Kimmy's flames were blown sideways towards some of the wooden crates. Whatever Tabitha's intent, chaos ensued as the crates caught fire, and one of Charlie's arrows was blown aside by the indoor gust.

"What are you doing?" Kimmy screeched.

"Sorry. I'm sorry." Tabitha's hands flurried about in a second incantation, ending her spell.

The creatures took advantage of the disorder and gathered themselves to attack. Evil laughs filled the room as a full dozen of them swarmed forward. Jackie shielded Bast and Art, who took advantage of the protection and slashed about with their blades. His broadsword gripped in two hands, Art brought his full strength in a single swing. The brutal attack decapitated one of the creatures and sliced through into another's chest. Next to him, Bast used his magical speed to good effect. Stepping to the side of one of his opponents, he thrust his sword through its body before he could turn to face him.

Zack fidgeted with his grip, trying to ready his staff, when one of the creatures leaped down at him from the top of the crates. He swung his quarterstaff down hard, striking the creature in the skull and it crashed, lifeless, to the floor. Zack noted, in thoughts detached from the moment, the sickening way its bones had crunched from his blow, but his attention was brought back to the room by the sight of yet more invaders crawling through the breach.

"I can't keep these shields up for much longer." Jackie steadied herself against a crate.

Zack took a step back so they were side by side. "Hold still."

He traced his fingers through the air and focused on the arcane words he had been taught, allowing their strange phonetic patterns to distract him from the real threat of harm in the room. Life flowed from him into Jackie and his muscles ached in fatigue. He was quick to break the channel, worried about rendering himself useless in this fight, but hopeful he had given her enough.

"Thanks, Zack." Jackie returned her attention to the fight, deflecting as best she could the invaders' attacks. Despite her best efforts, deep scratches could be seen on most of the defenders. Zack, Jackie and Charlie remained unharmed, the latter only because of the faithful protection of Max, who leaped forward to bite the throat out of the one creature who had dared threaten her human.

Kimmy fought her way to the burning crates and, despite the dangerous creatures gathering in the room, turned her back on the fighting to focus on another spell. Tabitha followed her, swinging about with her flail in an effort to keep the creatures at bay. The flail's head crunched against the neck of one of her foes, but another took advantage of her exposed flank to leap at her. Jackie's magic protection prevented the creature from sinking its fangs into Tabitha's neck, and it bounced off, hissing in frustration. Behind her, Kimmy used her magic to draw heat from the flames, extinguishing the crates before the fire could spread further.

Zack noticed three more of the creatures climbing on nearby crates and, as they launched themselves at Jackie, he threw himself at her, knocking both him and Jackie to the ground. The creatures' leaps took them over the pair and they landed on all fours, skittering to a stop on the ground. One of the creatures pointed towards the unguarded door out of the room and chittered to the other two before the three fled towards the exit.

Zack scrambled to his feet. "They're escaping!"

Bast and Art both rapidly incanted, while Charlie aimed, drew and fired. Bast's magic flared orange and one of the creatures fell to the ground, where it lay thrashing in an attempt to regain its feet. However, Art's spell had no obvious effect and Charlie's arrow thudded into the edge of a crate, missing its target.

The creatures had finally stopped entering through the breach, and Art and Bast flanked those that remained against Tabitha and Kimmy. Attacked from all sides, the invaders fell to blade and flail.

Jackie shot Zack an angry look and scrambled up to run over to the fallen creature by the door. On its back, it flailed at her with its claws and she thrust her spear through its chest, killing it.

Regrouped, the youths raced through the door after the two escapees. They stopped, surprised, finding one standing calmly in the hallway, staring in fascination at one of the torches on the wall.

"What's it doing?" Tabitha asked.

"So it did work. I hit it with my stupid spell." Art laughed before turning toward Kimmy. "I mean, it's no Dutch poetry…"

Kimmy stepped past him to the creature, killing it with a sweep of her axe. "Quick, let's find the other one."

They ran along the hall and up the stairs before coming to the first landing. "Which way now?" Bast peered down the branching paths.

"I don't know!" Kimmy replied, frustration clear in her voice.

"But I bet Max does," Charlie said, "c'mon buddy, which way did that thing go?"

Max lowered her head to the stone floor, sniffing all around until, with a single bark, she bounded up the stairs. Charlie led the others behind her. Upwards and upwards, they climbed. If Max was indeed on the trail, the creature hadn't strayed from the stairs, which suggested only one thing.

"It's heading for the exit," Bast said.

Two more flights of stairs and, panting, the teens reached the entrance room. Max followed the scent straight to the shadowy exit before Charlie called her back.

"What do we do now?" Art asked.

Before any of them could answer, a heavily accented voice called out from across the room. "Miss Kim, how did you fare?"

The group turned to see a middle-aged man striding towards them. He did not wait for an answer, gesturing at the light cuts most of them bore. "It appears your duty was not uneventful."

"No, Master Cho, it was not. A breach opened and lots of creatures swarmed in and attacked us."

Master Cho's face betrayed no reaction. "Describe these creatures."

"Small, about waist height." Kimmy gestured against her body. "Little wings and horns and covered in red scales."

Her mentor nodded. "An 'imp', I believe. It is hard to say, the magic can take many similar forms, but this one is relatively common. It is chaos given form, if on a minute scale. Did you defeat them?"

"Most. Nearly all of them," Art said.

The man did not take his eyes off Kimmy. "Most?"

"All but one," she said, "we think it escaped."

"Then your duty is not yet complete. Find it. Destroy it. Complete the Watch. Ensure the Silence."

"But couldn't it have come out of the Tower anywhere?" Tabitha asked.

He turned to face her. "Potentially, but most likely, it will end up where you all came from. Australia, yes? Its encounter with you will have imprinted that upon it, and these imps aren't intelligent enough to direct the doors. Now, enough questions. Go."

Kimmy turned and moved to the exit. The others hesitated a moment before following.

Master Cho cleared his throat and the teenagers stopped and turned back to him.

"I have not visited Australia, but I understand large medieval weaponry is not commonly carried around in public?"

They looked sheepishly at each other as they placed their weapons against the wall.

"How are we supposed to kill it?" Art asked.

"I do not care. Think of something." And with that, he turned and walked away.

CHAPTER 14
PURSUIT

They exited the tower, blinking in the glare of the late winter sun.

"Where to now?" Zack asked.

Charlie knelt down by Max. "How about it, girl? Can you still smell it?"

The dog yapped and explored the footpath outside the office façade. It wasn't long before Max barked once and moved in a particular direction. They followed; eyes peeled on their surroundings for any sign of the imp.

"So that was your mentor, Kimmy? Seemed like a bit of a jerk," Art said as they followed the trail.

"Actually, he's great," Kimmy said, "he treats me with respect."

"That didn't seem like respect," Zack said.

"Well, it does to me. He treats me like an adult. No coddling. Clear expectations. I like it."

"Good, that's good," Zack said.

"So what do we do when we find this thing?" Jackie asked. "Surely somebody has seen it by now."

"First things first," Tabitha said, "we need to find it. Then, as quickly and quietly as possible, we destroy it. After that, we can track backwards and try and clean up any mess with witnesses or evidence. But the longer it's out here, the harder that will be."

Max was taking them down along a major road, past shops and office buildings.

"I think it's going to be okay," Zack said.

"Why?" Art and Kimmy asked at the same time.

"Assuming Max is leading us the right way," Zack said, and was met by Charlie's questioning eyes. He continued. "And I think she is. Then nobody around here is reacting like they've seen a small monster running along the footpath. Look around."

The footpath outside the shops was filled with shoppers and other pedestrians and, as Zack said, nobody was behaving out of the ordinary.

"That's a good point," Tabitha said. "But that still leaves us with how we deal with it when we find it."

"I think Bast and Art hit it with the same thing they hit the other ones with," Zack said. "Trip it over, make it stupid. Neither of those spells look too flashy. Then we jump on it. Even if we wrap it up in Art's jacket."

"Hey!" Art said.

"Good plan," Kimmy said over the top of him.

Max and Charlie stopped at the doors to a three-story shopping mall.

"According to Max, it went in there," Charlie said.

"Oh no," Jackie said, "Max isn't allowed in there."

Charlie gave her an evil smile. "Sure she is. You leave that to me."

The others shared a doubting look as they followed Charlie and Max into the building. The dog stayed on the trail and they had rounded two corners when a security guard strode towards them.

"Excuse me, what do you think you are doing?"

"Shopping?" Charlie said.

"No pets allowed. You'll have to leave or tie it up outside."

"She's not a pet. She's my assistance animal," Charlie said.

The guard looked sceptical but unsure. "You don't look blind…"

Charlie raised her voice in outrage. "Did I say she was a guide dog? She's a seizure dog. I have epilepsy and she's able to sense a seizure coming and help me manage it. Or do I need your permission to have a potentially lifesaving animal by my side?"

The guard looked like he wanted to be anywhere else but there. "Well, no, that's quite alright, well, have a nice day." He strode away, pretending to answer his radio as he went.

Once he had gone, the others turned to Charlie in shock.

"Deadly, Charlie," Bast said.

She blushed and Zack found it hard to swallow.

"I'll admit," she said, "I've been thinking about how to get Max into places like this for a while. This seemed the best option. I hoped if I got frantic enough, they wouldn't ask to see any evidence. Anyway, we need to keep moving."

They hurried along behind as Max led them to a quieter corner of the centre, narrowing down the location of the imp to one of four shops.

"There are too many people around," Tabitha said, "there's no way we can do this subtly if it's actually in one of those shops."

"What if we get the place evacuated?" Kimmy asked.

"How? Even if we find a fire alarm and pull it, they'll probably come check it out before they evacuate."

"I'm not suggesting a false alarm," Kimmy's evil smile made Charlie's earlier one look saintly. "give me some cover and get ready."

The boys stood in a tight circle around Kimmy, making it hard to see the gestures that accompanied her quiet chanting. After a moment, a fire sprang to life on a bench across the concourse. The plastic bubbled and melted, carrying the fire along towards an indoor plant. In moments, smoke and flame were evident to all. Shoppers shouted and screamed and the teenagers joined in the call, urging people to flee. Charlie asked Max to follow the imp's trail again and, as their canine tracker led them into a video game shop, the centre's alarm system sounded the evacuation alert.

In the store, one startled staff member, maybe a year or two older than the group of friends, stood in indecision.

Kimmy and Tabitha shouted at him. "Run! There's a fire!"

He complied, stumbling out into the smoke.

"Okay, let's be quick," Charlie said, "it's got to be in here somewhere."

The group stepped into the store and spread out. Zack found himself, once again, painfully aware of how unprepared he was. He had no magic or weapon that could protect him. All he had was… Life.

"Hold on," he said, "everybody stand behind me."

Closing his eyes, he concentrated on Life. Straight away, he could feel his own and his friends' behind him. He narrowed his focus to the store in front of him, probing into the room. There was something else there. It was strange, unlike anything he'd felt before, but he was certain it was there. He opened his eyes and pointed in the direction of the service counter.

"It's over that way."

Bast and Art flanked around the counter, eyes scanning for a sign of the imp, ready to use their magic to subdue it. When they reached the counter, they glanced around before looking back at Zack.

"There's nothing here Z," Art said, "are you sure you…"

Before he could finish the sentence, a plush toy in the shape of an Italian plumber leaped off the counter and bit into his arm.

"Ahhh! Not again. Not again." Art screamed.

Bast snatched up a short metal rod from near the register. "Hold still, mate."

"You hold still." Art shouted, slamming his arm and his attacker down against the countertop. "Get. Off. Me."

With a screech, the plush toy fell to the ground and Bast brought the heavy pole down on its head. He struck it twice more before being satisfied that it was dead. The plush form rippled and returned to the shape of an imp.

"Oh thank god," Art said.

"What?" Zack asked.

"It was the imp. I was worried we had evil toys coming to kill us as well."

"Well go on," Kimmy said, "wrap it up in your jacket."

"The hell I will."

Tabitha pulled down a branded duffle bag from the wall. "Stick it in this."

"But that's stealing," Jackie said.

Tabitha laughed. "Jackie, we've committed arson, vandalism and violent assault. I think we'll be fine."

Art manoeuvred the imp's body into the bag before zipping it shut and throwing it over his shoulder. "Okay, one more stop before we go."

"What do you mean?" Bast asked.

Zack had followed his best friend's thoughts. "There are cameras all over this place, and after this strange fire, they'll be looking at them closely. We need to go to the security room and fast."

They all agreed, and set off running through the smoke, pausing for a brief moment to study the map at an information kiosk, before making their way straight to the Security office.

"How are we going to do this?" Zack asked.

"Get the girls to distract them for a few moments and I'll handle the rest," Art said with a confidence Zack suspected he didn't quite feel.

The door to the room was open as they approached and two guards were monitoring the evacuation through the monitors and over the radio.

"Help! Help!" Kimmy ran forward into the room. "There's so much smoke!"

The guard was forced to hold her by the shoulders as she ran towards him.

"It's okay, but you all need to make your way to an exit."

"We can't find an exit. We got so lost," she wailed.

Zack thought Kimmy was overdoing it a little, but the guards didn't seem suspicious. Then he noticed the second guard staring at the monitor with a blank expression on his face, pawing at the screen and a moment later, the guard speaking to Kimmy had the same look on his face.

Art stepped forward, speaking to the two guards. "Okay boys,

I'm the new boss. Head office sent me down and I need to use the computers, alright?"

The guards nodded. "Okay, boss."

"Good, good," Art sat down at the terminal. "Awesome! They're still logged in. I was worried I'd have to try and get a password out of them after doing that."

"So you didn't really have a plan?" Kimmy narrowed her eyes.

"Sure I did and it's working. Now leave me alone. I need to concentrate."

While Art focused on the terminal, Zack found himself standing next to one of the security guards. He looked into his dull and confused eyes.

"Loud noise," the guard said.

"Yes," Zack said, "loud noise. But it'll be over soon."

"Good. Don't like loud noise," said the guard.

"Yes. I'm amazing." Art stood up. "Today's recordings are wiped."

"Well done, Art." Tabitha said.

He blushed. "One more thing to do, everybody be ready to run."

He turned back towards the guards and incanted. The guards looked at him in confusion and, as he finished, each slumped a little.

"Okay, let's get out of here."

They all turned and fled through the smoke, towards the nearest exit.

Bast asked, "What did you do to them?"

Art grinned. "I wiped their memories."

"Completely?" Tabitha asked.

"Oh definitely not. I couldn't come close to that if I tried. I got the last ten minutes though. That should be enough."

"Awesome." Zack clapped him on the back.

The teens were feeling buoyant as they made their way back to the Tower. Junie and Master Cho were waiting for them as they entered.

"Did you find it?" Junie asked.

"Bast killed it." Art held up the bag.

"After Zack found it," Bast said over the top of him.

"Well, Max found it," Zack added.

Junie held up her hand. "Not all at once. Come and sit down and we can debrief with a little more decorum."

They followed Junie over to a small seating alcove and she motioned for them to relax. Taking a comfortable chair for herself, she invited them to describe their encounter. They explained, each occasionally talking over the other, while Junie listened with intent and without interruption. When Art finished by detailing his actions with the security guards, Junie gave a nodding approval.

"Very well done, Art. You've all performed well. I will admit there were more breaches than we expected today. That happens sometimes, but it often stretches our capacity to respond. I've seen the storeroom and you held yourselves impressively against the numbers that came through. It's disappointing one of the imps managed to push past you, but understandable. And from what you've said, you did particularly well cleaning up that error, including removing any evidence. The Silence and the Watch have been well served today."

Zack couldn't help himself from smiling at the praise and he wasn't alone.

"This was your first service and you don't need me to tell you that you have room to improve. Keep training, keep practicing and also take time to consider how to work with each other. Your mentors will want their own debrief next time you meet with them, but for now, go and enjoy your reward." She reached into her bag and pulled out a bundle of envelopes, passing them out.

While they interrogated the contents of the envelopes, Junie waved over Kristian, an old German man Zack had met a couple of times while studying with Sara. Kristian was not very talkative and he moved among them, using Life magic to close their scrapes and cuts. As Kristian turned his magic upon Zack, he could not help but follow the flow of Life, feeling the intricate way Kristian guided and focused it on his scrapes and bruises.

Zack bowed his head towards Kristian. "Thank you."

The older man bowed in return and left.

"Your reward is not limited to those envelopes," Junie stood. "The more you prove yourselves to the Tower, in both ability and trustworthiness, the more the Tower will share with you. Continue your service and you will have access to a world you can only begin to imagine."

And with that, Junie left the young mages alone. Zack laughed and realised he felt almost drunk. One by one, the others joined in until they were all laughing uncontrollably. In the space of an afternoon, they had fought monsters from another dimension, chased one through a shopping mall, setting fire to it in the process and now they each had hundreds of dollars in their pockets.

"Big day," Zack said.

Still laughing, they rose and left the Tower.

CHAPTER 15
EXCURSION

"The realms of magic surround us."

Junie lectured to the seven seated teens in an upper room of the Tower. Zack glanced around, seeing his friends transfixed to their Tower liaison and wished he could find his teachers at school as interesting. The end-of-year exams were approaching in a determined march and he still struggled to apply himself when there were more interesting alternatives.

"They are varied and beyond count, perhaps infinite. Some seem to flitter and change and it is difficult for us to understand anything more than the basics of them. However, some are stable and 'close' enough for us to find with regularity. The home realm of those imps you defeated is one such place. And it is where you will be going in a few moments."

Zack's hand sweated against the smooth wood of his quarterstaff and most of his friends were also fidgeting in nervous anticipation.

"We travel to these realms for a variety of reasons, but most commonly it is to increase our understanding of the threats we face and of magic itself, and it is an important part of your education that you become accustomed to travel between the realms. Your trip today is a training exercise, but keep in mind the dangers are real.

"The realm you will travel to, in many ways, is not unlike our own.

Physics works more or less the same and, to a lesser degree, so does Chemistry. But in other ways, it is vastly different. There is no life here as you would recognise it, no recognisable ecosystem or life web. It is a vast and violent hellscape, home to imps… and worse. For that reason, the Tower has labelled this realm 'Hades.'"

"Is it safe… for us to go there, I mean?" Zack snapped his mouth closed, feeling foolish.

"No, it isn't. But you will be accompanied by a more experienced member of the Tower. And you are not to venture too far from where we open the gate. Go in, look around and, if you are threatened, return. Erik will be your guide." She gestured to a man leaning against the wall to her right. "He has been in Hades a number of times."

Everything about this man screamed 'viking'; he had a tall, strong build, an immense light brown beard and he was holding a large battle axe. The impression held when he spoke in a deep Scandinavian accent.

"Pleasure to meet you all. Do what I say, when I say it, and we'll all be fine."

The teens nodded. Zack was too anxious to voice any of his questions.

Junie nodded to another woman standing nearby who approached the bare wall the teens had been facing. The woman incanted and traced the air with her fingertips.

Bast's eyes widened and he turned to Junie. "That's Movement magic!"

"It's very advanced Movement magic." Junie fixed Bast with a stern stare. "And you are not to attempt anything of the kind until you are far further into your studies."

Bast stood silently with the others as a swirl of familiar grey light appeared on the wall in front of the chanting woman. The swirl grew to a size that two people could walk through in comfort before it stabilised and the woman stopped chanting.

Junie motioned for the group to approach. "Go now and familiarise yourself with the realm. Be back within two hours. If we are forced to close the gate before then, hide nearby and wait."

Erik led the party forward through the gate. Zack's stomach lurched as he emerged, as if he had ridden on the most violent of roller-coasters. He steadied himself and looked around to get his bearings. The gate had opened on an elevated position, allowing a view out over the strange world. In every direction there was the same dusk coloured, gritty rock, with no sign of vegetation or soil. Above them hung a black sky, devoid of stars.

"If it's night, where is the light coming from?" Tabitha asked.

Erik shrugged. "Different realm, different rules. Look around, you barely have shadows."

The teens looked down and saw it was true. Although, as they moved, it was possible to see the faintest of silhouettes from all sides, as if there were many sources of light.

Erik pointed at an outcrop of boulders in the distance. "Let's go and explore over there. That looks as likely a spot as anything." He strode down the rocky hill.

Charlie caught up to walk along next to him, with Max bounding along beside her. "What exactly are we looking for here?"

"Some fun, I hope. There's bound to be some little beasties around," Erik said with a smile.

"I thought we were supposed to go back through the gate if we found monsters," she said.

"No. The key word was threatened," he patted the blades of his axe. "It'll take a bit to threaten me."

"Is it safe for us to leave that gate-thing open?" Bast pointed back.

"For us? Yeah," Eric replied as he walked. "You're the only Movement mage with us here, as I understand things. And I take it from Junie's comment that you don't know how to open them?"

Bast nodded.

"Even if you could, the Tower is so warded against breaches that only the most powerful could open one from here. Which means we've got two choices. Leave it open, or they shut it and open it for us at some agreed time. That second one is the fallback, but I'd rather not be stuck here waiting with a bunch of rookies. But don't worry, we won't be here long and we won't go far."

"You seem a bit relaxed for somebody travelling through Hell," Tabitha said.

Erik laughed. "It's not Hell, newbie, even if it looks a bit like it. Yes, travel far enough in any one of these directions and you'll come to a river or lake of lava; spend too long here and that chalky taste you have in the backs of your mouths will start to burn. But it is just another place. It's your first time, but after you've stepped through the grey a few more times, you'll be relaxed too. If you remember to keep that one safe, you'll be fine."

Zack blinked in surprise when Erik pointed at him. "Why me?"

"Because you're our Lifer, friend. Our medic. We keep you safe, you keep us up and fighting, everybody gets home with most of their parts."

Zack's stomach flittered. "Um, Junie did tell you I don't actually know how to heal yet, right?"

Erik shrugged. "Minor details. Let's keep moving."

The teenagers exchanged glances and followed along. After a few minutes, they reached the boulders.

"Let's hold up here," Erik said.

"Why here?" Art asked.

"Two reasons. First, we can still see our way out from here. It's your first time, so I don't want to let that gate out of my sight. Second, we might get lucky and run into some smaller creatures here. There's no real food web in Hades, or if there is, it's a messy one. Everything is food for everything else. As a result, smaller creatures spend their time hiding in places like this, with crags and little hidey-holes, preying on each other or waiting for an opportunity to attack something bigger."

"Like us?" Jackie asked in a squeak.

"They might try. But they never gather in numbers large enough to worry us. The temptation to feed on each other gets too high."

Bast cleared his throat. "You're not joking about this air. It's rank."

Erik nodded. "And it'll get worse."

"I could probably clean up a little bit of the air," Tabitha said, "but it wouldn't stay clean for long out here in the open."

Jackie looked thoughtful. "Maybe I could do something about that."

Without further comment she moved to stand in the middle of the group and chanted. A ripple of light sprang from her hands and poured up and out in every direction before falling to the ground, creating an all but invisible dome.

"Nice, Jack, but what is it?" Art asked.

Tabitha reached out around herself with her hand. "I can feel it. It's some kind of air barrier, keeping toxins in or out. That's awesome, Jackie."

Tabitha cast her own spell, weaving her hands around in front of her. Nothing was visible, but before long, Zack could smell the difference. The air inside had been cleaned.

Erik smiled. "Well done, girls. Okay, back to our reason for being here. All of these realms work on a different set of rules to ours. Sometimes it's obvious and sometimes it's not. It's up to each of you to use your senses, all six of them, to recognise the differences as soon as possible. It can be the difference between surviving and not. Try it here. The way the air feels and tastes, or did, at least. The way sound echoes. The way the ground feels beneath you. And above all, stretch out with your magic. How do the Air, the Earth, the Life around us feel? I can tell you from my own, the Water here is sparse, and where it is, it's putrid."

Each of his friends quietened and Zack pushed his senses out. Erik was right. This place was different and in more than the obvious, nightmarish-hellscape ways. Life here was strange; it hung in the air and the earth, lurking, almost aggressive. He shuddered and pulled back his sense, opening his eyes. His friends were still standing with their eyes closed, Bast and Jackie with their arms extended.

Charlie was the next to open her eyes and knelt to stroke Max's neck. "I know, girl. You're not the only one on edge."

Jackie opened her eyes next, wearing a furrowed brow. "Um… Erik?"

Before she could continue, Art's eyes snapped open. "We've got something incoming. A lot of somethings."

CHAPTER 16
SORTIE

Erik readied his axe. "Okay, weapons up. How many?"

"I'm not sure, heaps," Art pulled his sword from its scabbard. "Maybe forty? Or more? Coming at us from the other side of the rocks."

"Forty?" Erik asked. "There's no way they'd group up in those numbers. Your senses are probably confused here."

"Maybe?" Art said, "but either way, there's a lot of hungry coming at us."

"Okay," Erik took charge, pointing at Tabitha and Kimmy, "you two girls stand either side of me. Not too close now, I've got a wide swing with this axe. You two with the swords, one on either side of the girls, protect their flanks. Our Lifer and you, little one, behind me. And you, archer, fire at groups of them when you can, and otherwise keep them from circling around us. Understood?"

The youths murmured their confirmation. Zack wiped his hands down his jeans, but they remained clammy.

"There's one," Tabitha said, pointing at an ugly little face, its red scales almost camouflaged against the dull orange of the rocks. That face was joined by another, then another, until the rock formation looked like a strange shrub bursting with angry, squinting fruit.

"Imps it is then," Erik said. "I'll be damned if I know why there's so many, but we can take them if we stand firm."

Erik waved his hands over the ground in front of him as he spoke and a ripple of cold washed back over the group. "Don't step in front of me! I've iced up the ground."

To his right, Bast also wove a spell, speeding up his body, ready for the attack.

There was an eerie moment of silence, punctured only by the sound of sneakers and boots shifting on the rocky ground. Then, one of the imps screeched in a high-pitched voice followed by all the others and, as the eight humans stood against the barrage of sound, the creatures leapt to attack.

Charlie fired into the centre group of the imps. One fell with an arrow in its chest and was soon trampled by those that came after. That group faltered on the rocky ground in front of Erik, slipping on the conjured ice and the imps on either side strayed wider to avoid being tripped over by those that fell.

The wave of imps, easily the forty or so Art had divined, crept around the front row of their prey. Art and Bast stepped out, slashing with their blades. Art's target ducked under a blow that would otherwise have severed its head, but Bast skewered his own through its chest.

Tabitha and Kimmy also edged away from Erik and towards their own attackers. The chained head of Tabitha's flail whirred through the air before crashing into an imp's skull, sending it to the ground. Kimmy dashed towards two imps who were clumped together as one avoided the icy ground. She swung her axe hard and cleaved through one and into the other, dropping both with a spray of black blood.

Erik was also making swift, if gruesome, work on the imps that had fallen in front of him and slid within range of his own axe.

Despite this, the mass of imps pressed on. Most of the attackers jostled into each other and their sharp claws missed their mark. However, one, climbing its fallen companions, leaped at Kimmy, her guard left open by her savage swing. Slashing for her face, the imp crashed against a shimmering curve in the air.

"Thanks, Jackie!" she called out, reversing her swing to strike the falling imp square in its chest.

Art was not so lucky; the imp he had failed to kill latched onto him, biting deep into his shoulder. He cried out in pain.

"Hold still," Zack shouted as he moved forward, thrusting hard with the narrow of his quarterstaff. The wood slammed into the side of the imp's skull and it collapsed to the ground.

Blood stained Art's shirt as it flowed from the bite, but he gritted his teeth and swung hard at the next imp to approach him.

The waves of imps seemed endless, as more joined their brethren faster than even Erik could slay them. Still, the more experienced mage's formation and directions were holding up well against the attack.

Zack bounced on his feet, stuck uselessly at the back, while the front row stood firm, supported by Jackie's shields and Charlie's arrows. The most he could offer was a discouraging jab with his staff to any imp with ambitions to slip through.

Tabitha hissed as an imp clawed at her arm, distracting her from the spell she was trying to weave. She gave a wild swing at it. The weight of her flail sailed over its head as the creature dropped to the ground, dodging the blow that would have caved in its skull. She calmed herself and rewove the magic. This time, without the distraction, a short gust of wind picked up, blowing the small imps near her back over the ice, and sending them slipping to the ground.

Bast punched an imp with his rapier's wrist guard before slashing it across the throat. "Hold back, sis. I'm going to try something," he said to Kimmy before murmuring his arcane words and tracing patterns in the air with his free hand. The half dozen imps in front of them slipped over.

"Yes!" Kimmy took the advantage and swung out with her axe.

Whatever Bast had cast had taken a toll on him and the athletic boy's movements slowed down. Zack cleared his mind of distractions and drew Life from himself and the surrounds. With a wave of his hand, he directed it towards Bast. The familiar lethargy seeped into his body as Bast's movements sped up in turn. Renewed, Bast kicked an imp with the heel of his shoe before slashing a second across the throat.

The tide had turned, and chittering at each other, the remaining imps turned and fled.

"Don't let them get away. They could draw more down on top of us," Erik said, chasing down the last retreating creatures.

The teens in the front line charged forward and all but two imps fell to the ground. Charlie stepped to the side and drew back on her bow, aiming at one of the creatures as it clambered up the rocks towards safety. The arrow flew true and the imp fell limp to the ground. The final imp was now out of reach, but Erik spoke in arcane tones and, with a flick of his wrist, something cold and glittering spun through the air. The last of their attackers screeched and then went silent.

Erik turned and cast a surveying eye over the group. "Well, that was quite an ordeal. Is everybody okay?"

With the exception of Art, nobody had more than scrapes and grazes.

Zack moved over to examine his wound. "Hold still," he said, tearing a hole down the sleeve of Art's shirt so he could see better.

"Ow! Do you even know what you're doing?"

"Quiet, newbie," Erik said, "he's your Lifer, do what he says."

"Yeah, shut up and do what I say. Now stand still," Zack finished tearing away the sleeve before pulling a rolled bandage from his pocket. "Until I learn to actually heal, this'll have to do."

"Thanks, man. My very own first aid officer," Art winced as Zack tightened the bandage around his shoulder.

"Well, seems like you can't stop feeding yourself to monsters, so I'll have to be here to patch you up."

"I can't… Oww! I can't help being delicious. I also, apparently, can't help having a sister who'd leave her own brother open like that," he said, looking at Jackie.

She burst into tears. "I'm sorry, Art. I tried. There were so many of them, all at once."

Art brushed past Zack and wrapped his arms around her. "It's okay, Jack, I'm fine. I was just being a dick."

She sniffed. "But it's my job to protect you."

"It's your job to protect the group," Erik said, "and you did well at that. You all stood against far more imps than should have been together. Now, have a look around, see if anything stands out as strange."

"Strange?" Tabitha asked. "As in, out of the ordinary, in a hell dimension?"

"Yes. As important as learning the different realms, is being able to sift through them and see what stands out. You'll probably find nothing, but look anyway."

The teens split up and inspected their surrounds, most prodding at the demonic corpses littering the ground. Art grunted when he lifted his arm but, when Tabitha looked over at him, he forced himself to silence.

Zack wasn't sure what he was supposed to be looking for and instead turned his mind to the lessons Sara had taught him about injuries. While he assumed their physiology had to be different from human physiology, he was still surrounded by dozens of examples of wounds that, until now, he'd only seen in books or had been described to him. A narrow but deep wound from Bast's rapier. A ragged gash from Kimmy's axe. Shattered ribs from Tabitha's flail. Then he found a strange pattern of deep bruises that couldn't have been caused by this attack. At first he thought maybe Tabitha's chain had wrapped around the imp's leg, but the bruising seemed too old. Moving on to the next, there was a similar pattern of bruising around its chest. Three more times he found it, before remembering where he had seen bruising like that before.

"Guys, have a look at…" he said.

"That!" Bast cut him off, pointing up at the sky in excitement.

Charlie looked to where he was pointing, up and off in the distance. "Are they…?"

"Angels!" Bast shouted.

"Quiet," Erik said, but it was too late.

Seven flying humanoids gleamed brightly against the dark sky, broad white-gold wings beating through the air. One of them pointed in the direction of the Tower initiates and a second drew an item from its belt and held it to its mouth. The blast of a horn ripped through the silence and seven pairs of feathery wings flapped harder towards the humans.

"Run. Back to the gate!" Erik shouted.

Erik, so calm in the face of an imp horde, looked worried. Zack asked as he ran to keep up with him. "Why are we running from angels?"

Erik didn't stop to sling his double-bladed axe over his back and held it in one hand as he ran. "Have you all listened to nothing? This is not hell. What we fought were not tiny demons and those things flying towards us are not angels. Another year or so of experience and I'd consider standing and fighting them with you, but with you all as green as you are? If they catch us, they'll kill us."

Zack's feet stumbled on the uneven, rocky ground. Now they had left Tabitha's cleaned air behind, a caustic taste burned in the back of his throat. His legs ached, and the only reason he managed to keep pace with the others was they seemed to be slowing down as well. And they weren't even half the way back yet.

Max alternated between dashing ahead and weaving back to the group to run alongside Charlie.

"Run, Max," Charlie said between breaths. "Go ahead. I'll be right behind."

The dog hesitated for a moment and then bounded up towards the gate.

The angels were getting so close Zack could hear their voices.

"Come, brothers. Let us smite these foul devils."

Bast, who had been outpacing the group, turned and cast a spell, his fingers twitching back and forth. One of the angels bellowed as its wings were bound in an invisible force and it plummeted hard to the ground.

"No!" Erik shouted. "We'll never stop all of them. All you'll do is make them angry."

True to Erik's word, the remaining angels roared in defiance and sped faster on their feathered wings towards their targets. Zack risked a look over his shoulder and was shocked by how beautiful they were. They had toned muscles, gleaming skin, and were clad only in white linen skirts. Even their faces, while contorted in rage, were magnificent; they were like works of art come to life.

The gate was close now, but so were the angels. Zack could hear their wings beating in the air behind him. Two of the angels landed, the force rippling out like a meteor strike, and swept their broad wings forward. The rush of wind buffeted Jackie, Tabitha and Charlie to the ground.

Erik spun and hurled a conjured shard of ice at the nearest angel. The angel sprung backwards to avoid it. The other, however, faster than Zack could follow, drew a massive blade from behind its back. Gripped in the angel's two hands, the blade ignited in flame.

The girls scrambled to their feet and the angel strode forward and swung at them. Jackie summoned up a shield, but instead of blocking the blow, the arc of the angel's swing was merely knocked askew. Where the sword may have cut deep into Tabitha's chest, it instead landed high on her shoulder. She screamed in pain and the angel brought its blade around for a backswing. Art and Charlie grabbed her around the waist and carried her towards the gate.

Zack hesitated with Bast at the edge of the gate, worried about leaving his friends behind.

"Get through," Erik shouted, "and tell them to get ready to shut it."

Bast followed the order and Zack charged through after him, with Kimmy on his heels.

Back in the Tower, Bast turned to the woman standing by the gate. "We're being attacked. Get ready to close it."

Zack sprinted across to the stairwell. He tried to map his way through this part of the Tower and only made one wrong turn before doubling back and finding his way to Sara's quarters. He banged on the door for a moment before she answered.

He fought for his breath and, before he could explain, she stepped forward through the door.

"I'll come at once."

Sara, despite her age, moved with enough speed that Zack had trouble keeping up. The gate had been closed by the time they arrived, and Zack did a quick count to find everybody accounted for, including Erik. The large man was sitting with his back against the wall and his legs out in front of him. When Zack looked closer, he could see a dark red pool staining the stone tiles around Erik's right thigh.

Sara took less than a second to evaluate the situation. "Zack, apply pressure to Erik's leg and slow the bleeding. I will see to your friends first."

Zack knelt down beside Erik. Closer now, he could see Erik's heavy trousers had been burnt away in a wide radius around the wound. The exposed skin, where not covered in blood, was burnt and blistered. He pulled a bandage from his pocket.

"Sorry, Erik. This is going to hurt."

"It's all g… Ahhhhh!" the larger man cried out as Zack pushed down hard on the wound.

Sara had not taken long, but the cloth bandage was already soaked red by the time she arrived at Erik's side and Zack was sure he was paler.

Sara was unfazed as she inspected the injury. "I don't know whose idea it was to send these children out there with someone like you, Erik."

"Not children. Initiates," he said, but his voice was faint.

"Yes, well then. Teachable moment Zack; follow the flow of Life." Without any more instruction, she chanted, weaving delicate and elaborate symbols in the air with her fingers. Zack felt her draw Life from all around, including herself, but he paid closer attention to where it was going and what it was doing. The Target and the Intent. Compared to the Life magic he'd been using, both were so precise it was intimidating. He could well understand why he was not ready to do this himself. The veins, the muscles, the nerves, the skin; each were coaxed into rapid repair. Even the blood cells themselves were encouraged to multiply and colour returned to Erik's cheeks. Zack noticed that the burns remained.

As ever, Sara anticipated the question. "Those burns are all but impossible to heal magically, but they will heal naturally, given time."

Zack looked over at Tabitha. There was no sign of the sword wound, but painful blisters stretched from the base of her neck and down past her shoulder. She was putting on a brave face, but it was clear she was in distress and in no small amount of pain.

"Come, my dear," Sara said, "I should be able to do something about the pain in my quarters. Zack, help her up. You follow too, Erik."

Zack knelt next to Tabitha and slipped her unburnt arm around his neck. He eased her upright, allowing her to rest her weight against his and they followed Sara. Erik limped stoically behind.

Once inside Sara's room, Zack's mentor pulled some boxes down from a shelf. The contents looked more at home in a hospital, a strange juxtaposition to the stone walls of a magical tower.

"Two lessons today, Zack," Sara said as she drew medicines from the box. "First, there is much more to Life than wiggling your fingers and saying made up words."

Zack nodded. "And the second?"

"Unlike your friends, your work does not end with returning to the Tower. Now, watch closely."

Sara's sure and nimble fingers went to work.

CHAPTER 17

FRUSTRATION

It was a beautiful day in the last week of the spring school holidays. The September rains had dissolved into warm October sunshine with the lightest scattering of cloud cover creating the ideal weather for outside activities. One of these clouds shifted and a ray of sunlight reflected off the television screen. Zack, Art and Matt growled in frustration as their game was disrupted. Art forced himself out of the beanbag and pulled the curtain shut against the invading glare.

"Much better," Matt said, "I would have had you if not for that!"

"You wish," Art said, "Zack, can you let this fool know how thoroughly beaten he was?"

Zack held up his hands. "Honestly, I think the glare improved your game. You're both awful."

Art and Matt exchanged a brief look before they both leapt onto Zack, punching him in his sides. The attacks were in jest, but one of them found a bruise, high on the left side of his chest, where a training sword had avoided his parry a few days earlier. He held back a wince, but his eyes watered from the pain.

Matt stepped back, showing no sign of noticing Zack's discomfort. "I'm gonna get my mum to make us some nachos." He handed Zack the controller and left the room.

Art hadn't seemed to notice either and echoed, "Nachos" as he selected his character in the game.

While the game was loading, he looked over his shoulder and spoke in a whisper. "So, last night I went over to Tab's."

Zack's eyes widened. "Why?"

"She texted me. Asked me to come over straight away. Said it was an emergency."

"And?"

"Well, I had a quick shower, threw on a good shirt, and snuck out of the house. It was pretty late; a bit past eleven. I was kind of hoping it was her way of making a move. Maybe, since I've been picking up a little more..."

"More? You mean 'At all'," Zack said.

"Fine, been picking up a fair bit more lately. Maybe I'd made her jealous. The house is all dark when I get there and she sneaks me through the front door and into her room. I'm thinking, 'This is it!'"

"And?"

Art broke into a laugh. "And nothing. She wanted me to wipe her parents' memories. Turns out, after weeks of hiding the angel burns from them, her mum had finally walked in on her getting changed. They freaked out and Tabitha didn't provide a decent story behind the burns. They were going to take her to the hospital first thing this morning. Instead, she wanted me to creep into their room and take the memory away. I couldn't be precise enough to take that specific memory. I had to wipe out the whole evening, but she was desperate. So I did."

"Did it work?" Zack asked.

"How very dare you?" Art smirked, "Yeah, a lot of Mind magic is easier with sleeping targets. So, once that was done, I thought I'd try to press my luck a bit. Maybe she'd be feeling grateful to go along with how jealous I'd been making her."

Zack raised an eyebrow in question.

"Yeah. No. She's not interested. She was really sweet about it, totally not into it, though."

“You alright?”

“Yeah, I’m all good.”

“Gonna try again?”

“What? No! She’s not keen, mate. It’s a shame. She’s funny, tough, and hot as, but she’s not interested. Plenty of fish and all that, though,” Art unpaused the game, “still, felt good to ask her. You should try it some time.”

“It’s different, Tab is single.”

Art shrugged. “Speedbump.”

The connection splintered and Life rushed out into the room. Zack reached out with his Will and snatched as much as he could, but most of it flitted away like fireflies fading in the dark. He ran his hand through his hair in frustration before turning back to Sara, who was watching him in silence.

“I almost had…”.

“Almost is not good enough. When you are dealing with magic, almost is worse than nothing. Almost is packing a barrel with gunpowder and shrapnel and mishandling the match. Almost is dangerous.”

“I’m trying.”

“I know, Zack, but perhaps you are misspending your effort. The concepts. The techniques. These you seem to have in your grasp. It is focus you lack. You must rein in your thoughts,” Sara smiled, but there was a note of tension in her voice.

“Maybe it’s this specific channelling spell I can’t get right. We’ve been trying it for months. Can’t we move on to something else?”

“No. If you cannot master this, I cannot risk teaching you anything else,” Sara’s tone was firm.

“But the others are throwing fire and wind, casting shields and memory wipes.” Weeks of frustration came to the boil. “All I can do is keep them rested. I'm like a battery with a stick."

"Fire and Air is not Life. And you are not..."

"I'm not as good as them?"

"Those are not my words, Zack," her smile was gone. "Each of us is different, with different strengths and weaknesses. And Life is complex. The potential for failure is more severe. A large flame instead of a small one. A slowed down body instead of a sped up one. A storm cloud inside a library. Problematic? Yes. Dangerous? Yes. But nothing, nothing compared to misdirected Life."

"Can't you teach me something I can use to help my friends? If I'm channelling Life, can't that be weaponised in some way? Instead of passing Life around between my friends, I could have drawn it from those creatures. I could contribute."

"No!"

Zack had never heard Sara raise her voice before, but she did now.

"That is abomination. Life is not like other energies. When Life dwells within an entity, it belongs to that entity, be it person, dog or tree. That is what makes it Life. It must be freely given or it becomes corrupted. Toxic. And it will taint whoever wields it."

"I want to be useful. When we went to Hades, all the others did something useful, and all I could do was stand at the back." Tears threatened to come forward.

"You are not ready to do more, Zack. I'm not convinced any of you were. I don't understand why Junie decided to send you to that place. It is no place for children."

Zack stood up, anger surging forward to hide his tears. "We passed our tests. We're initiates of the Tower."

Sara looked into his eyes, not stirring from her seat. "Initiates, yes. Apprentices. Students. Children, who perhaps are being pushed too hard, too fast."

"I want to be able to serve better."

She crossed her arms against her chest. "Until you can find your focus, we will direct our attention to the principles. Otherwise, I can suggest the weapons room."

Zack's cheeks burned and he snatched up his bag. "I think that's a good idea."

He retreated through the door and sped down the Tower stairs. The weapons room, to his relief, was empty, except for the Commander and his soldiers. He dropped his bag in the corner and chose a quarterstaff from the racks.

"Commander, I feel the need to push myself today. Could I please train against two opponents?"

"Certainly," the golem said, "do you have a preference for their weapons?"

Zack walked into the middle of the room, shaking out his limbs. "Surprise me."

The Commander clapped twice and two statues stepped forward. The stone knight moved to retrieve a blunted spear while the terracotta soldier selected a wooden two-handed sword, almost as tall as Zack.

Zack and his opponents bowed and the fight began. He wondered how long he'd last against the two statues. He knocked away a spear thrust and spun into a double handed block of a downward sword stroke that would have otherwise landed on his shoulder.

He lost himself in the exertion and let go of his worries, allowing them to flow freely through his mind.

What was he doing? Was he wasting his time? He should be spending time studying for the exams that were a little over a month away, rather than failing again and again to construct a simple channel. Should he give up? His friends were accomplishing so much, why hadn't he? What was wrong with him? Why couldn't he clear his mind and focus like Sara had been teaching him? If he quit now, maybe he could rescue his impending exam failure. But if he did, he'd never catch up to the others. They would be off fighting monsters and saving the world, and without their 'Lifer' as Erik had called him. A Lifer with some band-aids, a small bottle of antiseptic, and no real healing magic. But what would quitting the Tower do to his friendship with Art? And to any chance he had with Charlie? Or hope of helping his grandmother?

His quarterstaff whirled in his hands like the thoughts did in his mind. His months of training and practice in this room surged through every limb. Each worry. Each fear. Each thought was punctuated by a parry, a switch of stance, a counterblow. His arms grew tired and his shirt clung to the sweat on his skin, but releasing his pent up stress was what he needed. He ducked under a sword swing and battered aside a low spear thrust. He spun forward, moving in between and past his two attackers, striking one in the back of its knee and the other in its neck. His wooden staff did no damage to the enchanted stone or clay, but the statues responded appropriately and fell aside. He ended his spin facing his opponents and stopped in surprise. Had he really defeated two statues at the same time?

He turned to face the Commander who gave him a single, respectful nod.

Zack smiled. "Again."

CHAPTER 18

END OF YEAR

Zack flicked through the practice Maths test in front of him and he realised he could do little over half of the questions with any level of confidence. He understood the concepts, but he hadn't practiced them enough. And Maths was one of his best subjects. He was doomed.

Art squeezed his shoulder. "Don't worry about it. I've got this."

"How?"

"I'm going to be awesome again."

Before Zack could demand more answers, Ms Agarwal interrupted, "I believe I explained this was quiet revision time, Arthur."

"Sorry Miss, I was saying I'm not feeling too well."

She gave him a look that did little to hide her doubts.

"No, I'm serious, Miss. Can I please be excused?"

"Very well. Straight to sick bay with you, then."

"Actually, Miss, I uh… I think it's more something I need to go to the gents for."

The class snickered and Art's cheeks flushed in embarrassment.

"Fine. Go." Ms Agarwal dismissed him with a flick of her hand.

After Art had left, Tabitha shot Zack a questioning look across the room. Zack shrugged in response, but as he turned back to his revision, his worry about what Art had planned, defeated any chance of productive work.

He had managed to make it about a quarter of the way through the test when the bell rang, declaring the end of school for the day. Art hadn't returned and Tabitha caught up with Zack on the way out.

"What was up with Art?" she asked.

"I'm not sure. He said he was…" Zack was interrupted by a clap on the back.

"Done." Art wore a triumphant look on his face.

"What do you mean?" Zack asked.

"Not here. Let's talk about it on the way into the city." Art led them out.

They loitered, as was their habit, behind the throng of students leaving the school on foot and bike, or to car and bus. When the seven of them were left, they started their walk towards the bus stop.

"Ladies and gentlemen, your hero… nay, your saviour, has delivered," he said with a flourish and opened up his backpack.

Despite their eye rolls, they shuffled in around him to have a closer look.

"Voila." He brandished a plain manila folder.

"And what's that supposed to be?" Bast asked.

"Oh, nothing. Just copies of the end of year exams for each one of our subjects. Yours too, Jackie, I felt generous."

After a moment of stunned silence, they all spoke at once, asking him how he did it.

"Simple. I walked into the different staff rooms, rummaged around in the desks and filing cabinets until I found them, took a few photocopies so we didn't have to share, and I left."

"And you didn't get caught?" Charlie asked.

"Oh, I got caught plenty of times. Gee caught me in the Maths room. Simmons caught me in Humanities. Pitt caught me three times in the science room, but in my defence, I was looking for five different exams in there; took me ages. None of them remember seeing me, though. Anyway, who wants?"

Art passed the folder around and they all rummaged through the pages to find the exams they needed, but Charlie hesitated.

“Is this okay?” she asked. “I mean, it’s definitely cheating.”

Art defended himself. “This is what Junie was talking about, that first night in the Tower. We can use our magic as we wish. And I wish not to fail.”

“Plus,” Bast said, “we’d all be doing better if we hadn’t spent so much time training at the Tower. This is how we balance it out.”

Kimmy scoffed. “You guys might have slacked off. Doesn’t mean we all have.”

“Fine. Then hand the papers back.” Art held out his hand.

“No way, I said I don’t need them to smash these exams. That doesn’t mean I don’t want them.”

“I guess that’s the only thanks I’ll get from you.”

Kimmy didn’t answer. She was already poring through the pages.

Charlie took a copy of each of her exams and, shortly afterwards, their bus arrived. The group was more or less silent as they read through their upcoming test papers. Zack claimed the seat next to Charlie, where he read through his Biology exam. Feeling his stress lessen for the first time in weeks, he saw her lips were pressed tight as she looked out the window.

“Are you okay, Charlie?”

“I’m not sure, you know? I get this is our reward for doing what we’ve been doing. But it’s one more thing that separates us from everybody else. I mean, we can’t share them beyond this group. It’s too risky, and I get that. But it’s still another reason to feel guilty.”

Zack’s gut tightened as he realised that he, once again, hadn’t considered Matt or any of his other friends. He looked at Charlie’s emotion-filled eyes. “I hadn’t considered that, and you’re right. But I suppose we need to think about what’s the alternative. Do we not cheat and fail? Do we stop training at the Tower until we graduate? A year from now?”

“No. I don’t want to stop,” she said, “and failing won’t help them. I guess I feel so guilty all the time and this is more fuel on the fire.”

“I feel that way, too. But maybe that’s a good sign. Maybe if we were the selfish people we're worried about being, we wouldn't be feeling this guilty."

"Maybe, Zack," Charlie turned back, looking out at the cars driving by, "but we haven't exactly done anything about it, either."

Zack munched on a piece of iced gingerbread and listened to the Christmas carols playing under the hum of conversation. His sister and cousins were discussing their summer plans, while his mother packed away the leftovers from the Christmas Eve feast.

His father approached with a pair of beers in his hand and offered one to Zack.

"No thanks, Dad." He would have liked to say yes, but he was exhausted. In the month since the exams, he had made no real progress with Sara, and so all he could do was keep his grandmother rested and alert. His entire body ached from the strain of maintaining the gentle flow of Life and he could barely sit up straight on the lounge.

Still, it was working. His grandmother sat listening as one of his cousins' toddlers was showing her his new remote-controlled dinosaur. She leant across and kissed his forehead before he ran off down the hall to play with it again. His grandfather hovered nearby, keeping watch over her as he accepted the extra beer from Zack's father.

"What are you lazing about for?" One of his uncles kicked his foot, attracting his attention. "Probably up all night with your computer games."

"Leave him alone," Zack's mother said. "He ran himself ragged studying this year and it paid off. Top ten in most of his subjects. We're very proud of him."

Zack smiled at her. He had almost grown accustomed to the twinge of guilt that accompanied her praise. Without Art's test paper crime spree, he wouldn't have stood a chance. He had spent that week practicing the tests over and over and drafting the best essays he could for English and Ancient History. And he'd managed some strong results. Which was especially good, because his lessons with Sara had gone nowhere. He closed his eyes and allowed the music to carry his worries.

"Zacharias."

He opened his eyes. The others had returned to the dining table for coffee and cake, leaving him alone in the lounge room with his grandmother. She beckoned him over.

He heaved himself off the lounge and knelt by her. "Yes, Babi?"

She took his hand in hers, holding it to her other forearm. "Thank you for this, Zacharias."

His heart sped up; his fatigue forgotten. "What do you mean, Babi?"

Her eyes narrowed. "I am dying, but I am not stupid. I don't know how or what you're doing, but I know it's you."

Zack opened his mouth, but no words came out.

"It's fine. It's fine. I'll keep your secret. You're a good boy, so I believe you are not doing anything wrong, whatever it is. But be careful. This, though, this has been a wonderful gift. Thank you."

"Of course," was all he managed in reply.

"Now, stop it for tonight. Deda is getting too worried. It's lovely to see, but he needs his rest too. Let me drift off now, please."

"Okay. Merry Christmas, Babi."

She kissed his hand before releasing it and let him go and then called out for his father to come and help her to her bed. His grandfather hurried to her side, scolding her for pushing herself too hard, and she showed him what she thought of that with a single silencing look. Zack joined his cousins at the table, exhausted, but pleased with himself.

At a Boxing Day party with his friends, Zack was on to his second beer and he was still pretty pleased with himself. Christmas day had been a laid back experience with his parents and sister, as had become a fairly recent tradition, and he'd been spoiled thoroughly. He'd spent most of the day playing his new computer games and a new board game with his parents.

Now, at a party with his friends that he hoped would become a new tradition of their own, he had to admit life couldn't get a lot better. A glance over to where Charlie was sitting with Dave forced him to correct himself, but he was still ahead overall.

The large backyard was crowded with happy teenagers, and the inclusion of at least a third of their classmates, as well as kids from other schools, restricted what Zack thought of as 'Tower-talk.' Similar to the exams, they were forced to be normal teenagers again. He sat with Art, Matt and Bast in a half circle of plastic lawn chairs.

"Forget about her tonight, mate," Art gestured with his bottle towards a group of girls across the backyard, "let's go try our luck over there."

"No thanks, Art. I'm good at the moment. Really."

Art looked at Matt. "C'mon, I need a wingman."

Matt looked at Zack and then Bast, the latter of which held up his hand.

"Sorry, bud. Wrong team." He patted Matt on the leg. "Go get 'em."

Matt dragged himself up and took a long draught from his beer. "Oh well, see you guys in a few minutes."

Bast laughed as the two boys walked off to join the girls. Zack couldn't hear the conversation, but within moments, Art was sitting next to a dark-haired girl with his arm placed casually around her. Matt was left standing before taking an awkward seat on the edge of a bench.

"Well, that went better than usual," Zack said.

"It did. You don't think he…" Bast left his thought unfinished, but Zack knew what he meant.

He looked around to make sure they weren't overheard. "No. He wouldn't use magic on a girl."

"Yeah. Christmas luck is all it is. Speaking of which, I'm off to find my own. I think I saw a cute guy in the lounge room and I'm going to go and strategically place some mistletoe."

Bast's departure left Zack on his own. He sipped his beer and scanned the backyard. His eyes were drawn, as ever, to Charlie. Devoid of distractions, his heart threatened to sink. He wished he could be more like Art, able to bounce his attraction from one girl to the next, but he was so stuck on Charlie. At times, when they were talking, particularly when he was able to cheer her up or make her laugh, he felt on top of the world, but knowing she didn't return his romantic feelings shattered him again and again. He had been interested in Charlie for years now, going back to when they met in the first year of high school. But she had always been popular and pretty and moved from one relationship to the next. Zack had never seemed to be in the right place, or maybe he wasn't the right type. From his perspective, Charlie seemed to be interested in guys who were different from him in many ways; they all seemed taller, stronger, more outgoing. And most of them were jerks, although he had to admit that Dave seemed okay. Zack couldn't help but feel lacking compared to them.

He'd emptied his beer while lost in thought and decided he wanted another. He wandered towards the laundry, hoping the remains of his six-pack had been left untouched. When Zack opened the back door, he found Kimmy confronting three guys he didn't recognise.

Kimmy eyed the three of them. "If you touch me again, you'll lose something."

"Aw, c'mon Kimmy, everybody knows you're up for a good time. Let's have some fun," said the taller of the three, a combination of ripped jeans and messy topknot that Zack wanted to name 'Kenneth'.

"I was already having fun, and I doubt you could add much to that," Kimmy turned to storm away.

"Slut."

With the uncomfortable knowledge that all three were larger than him, Zack stepped forward to stand next to Kimmy. "Not cool, man. Apologise."

"Or what, geek?" Kenneth loomed over him.

"Or nothing," Kimmy said, turning back around, "I am a slut. I'll sleep with whoever I want, whenever I want. Sometimes because I'm keen, sometimes because I'm bored and other times because it's a habit. But I wouldn't want to touch the three of you even if I had gloves on. In fact, there's only one guy here that is man enough for me." She turned and thrust her body onto Zack's.

Before he could think, her mouth was against his and he returned the kiss. His mind whirred in confusion, wondering why Kimmy was kissing him and whether he should be kissing her back like he was. His mind then went to his last kiss, over a year ago with a girl he met while away on holidays, before the taste of whiskey and cigarettes from Kimmy's mouth brought him back and he was suddenly conscious of where his hands were on her hips.

He was still lost in thought when the kiss ended and Kimmy turned back to the other three.

"So run away now, I'm busy. Plus, your shoe's on fire."

Zack and the others all looked down, and sure enough, the very top of Kenneth's sneakers were aflame. He pushed past Zack and Kimmy, shouting for help and his friends ran off behind him.

Zack tried to collect his thoughts. "Did you…?"

"Of course. Dickhead had it coming."

"Kimmy, about the ki…"

"Zacky, it didn't mean anything. I wanted to piss off those jerks and figured you deserved a little bit of a reward for sticking up for me. But you're not close to my type, and you're not interested in anybody that isn't Charlie. I know that. Hell, everybody knows that."

"Oh. Good, okay. Everybody knows that?"

"Next time though, go ahead and feel me up a bit, make it worth our while." And with a smile, she wandered off.

"Next time?"

But Kimmy had already left the room.

CHAPTER 19

BREACH

Charlie's face was alight with excitement as she looked out through the bus window at the German landscape being revealed by the rising sun. And despite his own excitement at being in Europe, Zack couldn't take his eyes off her. At the front of the bus, Art chatted away with the driver in fluent German, a language he hadn't known five hours earlier. Zack zipped up his thickest jacket as he stared outside at the snow on the passing rooftops.

Zack reviewed Junie's map for the fortieth time. As best he could tell, they would soon arrive in Lautberg, a small Bavarian village nestled on the edges of the Black Forest, not far from the red X Junie had drawn on the map. The mark represented the breach the group had been instructed to investigate. A small breach, she had assured them, but far from a training exercise. Go to the site, investigate, confirm whether it had remained open and destroy anything that had come through it. And above all things, maintain the Silence.

Relying on a paper map was frustrating, even more so when he could feel the weight of his smartphone in his jeans pocket. But without global roaming, the phone was useless, and without any passport, he'd been unwilling to risk buying a local SIM card.

Ten minutes later they arrived and the youths crossed their arms tight around themselves as the winter cold assaulted them upon exiting the bus. The centre of the village bustled with life.

"Something's not right here," Jackie said, looking around.

"Well, we don't know what's normal for them," Bast said, "I mean look around, apart from the cars, we could be back in time."

Art shook his head. "No, Jackie's right. I'm getting waves of anxiety from every direction. Hang here, I'll go find out."

"Be subtle," Tabitha said.

"Girl, I'm smooth as." He smiled over his shoulder.

"Smooth like an immature arse" Kimmy muttered to herself, causing Charlie to laugh.

Art trotted over to a young man who was pulling open the shutters of a corner store.

Zack stuck his hands as deep into his pockets as he could, wishing he had packed gloves. Tabitha's advice to pack warm clothes had come that morning, attached to the news Junie had a job for them. Two weeks into the school year, Sydney was still in the firm grip of summer, so Zack had to hide his winter clothes at the bottom of his bag as he left to 'sleep over at Bast's house'.

Art returned to his friends. "Well, it could be a coincidence, but a boy went missing last night. A baby, actually. He's like nine or ten months old. Are kids still babies at ten months?"

"I think we have to assume it's not a coincidence that a child is missing so close to the breach. Do you know where he went missing from?" Charlie asked.

"Yeah, it's a house out that way. On the outskirts, on the edge of the forest."

Zack studied the map. "That matches the direction of the breach too, I think."

"Alright," Tabitha said, "so what's the plan?"

"Do we go and help look?" asked Jackie.

Kimmy grimaced. "I'm not sure. Our job here is the breach, not the kid."

"You're not saying we should leave the baby out there," Charlie said.

"No. But they'll have heaps of people looking for it."

"Yep," Art looked uncomfortable with being on Kimmy's side, "they're going to start a proper search party in an hour or so, as soon as it gets a bit lighter."

"A baby going missing is real-world stuff," Zack said. "I'm not saying it's not magic related, but we have to be really careful here. Bunch of foreigners show up when a baby goes missing? Looks dodgy."

"But we just got here," Jackie said.

"Still suspicious enough for us to be questioned. And we don't have passports, or any proof of how we got to Europe to begin with. I think it all goes downhill well before we get to prove we got off the bus after the kid went missing."

"Not to mention most of us have a deadly weapon hidden in our bags," Tabitha added.

Zack had almost forgotten that. He and Jackie had opted for stout wooden staves that he hoped would pass as walking sticks.

"I think they're right," Bast said, "so, where does that leave us?"

"Let's get out ahead of the search party," Tabitha said. "If there's something else out there, we want to find it before them. If we find the baby first, we work out what we do then, otherwise, we stick to the job."

The group set off in the direction of the forest. There was a scattering of others around, which they assumed were heading to the house to join the search party, but when they saw two police cars up ahead, the teenagers left the direct path and skirted around and into the woods.

The trees were old, thick and close enough together to create a dense canopy. It left the forest floor mostly dry and free of snow, but it also made it dark. The map soon became useless and every direction looked the same. While they were confident they could find their way back to the village, any navigation beyond that felt unlikely.

"So, what do we do now?" Bast asked.

"Zack, do you think you could try and find the baby, like you found the imp in the store?" Art said.

"I thought we agreed we weren't here for the baby," Kimmy said.

"It's still our best lead on the breach," Art said.

"He's right," Zack said, "I'm not sure I can, but I'll try."

Zack centred himself and closed his eyes. Reaching out with his mind, he searched for Life and was almost drowned by it. He had never been in the presence of the sheer amount that was here in one place; the trees, the moss, the insects, the birds, rodents, even in the soil. It was dizzying. He took a deep breath and tried to filter it out, the way he had learned to filter out his friends. He discarded the trees and the smaller life, then the birds and animals. He pushed his mind out further, seeking something that didn't belong. He could feel the strain building, like trying to lift a heavy weight, but nothing was out of place, so he pushed harder. The strain was joined by a sense of vertigo and his legs wobbled. He knew he couldn't push more than a little further without harming himself, but, as he fell to his knees, he felt it; a something.

With one hand on the cold soil to steady himself, he pointed with the other. "That way."

Kimmy and Bast charged off in that direction, followed a moment later by Tabitha, Charlie and Max. Art and Jackie hesitated, kneeling beside Zack.

He shrugged them off. "Go, they'll need you. The kid's not alone."

The siblings ran through the trees in pursuit of the others. Zack took a deep breath and pushed himself up. Traces of colour swam across his eyes, but with the help of his walking stick, he levered himself onto his feet and staggered after his friends. Half balancing, half bouncing off trees, he managed to catch up to the others when they stopped, crouched and hiding behind some foliage. He leant, gasping for breath, against a trunk next to Art. He blinked to clear his blurred vision and look ahead at what had given his friends pause.

"Am I seeing this?" he asked Art.

"If by 'this', you mean four fairies skipping through the forest with a toddler? Then yeah, you're seeing this."

The infant, barely able to walk, was being held upright by a pair of fairies on each side, giving the appearance of a pleasant skip through the forest. The child didn't appear to be in any distress, with a broad smile resting on his face.

"So what's the play?" Bast asked, "we go grab the little fella?"

"And we destroy the fairies," Kimmy said.

"Are we sure?" Charlie asked. "It's not like they're…"

"Angels?" Tabitha offered.

"Well, I was going to say imps," Charlie said.

"Exactly," Tabitha said, "we know now, whatever they look like, they're magic and, worse, they're in our world now. The job is to destroy them. We all ready?"

They rummaged through their bags to pull out their weapons, while Jackie and Zack shifted their grips on their walking sticks. Ready, they nodded to each other and stepped out from behind the trees.

The fairies met the appearance of the teenagers with mischievous laughter; however, when their eyes shifted to the weapons in the youths' hands, they chirped at each other in an oddly musical tone. The four fae creatures broke away from the child and spread out to confront their attackers. One gestured towards a nearby tree, and an angry hum came from it in response as a beachball-sized swarm of bees erupted from inside a hollow in the trunk. The swarm moved like a cartoon towards Kimmy, who screeched and ran in the opposite direction, with the bees in pursuit.

Before the others could move to her aid, a second fairy cupped its hands and made a cooing sound into the forest. There was a crashing noise as three massive, wild boars charged from behind the trees.

The fairies laughed as the teens backed away, unsure of how to approach the tusked beasts. Max barked at the boar closest to Charlie and flanked around it, while the other two boars charged Bast and Tabitha.

Bast leapt out of the way and the boar squealed in frustration as it careened past him, scrambling to halt its charge. Tabitha followed Bast's example, but her foot hooked itself under a root and she stumbled to the ground in the path of the angry pair of tusks. She screamed, but her cry was met with a grunt from the boar as it crashed with force against an invisible wall. Jackie groaned from the effort.

Art made a move towards the nearest boar with his short sword ready.

Charlie called out to him, "Don't hurt them!"

"What?" Bast and Art both looked incredulous.

"Distract them for me. I've got this," she said.

Zack's breath had steadied and he ran towards Tabitha to help her up. Charlie stepped towards the boar Max had turned around, with her arm outstretched. The boar's ears pricked up and it sniffed the air, but its body language changed as Charlie approached and she placed her hand on its side. The animal relaxed and sat down on the ground. She moved around it, patting its head to keep it calm. Charlie stepped back, holding a string of pale forest flowers that had been tied in a crown around the boar's head. The animal's eyes seemed to clear, although the calming effect of her spell remained and the boar lazed on the forest floor.

The others were attempting to distract and confuse the remaining boars by circling around them and shouting. It was mostly working, as the boars looked from person to person, unsure of what to do.

"I think it's the crowns," Charlie said.

"Crowns?" Art's face was wrinkled in confusion.

"The flower circles on their heads. I think they're magical or something," she held one aloft.

Art concentrated for a moment. "She's right. There's some weird magic on those flowers, and it feels a bit like Mind magic, I think."

"So we have to wrestle them and pull it off?" Tabitha was limping a little from her hard fall.

Kimmy circled back around, still pursued by her apian attackers. Each hand was filled encased in conjured fire and frantic, she waved her arms around to keep the swarm away. "What gets rid of bees?"

Zack said the first thing that came to mind. "Smoke?"

Kimmy kept running. "I can do smoke!"

Zack worried Kimmy was going to burn the forest to the ground, but his attention snapped back as a boar charged at him. He dove out of the way, but timed his jump late and, while he missed the tusk, the boar slammed him aside with the weight of its body and the wind rushed out of him. Bast stepped past him, reaching out towards the boar while chanting.

"Got it," Bast said.

Zack looked over his shoulder to see a circle of flowers hovering in the air. The uncrowned boar fled deeper into the forest.

Bast grinned. "That was hard! Thanks for slowing it down with your..."

His smile turned into a look of pain as one of the fairies flew in behind him and sliced the back of his calves with its tiny blade.

Kimmy finished her hurried incantation, distracted by the pain from bees that had avoided her ineffective flames, and the fire in her hands turned into plumes of smoke. The grey clouds engulfed the swarm and within a few moments it ceased its attacks and dispersed.

Tabitha tried to blow the flower chain from the third boar's head with sharp gusts of summoned air, but the flowers were woven too thickly into the boar's fur and, apart from a gentle wobble, the crown stayed firmly in place. Charlie approached the boar, which was thrashing against Jackie's shield. She repeated her previous calming magic and as soon as she had finished, Tabitha jumped forward and yanked the flowers clear.

With their animal proxies neutralised, all four fairies joined in the attack themselves. They dived in and out at almost impossible speed and slashed at their human targets with their miniature but sharp blades. One slammed into Jackie's magical shield and, as it hovered in a brief daze, her brother sliced it in half with his short sword. A second fairy was faster and thrust its tiny sword into Jackie's shoulder. Zack and Tabitha chased after it, swinging their weapons, but it jetted up into the air outside their reach, laughing.

A few metres away, another fairy lured Max toward it, singing softly to her, and the dog stepped closer as if in a trance.

"Charlie, Max!" Zack shouted.

Charlie screamed out to her companion, "Max!"

Her voice shattered whatever fae enchantment was falling over the dog. A brief look of surprise crossed the fairy's face as Max leapt forward and snatched it out of the air and into her jaws.

The remaining two fairies turned to flee into the trees, but Bast and Tabitha stepped forward.

"I've got the one on the right," Bast said.

Both made quick incantations, their fingers moving through the air. The fairy on the right went rigid, as if it had been wrapped up in twine, and fell to the ground.

A sharp bang ripped through the air next to the fairy on the left. Its hands clutched its ears, while its wings beat uselessly in the air. It fell hard to the ground beside the other.

"Quickly," Tabitha said, and Art and Zack charged forward, killing the prone fae before they could recover.

Zack forced himself to look away from the broken body of the fairy he had struck and saw Kimmy staggering through the forest towards the others.

"Are you okay, Kimmy?"

Kimmy looked over in his direction, but seemed to be unable to see him. Her mouth was wide open as she gasped for air with shallow breaths. He dropped his walking stick and ran, reaching her in time to catch her as she fell to the ground, fighting for breath.

CHAPTER 20

RETURN

In the tree-filtered morning light, Zack could see Kimmy's exposed skin was covered in hundreds of bee stings, as she lay on the ground struggling for breath.

"What's wrong?" Tabitha ran up behind him, followed by Art and Bast.

"Bee stings. A lot of them," Zack's mind was racing.

"Is she allergic or something?" Art asked.

"I think everybody is allergic to this many stings. Now quiet and let me think. Sara's discussed this with me in theory, but I've never actually done it."

He closed his eyes and focused on his memory of the lesson: The Source, the Intent, the Target. The Source? Plenty of Life here to draw on. The Target? Kimmy's cells, being attacked by the bee toxin. The Intent? Neutralisation of the toxins. This was far more precise than anything he'd tried before. He could hear Sara's instructions in his mind, but he could also hear her warnings about trying untested magic.

"I don't have a choice," he wasn't sure if he was speaking to his friends, himself, or to Sara's voice in his mind.

Zack knelt down beside Kimmy's gasping body and wove his hands and fingers, taking great care to make the precise forms he had been taught. He knew there was nothing magical about the gestures; Sara had been honest in a way none of the other mentors seemed to have been, but the pattern of movement kept his mind focused on the task. He forced his mind to stillness: there was no cold winter air, no worried friends, no gasping, dying Kimmy. There was only the Source, the Intent and the Target. His mind flowed through the Life into Kimmy's cells, seeking out the right ones to harness and fight the bees' toxin. Uncertain, but calm, he allowed the Life to lead him, and when he found what he hoped was the right Target, he relaxed and allowed the Life to flow. Kimmy's breathing returned to normal, and the harsh redness of the stings calmed. He dropped his arms to his sides and his spirit was buoyed as Kimmy smiled up at him.

Art patted him on the shoulder. "Good work, Lifer."

Bast and Tabitha helped Kimmy up and Art did the same for his best friend. Their attention was drawn to Charlie, who was attempting to pry a dead fairy from Max's jaws.

"Drop it," Charlie said. Their eyes met in a brief battle of wills and Max reluctantly gave up her trophy.

Charlie rubbed her muzzle. "You did great, Maxie, but I don't know what eating this thing would do to you." She held the fairy at arm's length. "Um, what do we do with this?"

"And what do we do with him?" Jackie pointed to the toddler, who sat on the ground, watching them.

"Do we take him back to the village?" Art asked.

"That could give us more attention than we really want," Kimmy said.

"We can't leave him here," Charlie said.

"What if we walked him closer to the village, and then we take off to avoid the search parties?" Bast asked.

The others nodded in agreement.

"And these?" Charlie shook the fairy in her hand a little more than Zack thought was necessary.

"My mentor mentioned burying creatures she'd fought," Zack said. "But I don't think we could do that in time, and we can't hide them. They clearly smell enough like food to attract animals."

"I guess that leaves only one option then," Tabitha said.

"What?" Kimmy asked.

Zack grimaced. "We're going to have to take them with us."

Kimmy's jaw dropped open. "How?"

"They aren't that big," Bast said, "I'm sure we could wrap them up in our spare clothes and stick them at the bottom of our bags."

Zack opened up his duffel. "Let's try and get them all into mine. That way, we've only got the one bag to worry about."

The boys pulled out the summer clothes they had worn to the Tower that morning and wrapped up the bodies. It was unsettling to do, but Zack focused on the necessity of maintaining the Silence.

Once his bag was packed, not a lot heavier than before, they began the slow walk back to the village. The little boy seemed quite happy to walk along, holding hands with Jackie and Tabitha.

They hadn't gone far when Kimmy said, "I wonder what the fairies were going to do with the little guy."

"Well, it looked like they were bringing him back," Bast noted.

"Weird," said Kimmy absently, scratching at the bites on her neck.

Something clicked in Zack's head.

He turned to face Art, whose expression suggested he had had the same thought. Without speaking, they both reached out with their sense, investigating the toddler with Life and Mind.

"Changeling!" they said in unison.

"What?" Tabitha asked.

"That's not the missing boy," Art said.

Jackie snatched her hand away. The others all looked at him in confusion.

"In stories about fairies, there are these things called changelings," he said. "Basically, fairies steal children and replace them with things that look like them. And, while I didn't notice it at first, that thing there doesn't have the same kind of Life in it that the rest of us do."

"Or the same Mind," Art said.

"No," Tabitha said. She looked down at the child and it peered up at her with a far too knowing smile before bursting into harsh laughter.

Tabitha wrenched her arm away and it dropped to the ground, still cackling.

"So, what do we do now?" Jackie asked. "And where's the real baby?"

"Well, we can't take it back to town, obviously," Art said, "I think we need to take it back to the Tower. Maybe Zack and I are wrong and this is the baby, and they can fix him up and we can sneak him back. Maybe the baby's been taken back to whatever magical realm these things come from, or maybe it's out there somewhere. But we can't stay here any longer with four dead fairies, miss queen of the bees, and whatever this thing is."

Kimmy growled at Art's description, but she looked flushed and tired.

"How do we get him out of here, then?" Tabitha asked.

Art took a breath. "Well, unless somebody has a better idea, I could put it to sleep and stick it at the bottom of my bag."

They all looked horrified.

"Look, I'm all ears if anybody has another suggestion, but I can keep it asleep until we get to the Tower, and I can convince anybody who gets too close not to look in the bag. Either way, we need to decide now."

When no alternative was offered, the others agreed, and Art used his Mind magic to send the creature into a deep sleep. Zack pulled a bandage from his pocket and carefully wrapped it around the creature's head, covering its mouth. They all looked as uncomfortable as Zack felt, but there were no objections, and he made sure the creature's nose was clear. Together with Art, they slid the sleeping body into the taller boy's bag and zipped it almost all the way closed.

"This is all kinds of messed up," Bast claimed the map from Zack, "I think we avoid going back to town. It'll be a longer walk, but we'll hit a major road if we head this way." He pointed through the trees.

They all agreed and they followed Bast's direction.

Charlie sidled in next to Zack. "How did you know that stuff about change… changers?"

"Changelings," he said, "and, I don't know, I've always liked reading about that kind of stuff, magic and monsters and adventures. I'm a geek, remember."

"Well, we're lucky you did. Can you imagine if that thing had got back to the village?"

He blushed at the praise and then blushed more when he realised he was blushing. "Well, we don't know that Art and I are right. I mean, they're just stories."

"Maybe," she said, "but maybe that's where all these stories come from. As well as stories about hell and devils and angels and things."

"Yeah, maybe," he'd had similar thoughts.

"You must be loving all this, then?" she asked. "You've been reading stories about fighting monsters and now you're living it?"

"A bit," he had to admit that parts of this new life had felt right out of some of his books, "but I don't remember the heroes of any of my stories carrying around a bag of fairy corpses."

She stared down at his bag and fell quiet. Zack screamed at himself in the silence of his mind.

The rest of the trek through the forest was uneventful and, as the sun rose, the teens were grateful for the slight rise in temperature that accompanied it. However, they were still cold and exhausted by the time Bast led them to the road on the map. They followed the road and made their way to another town where Art bought them each a bus ticket, and spent some extra Euros on some pastries from a nearby bakery. Zack noticed he was more subdued than usual and they sat down together at the bus station.

"You alright, Art?" he asked.

Art rubbed his temples. "Yeah mate, but it's a bit… I don't know if 'tiring' is the right word, but maybe 'wearing'? Keeping this sleep spell going is tough. I've never held magic for this long. I can do it, but I can't wait until we're back."

"Right, well, if you need a little extra juice, let me know."

"You're up to it? Even after what you did for Kimmy?"

"Yeah, that wasn't too tiring, more tricky. Threading a needle in the dark kind of tricky."

"Well, whatever it was, it was awesome."

"Hey, I'm glad to be useful for once, instead of staying at the back and offering some band-aids at the end."

"Well, you found the fairies and saved a life. I think you've done alright. And I'm really glad Kimmy is okay."

Zack raised an eyebrow, wondering if his friend had now shifted his romantic interests after Tabitha's rejection. "Really?"

Art broke out into a massive grin. "Yeah. If she had been really hurt by those bees, I wouldn't be able to laugh at the image of her being chased by them."

Jetlag or, perhaps more accurately, magical-portal-lag, was catching up to them, and while Zack worked to keep himself and Art awake and alert, the others took the opportunity to snooze as the noon sun streamed through the train windows. A little under twelve hours since they'd departed it, Munich station came into view. Art and Zack roused their friends and the group disembarked the train to make their eager way through the streets and back to the Tower.

The foyer was empty when they arrived. They looked at each other, unsure, before Tabitha called out, "Um, Junie, we're back."

It was Sara, however, who stepped out from where she had been sitting. "Junie is not here. I offered to look out for you if she had not returned by the time you did." She gave an extra smile to Zack. "How did you fare?"

"We killed four fairies," Tabitha said. "They had kidnapped a child. We thought we'd found it at first, but… Art, you'd better get it out."

Art rested his bag on the ground and opened it. Taking care, he pulled the sleeping creature from the bag and laid it back down on the ground.

Sara's eyebrows furrowed for a moment, but then she nodded. "And you correctly determined that it is not the kidnapped child? Well done."

"So we were right? It's a changeling? Then where's the real baby?" Zack asked.

Sara frowned. "Most likely, he is back in this creature's realm."

"Is there a way we can find him?" Jackie asked.

Sara was silent for a moment. "Yes. But you must consider that is not necessarily our role here in the Tower. We maintain the Silence and the Watch. Destroying the fairies, capturing this creature, these tasks achieved this. Entering the fae's realm to rescue the child would not, and it would be very dangerous."

"But it's a baby," Charlie said.

"We have to try, Sara," Zack said.

His mentor smiled at him again. "Of course you do. And the Tower will help. I simply make the point that you do this at your own direction, not at the Tower's. But first, were any of you harmed?"

"Bruises mostly," Tabitha said. "But Jackie and Bast were stabbed by the fairies, and Kimmy was stung by a lot of bees."

Sara moved straight to Kimmy's side and inspected the stings. "Are you alright? How is your breathing? Are you in any pain?"

"I'm okay… Sorry, I don't know your name."

"Sara."

"Sara. Zack did something and the pain went away. Still itches though. And I feel a little warm."

Sara held her hand over Kimmy's forehead. "You are not 'a little warm,' you are burning up. Zachary, what precisely did you do?"

Zack rushed to her side. "When we were discussing poisons and venoms, you mentioned the lymph nodes were vital. So, I fed Life into them to give them a boost."

Sara's expression darkened. "You were not ready for this level of magic. We were discussing it in theory only."

"It was difficult to breathe," Kimmy said, "he saved my life."

"Perhaps, my dear. But what he also did was suppress your immune system to such an extent that you are at a risk of infections from the sting wounds themselves as well as anything else with which you've been in contact."

The blood drained from Zack's face. Sara worked her own magic over Kimmy and, within a few short moments, Kimmy's colour returned to normal and her skin was healed.

"I'm sorry. I thought she was going to die," Zack said.

"And she may still have," Sara said. "You must all understand the dangers of using untrained magic. This could have had a very different outcome. This is not a game."

She moved away from Zack and Kimmy and on to Jackie and Bast, repairing the wounds he had tended with rough bandages.

"We will discuss this later, Zack," Sara said. "Now, quickly, follow me if you are certain you want to rescue this child."

When none of the teens spoke to the contrary, she nodded and they followed her up the stairs. The path Sara took was familiar to Zack, and he thought they might be heading to her quarters, but she soon deviated and led them towards the Movement school. She stopped outside a door and knocked with polite impatience.

Bast muttered under his breath, "This should be interesting."

The door opened and a man with curly blonde hair and appeared to be in his forties looked at Sara and the teens behind her. "Yes?"

"Liam, would you kindly come and help with a gate?"

"And to where would this gate lead?" Liam spoke in a lazy Irish lilt.

"I'm not sure, but we have an anchor." She gestured to the sleeping changeling Art was awkwardly carrying.

"And why are you taking them through a gate?" he asked.

"I'm not; they'll go on their own. They are trying to rescue a child that was taken and replaced by this creature."

Liam rolled his eyes. "Seems like a waste of time to me, and dangerous. The Watch has been met. This serves no purpose."

Kimmy opened her mouth to speak, but Sara beat her to it.

"They neither seek nor require your permission, Liam. I simply came to you first out of courtesy as a mentor to one of them, but if you are too busy, I will find another."

He brushed off her tone. "No, no, I'll not have it be said I'm derelict in my mentoring duties. Come along then." And he strode past them and up some stairs.

The group looked at Bast, who shook his head and followed the two mentors. They arrived in what Zack thought of as the gate room, from where they had previously travelled to Hades.

There was a stone table near the centre of the room and Liam gestured towards it.

"Place the anchor on the table."

As Art gently placed the sleeping changeling on the stone, Liam approached it.

"Seb, see if you can follow along. You aren't remotely ready for this kind of magic, but you may find you learn something if you look closely enough."

Tabitha and Jackie looked at Bast, concern showing on their faces. Bast showed no sign of shock at the dismissive tone or his least preferred name shortening his mentor was using and was instead watching on with intent.

Liam concentrated with one hand resting on the prone creature. After a few moments, he stepped away and addressed the group.

"I have located this thing's home realm. Opening a gate there will not be too challenging, but that is where the easy part ceases. My understanding is you have only travelled to Hades, no other realm?"

They nodded.

"Hades is a large realm, and it is also stable and close to ours. While it is different, it also holds many similarities, fundamentals like distance, energy, consumption. This creature's realm is not like that. It is more different from Hades than Hades is from ours. It is a small thing and dynamic. It moves back and forth away from our realm so much that I don't think we've named it, or if we have, I certainly haven't taken the care to learn it. It is a Fae realm, and the rules within it are bizarre and inconsistent. Gravity probably works, most of the time, there's likely something breathable in the air, but apart from that, leave your assumptions of Physics, Chemistry and the rest of what you take for granted here in this room before you go. Other rules apply though: Eat and drink nothing you find or are offered. Take nothing you have not earned. If you find yourself on a path, do not stray from it. And once you make to leave, do not look back."

Kimmy snorted. "That sounds like something out of a storybook."

Liam looked down his nose at her. "Indeed. Like something out of a fairy tale. Still, this isn't official Tower business, so take my advice or don't."

He strode away and began conjuring a gate.

Sara turned to Kimmy, lowering her voice. "Take his advice."

An oval of shimmering grey light opened and Liam ushered them through. Zack heard Sara wish them good luck as he walked through the gate and his feet stepped down into soft green grass.

CHAPTER 21

FAIRY TALES

The teens, with Max in tow, stepped out of the grey light of the gate into a lush meadow. They stood in what appeared to be a field or clearing, ringed by dense mist outside a radius of ten or so metres. In the centre of the clearing was a single hill, unremarkable except for a wooden door on the side.

"I kind of see what he meant. This place is a little bit strange," Art said.

"Remember what Erik said in Hades, though," Tabitha responded. "Before we go any further, have a really good look at what feels different about this realm, including with our magic sense."

Apart from the obvious things that were strange about the clearing, Zack tried to look closer. Light had the same weirdness as in Hades and seemed to be coming from somewhere unseen, filling the clearing with a kind of twilight. The ground felt normal under his feet, the air smelt and tasted of the outdoors; clean, similar to where they had encountered the fairies in Germany, and there were no sounds to speak of except his friends. He closed his eyes and extended out in search of Life. He recognised it immediately, similar to home, more so than it had been in Hades, but with the same strange tone he had sensed when he first discovered the changeling. It was hard to put into words, perhaps a flightiness, as if even the grass itself would dart away if he gave it too close a look.

He opened his eyes and the others did the same.

"I can feel it," Bast said. "It's strange alright. Movement is here, but it's different, like everything is dancing or skipping or something."

Tabitha nodded. "Air too. I was going to say it was alive, but I think I'm feeling what you are. It's got this kind of whimsical energy to it, like it wants to play."

The others nodded in agreement.

"So, I guess we're supposed to go through the door," Charlie said.

"Do we have another option?" Kimmy asked.

"Well, there's the mists, or back through the gate," Bast said. "But I think the door's the way to go."

Tabitha turned to Art and Zack. "Well, you two are the fairy experts. What do you think?"

Art laughed, but Zack was a bit nervous about being put on the spot. "The door does seem the obvious choice. What do you think, Art?"

Art stopped laughing and approached the hill. "Yeah, I think the door is the way to go, but I've got an idea. There's something about the way Mind feels here…"

He walked up to the door and rapped against the wood with his knuckles. "Excuse me, could we please come in?"

After a brief moment, the door opened, although it appeared nobody was on the other side.

Art's eyes were wide and alight as he entered. "This place is awesome!"

The others exchanged nervous looks, but followed him through the doorway and down the rough stone steps that lay beyond. Inside, the light was warm, orange and flickering, as if from gentle torch flames that nobody could see.

The steps descended twenty or so metres before flattening out into a short hallway. Ahead of them, the sound of joyous folk music could be heard and the teens looked at each other, unsure of how to proceed. When no other option presented itself, they crept down the hallway and into the room beyond.

If finding the fairies in the forest that morning had made Zack doubt his eyes, he could do little now, but call all his senses as liars. The teens entered what appeared to be a grand festival hall in the height of a celebration. Rows and rows of broad wooden tables, lined with benches, crowded the room and were filled with food. There were plates of apples and pears, potatoes and carrots, and large cuts of roasted meat. Tapestries and ribbons hung from the high ceiling in yellows, oranges and reds, accompanied by leaves and flowers of the same colour.

But these sights were almost mundane compared to the celebrants. Fantastical creatures, right out of story books Zack had read as a child, filled the room; centaurs stood beside sitting satyrs, pewter steins of frothing drinks in hand. Elves danced between the tables, while others played along with flutes and pipes. A gnome climbed up from bench to table, to tear the leg off a roast turkey and fairies, similar to those they had seen this morning, flitted through the air.

The youths looked at each other in shock.

"We can't fight them all. There must be hundreds in here," Kimmy said.

"I don't think we'll need to," Art said, "we follow the rules and be polite at all times."

"Is that a go at me?"

Art rolled his eyes. "No, but I'm trying to say, if we play the part of guests, I think we'll be safe."

Zack was still absorbing the sights and sounds of the room. It occurred to him it was impossible. They had not descended low enough for these high ceilings to be underground, and this room would not have fit inside the hill. He chided himself that he shouldn't be surprised by this, but it was one thing to be told you were in a place that didn't obey the laws of reality and another to walk through it. He was about to say something when he spotted something across the room.

"Look, another door," he said, pointing.

Charlie looked down. "And this carpet roll could be a path of some kind, Liam mentioned we should stick to a path, and it leads right up to that door."

"But what if the baby is in here?" asked Tabitha.

"I'll ask," Art said.

"Art, no!" Bast said, but it was too late.

Art took a few steps down the carpet and tapped a chubby looking satyr on the shoulder. "Good evening, sir."

The satyr looked over his shoulder at Art and smiled broadly. Without putting down his mug, he swivelled around on the bench, tucking his goat legs up over the wood so he was still seated, but facing the teen.

"Hello there, young man," the creature replied in a rich voice, gesturing at the contents of the table behind him. "Have you come for the festivities? There is food and drink for all."

"That is too kind, my good sir," Art said. "Perhaps later. At the moment, my companions and I are searching for somebody, an infant boy. Do you know, perchance, where we might find him?"

The satyr stroked the tuft of hair at the end of his chin. "I certainly haven't seen one. No, no, Autumn is not a good time for a baby, the food is too strong, the music too loud. Try again in the Summer."

Art looked puzzled as the conversation slipped away from him. "Um, thank you for your time."

The satyr's laugh came all the way from his hooves. "No shortage of that here. Are you sure you wouldn't like a drink?" He thrust a pitcher at Art.

Art backed up. "Not right now, thank you again."

Art continued walking and the satyr turned back to his celebrations with a shrug. Zack and the others caught up with him.

"Why were you speaking that way?" Tabitha asked.

Art laughed. "It seemed appropriate. I'm trying to fit in."

Kimmy half whispered, "Such a geek."

"I don't know what good it did," Art said, "I don't know if he knows what he's talking about, but if it's Autumn here, we can't wait around for Summer until a baby shows up."

"So what do we do?" Jackie asked. "Look around here for the boy? Or go through that door?"

"I think we try the door," Tabitha said. "If this is a path that we're on, we shouldn't leave it to look under every table. But keep your eyes open."

They moved together across the room. Creature after creature, elf after fairy after centaur, offered them food and drink as they waded through the celebrations. Each time they followed Art's lead and were polite as they declined. Zack was nervous at first that repeated denials would result in some consequence, but the celebrants appeared too involved in their own festivities to worry about them.

While scanning the room, Zack noticed something between the throngs of revellers; first one, then another, until he had counted a dozen or so scattered across the room. He slipped in next to Charlie and was about to speak when she spoke first.

"I see them too, Zack. Who do you think they are?"

Sitting alone at some of the feast tables were several humans. The majority were men, but at least four were women, most either looking down at the tables in front of them or watching the teenagers with strange expressions on their faces.

"I don't know, but I think we should be careful around them." Zack couldn't explain why he felt that way. There was something in the back of his mind, half remembered, that suggested these humans were more dangerous to them than the magical beings all around them.

Charlie nodded in agreement and stroked Max's neck for comfort as they walked.

A few minutes later, they arrived at the door. Art approached. "Excuse me. Could we come through, please?"

The door remained silent and shut. Kimmy rolled her eyes and muttered, "Idiot" as she pushed past him and opened the door.

"What? It worked last time."

A burst of cold air rushed through the door and they hurried through, snow crunching beneath their feet. This new room was far colder than the last and, as an icy wind slammed the heavy door shut behind them, they found it was also pitch black.

"What do we do now?" Bast had to shout over the wind.

"Do we go back?" Charlie asked.

"No," Art said, "we need to keep going."

"Which way then?" Bast asked.

"There's something out there," Jackie said. "I can hear them, feel them, skittering around."

The youths fell silent and they could all hear it, too. There were things out there in the dark and they were circling, drawing closer.

"We need light. Now!" shouted Tabitha.

Kimmy chanted and fire roared to life in her hand. The others had been looking in her direction and the burst of light pierced their eyes.

While blinking away the tears, Zack heard frightened hissing coming from out in the shadows and the skittering sounds retreated. "Good work Kimmy, they don't seem to like that."

With the danger reduced, the group took a few moments to look around. Kimmy's flame did not stretch far into the darkness, but in the shadows beyond, they could see dark, lifeless trees and snow dusted stones.

"Where are we now?" Bast asked. "If the baby is in here, I don't think he'll have survived."

Zack's mind flashed with an idea. "I think we're in Winter."

"So?" Kimmy asked.

"We've been told the rules are different here. I think the seasons aren't times here, they're places. Remember what that satyr told Art? He said the baby wouldn't be in Autumn, it would be in Summer. That room back there was all decked out in harvest feasts and yellows and oranges. This room is all snow, wind and darkness. We need to find our way through to Summer."

Charlie squinted at him in the firelight. "Are you sure?"

He smiled back. "Not in the slightest. But it does make a bit of sense."

Art clapped him on the shoulder. "I concur with my fellow fairy tale expert. We need to keep going forward towards Summer."

"So, which way?" Bast asked.

They all looked around, straining their eyes in the gloom at the edge of Kimmy's flame light.

"Here. It looks like there's a rough path marked out with clumps of stones," Charlie said.

The others followed her lead, moving in a tight pack near Kimmy.

Charlie pointed again. "There's another clump. Yep, this is the path."

The teens moved as one down the path in the dark, huddled together for warmth and the security the light brought. The wind and their own footsteps, crunching down on the icy snow, covered any sounds of their shadowy stalkers, but Max's bared teeth and twitching tail said they were not far.

With no reliable gauge of time's passing, it was hard to measure how long they walked through the cold wind. It may have been half an hour or three. They were cold and tired, following what they hoped was the path from one clump of stones to the next. The only thing that prevented Zack from voicing his worries that they were not, in fact, on the path, was that he had no better alternative in mind. That and it had been Charlie's idea to follow the stones.

However, his fears were somewhat allayed when the snow began to give way to raised stone tiles, and a shadow appeared at the edge of the gloom. It took shape as Kimmy moved toward it with her light and seemed to be some kind of raised platform of stone and ice. On it rested an enormous double throne which, from the glittery reflection of the flame light, appeared to be made of dark ice. Sitting on the thrones were two giant figures.

Kimmy, surrounded by the others, crept forward, further illuminating the occupants of the thrones. To the left was a huge figure of a man, snow-white beard, unkempt and knotted down to his lap. He wore dark armour-like garb that may have been metal or ice and in his hand he clutched a jagged spear of similar material. On his head was a jagged ice crown. His companion was a waif thin woman, her hair as long and white as his beard, but better kept. Her dress was a composite of silvers, blues and whites. Both sat with their heads slumped down.

"Are they dead?" Kimmy asked.

Zack could feel the Life inside them, but it was still and dormant, like it was waiting.

"They're sleeping," Art said, "or something like it, anyway."

"Maybe we should wake them," Bast said, "ask them if they know where the baby is?"

Jackie shook her head, her eyes wide. "No. I can feel the danger radiating off them. We shouldn't wake them."

"But the path ends here," Bast said.

"Then let's look around," Tabitha said.

The need to stay within Kimmy's light made the search difficult, but it wasn't too long before they had found a door hidden behind the thrones.

"Next stop, Spring," Zack said, "hopefully it'll be warmer."

Yellow light poured through the door as they opened it and stepped through onto grass strewn with wildflowers. The air was warm and rich with the scent of flowers and Max, relieved to be free of the cold and threatening winter, bounded through the grass. A vibrant canopy covered the sky in a loose lattice that allowed light to stream down onto a path winding through the thick trunked trees that held it up. The cold melted from their bones and Zack had a momentary impulse to chase Max through the wildflowers.

"This is much nicer," Tabitha said, "still, we're on the job. It looks like Zack might be right about this and the baby is going to be in Summer, but everybody keep an eye or ear out as we go, just in case."

The teens started down the path. Butterflies flitted between the trees and birds sang unseen from the higher branches of the canopy. Zack had the sense there was other Life here too that flitted about out of sight. Further down the path, the sense of this presence increased, and so he was distracted when he saw a satyr approaching from the left amongst the trees. It didn't appear to be hostile, but there was something different about this figure than the ones they had seen at the feast tables, something more vibrant. Movement from his right revealed a centaur, and then a leaner figure, like an elf wearing the colour of the spring leaves, also approached the group.

These figures were unarmed, but they moved with an intent that sent a shiver of alarm through Zack. He was about to say something when he noticed another figure slip from the tree closest to him. Her body, somehow both thin and curved, was the colour of an oak tree and covered with the barest modesty in wispy green silk. Deep green hair in tight, short curls bobbed like coiled springs as she slinked toward him, her amber eyes fixated upon his.

The remains of his earlier alarm called out to him and he turned away from her to his friends. More creatures joined them on the path. Art was smiling at a young woman with green skin and flowers growing from her long brown hair. Charlie's arm was being kissed by the satyr Zack had first spotted while another was approaching Jackie, who was responding with a deep red blush. Tabitha was approached by the verdant elf, while Bast was running his hand over the rippling chest of a third satyr. Lastly, Kimmy was kissing the centaur, while a second elvish figure nuzzled into her neck.

Zack heard Tabitha call out, "Uh, guys?"

A gentle hand touched his cheek, drawing his attention back to the alluring amber eyes and a pair of delicate lips that were reaching up for his. He leant down to meet her and kissed with a passion she returned. His hands moved to her hips and he held her body against his.

"What are you guys doing?"

Zack could hear Tabitha shouting as if at a distance. He wondered where she was going, but as his paramour's hands grasped under his shirt, he returned his attention to more pressing concerns.

"Are you freakin' serious?"

He wished Tabitha would go away. Zack could feel the others nearby too, but he was lost in his shared passion. His lover drew him down to the forest floor and climbed on top of him, pressing her body against him. He responded, losing his fingers in her curls and burying his face in her neck.

"That's it!"

He had a vague awareness Tabitha was chanting and was happy she had found something to busy herself with while he continued with more important matters. His hand had found its way to the petite thigh that had straddled him with such eagerness, when he smelt something odd. No, not odd, off. A rank stink, like garbage that had been burnt and then wet, charged up his nostrils and he blinked the tears out of his eyes. The beautiful face, so intent on kissing his a moment ago, wrinkled in disgust. She retreated from him, back to the trees and he sat up, looking around. There was a slight green tint to the air and the woodland creatures had retreated from their human partners to the safety of the trees. In the centre of the teens, who were in various states of indecency, was Tabitha, arms waving in control of her spell and eyes furious.

"Are you all quite finished?"

Kimmy buttoned up her blouse with a casualness that may or may not have been forced. "Relax, Tabs, it was a few kisses. That horse guy was cute."

"A few kisses?" Tabitha's knuckles went white as she squeezed her hands into fists. "Kimmy, you've been all over those things for close to twenty minutes!"

The others looked at each other in shock, except for Jackie, who hadn't taken her eyes from the ground at her feet.

Art forced a laugh. "That was some pretty intense magic."

Charlie looked at Tabitha. "Why didn't it affect you, then?"

"Maybe because I think with my brain and not what's in between my legs? Ugh!" Tabitha started off again down the path.

Zack could feel his cheeks burning and fell in beside Art as they followed Tabitha.

Art made a show of scraping the top of his tongue on the roof of his mouth. "I swear I'm going to be tasting Tabitha's spell for a week. This is awful."

"Still, lucky it worked."

"Well, honestly, I could have used another ten minutes or so. Speaking of which, mate, fly check."

Zack made a quick fumble at his jeans' zipper, setting off a fresh wave of blushing. After correcting his fly, he joined the others in their silent march behind Tabitha. He couldn't shake the feeling he'd embarrassed himself in front of Charlie; intellectually, he knew the others, including Charlie, had been caught up in the same magic he had, but that didn't change the fact he felt like he'd lowered himself in front of her. Zack risked a glance in her direction and caught her staring at him before they both looked away and continued down the path. He was so lost in thought, he almost walked into Tabitha, who was waiting next to a door cut into a large oak tree. Her arms were crossed tight.

"Have we all had our fill of Spring?"

Art opened his mouth to say something, but met Tabitha's determined stare and shut it again without a sound.

"Okay then, let's get that baby," Tabitha opened the door and they stepped into a grand throne room.

CHAPTER 22

COURT OF THE SUMMER QUEEN

Dense ivy clung to the stone walls and rich carpets of green and yellow covered the floors. At the end of the room, in thrones that matched those they found in Winter, sat two regal figures. Around the thrones, a few dozen fae creatures were gathered in attendance, and all turned to look at the youths as they entered.

In the left seat sat a tall man, his ageless face framed by pointed elven ears and a golden crown on his brow. He eyed the approaching teens with cool curiosity, his right hand near the hilt of an ornate blade. That was all the time Zack's eyes could spend on him as they were drawn to the figure's companion.

On the right-hand seat sat a woman that tore Zack's breath away. She looked down on them with a curious smile and eyes that gleamed with the warmth of a summer's afternoon. Rich, auburn hair cascaded around her golden crown in a thick tangle of curls, hiding what Zack assumed were a pair of pointed ears to match her companion's and she was dressed in a flowing gown of rich greens and yellows.

On her lap sat a human child that looked identical to the changeling. Or rather, Zack thought to himself, the changeling had looked like him.

The teens hesitated, unsure of how to proceed and the woman waved to them with a flourish of her hand.

"You have conducted yourselves in good faith. If you seek an audience, you may approach. As queen of this domain, I offer you sanctuary."

They exchanged glances before walking toward the throne, stopping in a gap between the gathered attendants.

Art took a breath and took an extra step forward, dropping into an attempt at a gracious bow. "Thank you for your hospitality, your Majesty."

The queen maintained her curious smile, playing with the child's fingers. The infant seemed happy with the attention and looked to be in no distress.

"And what brings seven young mortals to my domain?"

"That human child, your Majesty. We seek to return him to his family."

The queen sniffed at him. "That will not do. I have grown fond of him."

Art paused to consider his next thought and none of the others stepped in to speak in his turn. After a brief moment he said, "But he does not belong here, your Majesty."

She arched her brow. "Surely, as queen, I am the authority of what does and does not belong in my realm?"

Art gulped. "Apologies, your Majesty, I simply meant that his place is with his mother and father, who miss him."

"As I will miss him if you take him away. And my loss will be felt longer than his parents'. Your lives are all so very short."

Kimmy stepped forward and Zack's stomach tightened in anticipation. "You and your fairies stole him."

The queen held up her free arm in a delicate shrug. "Be that as it may, he is here now and here he is mine."

Art inched back in front of Kimmy. "Is there something we could offer in exchange?"

The queen's eyes sparkled with interest. "A trade? Interesting. I don't suppose any of you would take this child's place? You are older, but I think, perhaps, filled with far more potential?" Her gaze lingered over each of them in open and unsettling appraisal.

"Uh, no, your Majesty. But perhaps we have something else of interest." Art gave his pockets a frantic pat.

"Would you like this watch, um… your Majesty?" Charlie asked.

The queen dismissed it with the barest of glances. "I have no interest in time."

"I have this necklace. It's silver." Bast held it up and away from his neck with his thumb.

The queen gestured, in silence, to her more impressive array of ornamentation.

"We have some money?" Tabitha asked.

The queen looked away; her interest lost.

Zack had a flash of inspiration and while his idea terrified him, he looked at the child in the queen's arms and decided he needed to try. He pushed the question out of his mouth before his brain could stop him.

"Could I offer you a dance, your Majesty?"

The queen turned back to face him, her eyes curious. "You are offering to dance with me in exchange for the child?"

"Yes, your Majesty." He swallowed with difficulty.

"Are you a good dancer, mortal?"

"No, your Majesty."

"And yet you offer it as fitting recompense for taking this child from me?"

"Yes, your Majesty." The heat radiating from his cheeks burned.

The queen appeared to mull the idea over for a few moments. "Very well, I tentatively accept. On the proviso, of course, that the dance must be sufficiently pleasing to warrant the loss of my dear little companion. Agreed?"

"Agreed, your Majesty." Zack hoped he only imagined his voice breaking in response.

The queen placed the child into her companion's arms. He smirked in Zack's direction before supporting the infant on his lap. The fae monarch rose from the throne and sauntered down the dais towards Zack with a grace that almost made him feel dizzy to watch.

Zack's legs felt heavy, his hands sweaty and he noticed now, adding to his discomfort, that the queen was a good deal taller than he was. Pushing half a mouthful of saliva down his dry throat, he wiped his hands on his sides and forced himself towards the queen. When the two reached the centre of the circled crowd of onlookers, a dozen or so of the attendees began to play a selection of string and woodwind instruments. Zack paused, listening to the rhythm and flow of the piece, before taking a deep breath and bowing to the queen. She curtseyed in return, and he approached, offering her his hands. She accepted his left hand in her right, and his right around her waist.

While her hips were higher against his body than would have been preferable, he had been taught to dance from a young age by his grandmother and, with that thought, the height difference was no longer strained. It was familiar.

He grasped for that feeling, focusing on the memories of his grandmother, as he led the queen of a fairy-tale kingdom in a dance. Zack had no delusions his performance could be rated as spectacular, but he was content to settle for not being a spectacle, and so far he'd managed to avoid stepping on the queen's feet. He faltered for a moment, however, when he met her eyes. She was beautiful, beyond doubt or comparison, but that was not it. Instead, it was the look on her face, a mixture of curiosity and bemusement.

"Easy, child," she smiled as he recovered from his awkward step, "you do not wish to shame her, do you?"

"Who? Uh… your grace?" he asked.

"The one who taught you these quaint manoeuvres. A matriarch of some kind."

Again, he almost stumbled. "You can read my mind?"

"Not your mind, child, your heart. I can feel what you feel for her: the love, the awe, the nostalgia, the determination, the fear… she is dying, isn't she?" The queen's face held no sadness or sympathy, but rather she looked like somebody trying to determine the citrus notes in a new wine.

Zack's shock gave way to his resolve. "Not any time soon, if I can help it."

"It is all 'soon' for you mortals. You must seek life's worth from some other measure than time."

"Is that why you accepted the dance as payment? For my emotions?"

"Indeed, child. Not that your simple dance is entirely without its charms, but alone it would be poor compensation for the loss of that little one. Now, come, let us make this more interesting."

In response, the instrumental music increased in tempo.

The queen's hands tensed around his waist, as she took a non-lead lead of the dance. He moved his feet faster to keep up with hers and they whirled around the courtyard with her shared grace. Out of the corner of his eyes, he caught glimpses of his friends watching on, but he kept his focus on the dance. Before long, sweat trickled down the back of his neck, but at last the music slowed and the two dancers followed its lead.

"There, that should impress your companions," the queen said.

Zack couldn't help his eyes from flickering over to Charlie, who was watching the dance intently, an unclear look on her face. Perhaps surprise or shock.

The queen chuckled and her smile grew wider. "Ah, her? And unrequited at that?" Her eyes sparkled. "My child, you are delicious. Are you sure I cannot convince you to stay a while?"

Zack's cheeks were ablaze. "Ah, no. Thank you, your Majesty."

The musicians brought their piece to a gentle close and the two dancers parted.

"A shame," the queen said, curtseying again in response to his bow. "But my word is true." She stepped up to her throne and claimed the child from the man. She ran the side of her hand down the infant's face before handing him to Zack.

Zack attempted an awkward, shallow bow while holding the little boy. "Thank you, your Majesty."

She gestured towards the door they had entered. "You may leave, if that is your wish, but you are all welcome to return if you do so in good faith."

The others bowed and turned with Zack towards the door.

They had only taken a few steps when the queen said, "One more thing."

Zack started to turn back.

"Do not turn around!" Tabitha hissed before she raised her voice, still facing the door. "Yes, your Majesty?"

Zack was not sure if he could hear a hint of laughter in her voice. "I find that the dance earned a small boon beyond the return of the child, so hear this: something is coming for you, something very old, something very hungry. Prepare yourselves as you can."

"Th… thank you, your Majesty." Tabitha moved to the door with the others following behind her.

Before they walked through the door, Tabitha said, "I trust you all can control yourselves in spring this time?"

But the door instead opened on the grassy, mist-encircled hill top, the faint shimmer of the gate a few metres away.

"Well, that was easy," Art said.

Jackie didn't look so sure. "Bast, are you able to check if that's the same gate?"

"Good idea, Jackie." Bast approached the gate with his hand out. He paused for a moment. "With the massive asterix that I don't really know anything about gates, this one feels right to me."

"Good enough for me." Kimmy stepped through.

The teens waited for a moment before her head emerged back through.

"Yep, we're home."

CHAPTER 23

COST

The others filed in through the gate, Zack still focused on holding the rescued infant against his chest. The tension he'd been holding in his neck since receiving the baby relaxed the instant he stepped on to the Tower's familiar stone tiles.

Sara approached him, taking the baby from him with an easy confidence and giving him a quick examination. "Is all well?"

"I think so."

"Good. We must continue our discussion about your use of magic, but you have all done good work here."

"Yes, we're all very proud of everybody for not dying," Liam yawned before gesturing for Bast to come closer, "now Seb, attend this. I am going to teach you how to close a gate. Everybody else, step away."

Zack moved over to where Art was leaning against a pillar.

"I didn't know you could dance, man," Art smiled at him.

"Don't know that I proved I could."

"Looked good to me and it got us the kid. Where'd you learn?"

"My grandmother taught me when I was little."

"Well, you did her proud, mate."

The two boys watched as Liam instructed Bast on how to close a gate. He spoke in harsh whispers and with precise hand motions.

"I don't know how he puts up with it. The guy's a dick," Art whispered.

"Not sure he has a choice if he wants to keep learning. I don't think there's a mentor appeal process."

"Still sucks."

"Yep."

The gate shrunk in on itself until it was a tiny grey dot and then nothing. Liam stayed silent, but Bast looked pleased with himself.

"Sara, should we take the child home now?" Tabitha asked.

Sara shook her head. "No. Liam has offered to take the child home. The group of you travelling again through Germany, this time with a baby that has been missing for so long, would draw far too much attention. Liam can arrange for the child to be found safely."

"I will not have you children endanger the Silence," Liam took the baby from Sara, "and also, it would do to be acquainted with the area should this child manifest any magical potential as he ages."

As the Movement mentor strode from the room, Jackie whispered to Sara, "Will the baby be safe? With him?"

Sara smiled. "He may not be the kindest of people, Jackie, but he is not a monster. Also, the Silence will be best served by the safe return of that little one to his parents. He will be well."

"Well, in that case, I think we'd better go," Kimmy said. "I don't know exactly how long we've been gone, but I'm sure it's been a while."

"Indeed. Junie will require a full debriefing, but it will have to wait for another time. You have all done very well today."

The youths collected themselves and walked to the stairs. Sara motioned for Zack to linger. He left the others and followed his mentor back to her study. When they entered the room, Zack remembered the Queen's last words to them.

"Sara. We spoke to some kind of Fae Queen when we were rescuing the child. As we were leaving, she gave us a warning. She said something is coming, and that we should prepare ourselves."

Sara turned to face him; her face strained. "Zachary, this is precisely what I have tried to warn you about. These creatures are the embodiment of chaos. She was likely trying to trick you, distract you or worse, entice you back to her realm. And it is hardly a great revelation. 'Something' is always coming. It is the nature of magic to try and breach our realm."

Zack's cheeks burned.

"You are displaying a concerning lack of judgement in these matters. Trusting magical creatures. Using unpracticed magic. Where is your mind? Helping that boy, saving your friend, your heart may be in the right place…"

"It is."

"That is worse. The best of intentions will only lead you to destruction faster than none at all unless you start using some judgement."

Zack stood in silence, unable to meet her eyes with his own.

Sara leant against the wall with an outstretched arm, her other hand rubbing her brow. "Go now, Zack. Be happy with what you managed to achieve today and leave me to think on this."

"Oh, okay," he closed the door behind him.

The others waited for him outside the Tower and he gave his eyes a quick wipe before he joined them. He trailed behind the others as they walked and Bast dropped back to join him.

"You alright, dude?" he asked.

"Yeah, just caught a bit of a serve from Sara." Zack noticed that Bast's expression was more serious than usual. "What about you?"

"Yeah, fine. Still getting over what happened in Spring, I guess."

Zack nodded. "You're embarrassed too, huh?"

Bast spun to face him. "Embarrassed? Nah, I'm pissed off!"

"What?"

"Zack, what happened to us in there was not okay. That was assault. You get that, right?"

Zack squinted. "No, it wasn't. I remember, I was, um, really into it."

"I don't think it matters what your body did or how good it feels. If some guy, or girl, slipped something into your drink, it might feel good. This feels like that to me," Bast put his hand on Zack's shoulder. "I'm not trying to say how you should feel. But I don't think any of us should feel embarrassed. This is something that was done to us."

The two lapsed into thoughtful silence as they walked.

A short time later, Zack climbed onto the bus home and collapsed into the seat next to Tabitha. Charlie, Kimmy and Bast had spread out along the back seat and the two siblings were sitting diagonally across from him, staring with wide eyes at their phones.

"That is a lot of missed calls," Art whispered.

Jackie nodded in silence.

Zack closed his eyes, thinking over what Bast had said, when another thought came to him. "Tabs, can I ask you something?"

"Sure." She sounded as tired as he felt.

"In Spring, how come you…" he struggled to find the right words.

"How come I didn't join in on 'Fairy Grope-Fest-Palooza'?"

"Uh, yeah?"

"Well, I think it's because I'm Ace."

"Yeah, obviously, you're awesome, but I mean, how did it not affect you?"

"Thanks. But that's not what I meant. I'm Ace, as in asexual."

"Oh. So you're not…" Again he struggled.

"Sexually attracted to anybody? Nope. I thought Art would have told you."

"Art knows?"

"Yeah. I asked him over last month to help me with my parents. Poor muffin thought I was hitting on him. I told him then."

"He told me he struck out, nothing else."

She smiled in Art's direction. "He's one of the good ones. Kimmy's got him so wrong."

"Well, we're damn lucky you were there with us, Tabs. Otherwise we'd probably be stuck in Spring forever." Zack shivered despite the stuffy heat of the bus.

Tabitha nodded and closed her eyes again as she rested her head on the side of the bus. "You know, I'm pretty happy with who I am, really. I'm still working it out, but I'm comfortable with it. There's always been a part of me though, just a small part, that wondered, just maybe, if that bit of me was broken," she snorted, in a soft laugh. "Screw 'broken', I'm a freakin' superhero."

Zack smiled in return and closed his eyes, trusting Art to wake him up when they reached their stop.

Lining up outside a classroom waiting for a Maths teacher to arrive seemed to be the most surreal kind of dull compared to his weekend's activities, and a double of Maths on a Monday morning was certain to be dull. He was about to suggest this to Art when he noticed a scowl on his friend's face.

"You alright?"

"What? Yeah. Didn't have a great night last night."

"Even compared to," Zack looked around to see if they were being overheard, "everything else we went through?"

Art laughed. "Speak for yourself, mate. Fond thoughts of those elven nymphs helped carry me to sleep last night. No, it was getting home to two pissed off parents that was the crappy part. They'd been trying to check in on Jackie and me for hours and they lost it at us when we got home."

"Yeesh, sorry mate."

"Oh, that's not even the worst part. I figured 'Hey, we were on Tower business, that justifies a little cheating here.' So I waited until they got distracted and I wiped their memories. A little bit. Enough so they forgot they were angry. Easy days. But then Jackie goes off her brain at me. Quietly, of course, so mum and dad couldn't hear. She made me promise never to mess with their minds again. She's still pissed, even though I promised."

"She might have a point."

"Why? So I should have let my parents stay angry and remember being worried about us? While we were off saving the world? It's not fair. There's all these rules for who I'm allowed to use my magic on, but nobody is telling Kimmy who she can set on fire."

"I'm pretty sure we'd be pretty vocal on who Kimmy can set on fire."

"I've actually been very clear with Kimmy regarding that," Tabitha said.

Both boys jumped, not having noticed Tabitha slip into line next to them.

She tutted. "Good work on the Silence, gents. Not noticing who could hear you."

"I feel like conversations about Kimmy potentially burning people aren't really that uncommon," Zack said, as they filed into the room at the arrival of the teacher. "Anyway, you're cutting it a bit fine."

"Yeah, I swung by the T… office. Checked in with Junie and gave her a quick debrief. She'd like us to swing by on Friday and pick up our pay. We're getting two grand each."

Art's eyes lit up and Zack knew he was already spending the money in his head, probably several times over.

"Did you mention the queen's warning to Junie?" Zack asked as he sat down next to Tabitha.

"Yeah. She said not to listen to it, that it was probably made up to trick us into staying or something."

"Sara said the same thing to me."

"They have a point," Tabitha said, "those things aren't really alive. They're lifelike forms the magic takes, so who knows what their motivations are."

"The queen seemed real to me," Zack said.

"Well, yeah, but you were all up close to her. Might have played with your mind. It really wasn't safe for you to have done that. I mean, think about what those things did to you in Spring. Oh, and remember those people we saw in Autumn?"

"Yeah?"

"Junie says they were probably people who broke the rules. Maybe they stepped off the path, ate some food, or turned around once they had started leaving. We can't trust those things, even the ones that seemed friendly."

Zack didn't know how to respond to that.

"Look, you got the kid out. That was great. But we need to be careful, that's all."

Zack turned to Art for support. "What do you think?"

Art paused before answering. "I think I've got enough for a new phone and a leather jacket."

Zack sighed and opened his text book.

Zack took a deep breath before knocking on the door.

"Enter," Sara called.

Zack opened the door and peered in. "I'm here for my lesson, if that's okay?"

"Of course it is, Zachary. Please sit down."

When he did, Sara rose and fetched a textbook from one of the shelves. He had been hoping for a more practical lesson, but kept his disappointment to himself. Until, that is, he recognised the book; a Biology textbook they had covered months ago.

He groaned. "We've read this one before."

"And we will read it again," Sarah said, "the fundamentals are everything."

"We're going backwards. Am I being punished?" Zack's stomach twisted and ached.

"No. But I have taken some time to consider your lessons. Your quick grasp of the first few tasks led me to push you too hard, too fast. We're going to slow down."

"So I am being punished."

"If you insist on seeing it that way," Sara shook her head, "between your inability to focus long enough to complete complex magic and your recent errors of judgement, you leave me little choice."

Zack struggled to find any words of reply.

"So, shall we begin?" Sara opened the book in front of him.

"Yeah, okay."

Over the next hour, an hour that felt closer to three, Sara moved with a methodical pace through the basic principles of Life. Zack tried to pay attention, but nothing Sara was teaching him seemed new. He spent most of the lesson fighting the urge to check his watch.

Defeated, he walked down the stairs and into the foyer. Kimmy and Bast were already there, waiting for the others. Kimmy was pacing back and forth and it wasn't difficult for Zack to see she was angry about something. Bast met his eyes and gave a sharp shake of his head to warn him off.

When the others arrived, Kimmy stormed outside and they followed behind.

"That was a freakin' joke!"

The group stared at her. Nobody dared speak.

"Do you know what I got to spend forty minutes doing? Practicing my sparks. Master Cho said it was to ensure I was being efficient with my energy. That's crap. I mastered all that months ago. And he gave me a hard time about Spring. I wonder how he found out about that?" She turned to glare at Tabitha.

"Junie asked me what happened on the mission," Tabitha said, "am I supposed to lie?"

"So you're our spokesperson now, are you? Our referee? I don't perform how you'd like and I get a remedial lesson?"

"Oh, come on," Tabitha said, "I'm sure it's not like that."

"I don't know, Tabs," Bast said, "I wasn't sure until what Kimmy said, but my lesson was back to basics as well. Anybody else?"

Zack murmured his agreement alongside Art, Charlie and Jackie.

"See!" Kimmy jabbed at Tabitha with her finger. "Are you happy now?"

Without waiting for a response, Kimmy stormed off down the street.

"I'm sorry," Tabitha called after her, before turning back to face the others. “I’m sorry. Junie asked what happened and I told her.”

The others shrugged and walked off after Kimmy. Zack lingered for a moment, letting Tabitha fall in beside him. She looked at him with tears in her eyes.

“She’ll cool off,” he said, “and I can’t blame you for my lesson. I’m pretty sure Sara’s been planning to take me back to square one for a while now.”

They walked to the bus stop in silence.

CHAPTER 24

STRAIN

Zack slid his books into his bag as the school bell rang for the morning break. He'd woken up exhausted after a night spent thinking about how the Tower mentors had pulled back on their lessons and forty minutes of trigonometry hadn't improved his mood. He waited for Art to gather his folder and sought eye contact with Tabitha. She hadn't sat with them, which was not that out of the ordinary, but as she fled the room, he thought she might still be feeling guilty about the previous night.

By the time Art was ready, even Ms Agarwal had left and the two boys shuffled together towards the quad. From the steps of the Maths block, they looked over at their usual bench. It was empty.

"Where do you think everybody is?" Art asked.

"My guess is nobody wanted to be around Kimmy and Tabitha."

"Not even Kimmy or Tabitha," Art said with a soft chuckle. "Oh, hey. Look over there."

Zack's eyes followed to where Art was pointing. Charlie and Dave were sitting at a bench in between two buildings. Even from that distance, it looked like an uncomfortable conversation.

"Where's Matt?" Zack asked. "He wouldn't be trying to avoid Kimmy and Tab."

"Not Tab at least," Art said. "I saw him come in this morning.

He'll be around somewhere."

The two boys wandered around the school in search of Matt. The break was almost over before they found him, sitting in a circle with some other boys, playing a trading card game.

Art moved behind him. "Hey mate. We were looking for you."

Matt didn't lift his head. "Well, you found me."

Zack heard the tone in his voice, but Art continued. "Whatcha up to?"

"Playing a game."

"Oh. We were wondering where you were."

At this, Matt looked up. "Really? You were wondering where I was? Funny."

Art scrunched up his face in confusion. "What's that supposed to mean?"

The bell rang and the others in Matt's circle snatched up their cards, looking grateful for the excuse to move away. Matt left his cards on the ground and stood up to look Art in the face.

"What it means, Art, is I find it funny that for once you're the one wondering where his friend is. For example, I haven't been sitting with you at recess or lunch for about two weeks."

Matt's words landed on Zack like one of the Commander's statues had knocked him in the head. His mind raced, trying to prove Matt wrong, but it was true.

Matt continued, "I got sick of conversations that ended the moment I walked up. Sick of going home from school alone. Of logging on and finding both of you offline, night after night. I don't know when it happened, but you guys decided you didn't want to hang out with me anymore."

"It's not like that," Zack said, "we've been focused on studying and…"

"You're a crap liar," Matt said, "and even if I did believe you, why not ask me if I wanted to study? You've been cutting me out for months. Well, I get it, I'm cut. I gotta get to class."

Zack and Art watched in stunned silence as their oldest friend turned his back to them and walked away.

Shock gave way to guilt and Zack spent the next two lessons lost in thought. When the lunch bell rang, he still sat, staring at his desk, until Mr Hancock cleared his throat. Oh, Mr Hancock, Zack thought, so this had been English class then. Zack took the hint and headed out into the hallway.

He couldn't face another empty bench, or the inevitable conversation with Art about Matt, not yet anyway. Instead, he sought refuge in the library. Zack tucked himself away in between the stacks and out of the sight of the librarians. He hadn't had much of an appetite all day, but he decided he needed to eat something. He reached into his bag, tore off a corner of his sandwich and chewed without tasting it.

The library was quiet and he closed his eyes, letting his thoughts and worries loose in his mind. Matt was right. Art and he may not have been explicit with each other, but they had been excluding Matt from their lives. Yes, the pressures of the Tower had taken up a lot of time, but if he was honest with himself, they had put in little more than a token effort of maintaining their friendship with Matt. Under the all-consuming focus of the Tower, their friend had become one of the 'others' and Zack had done nothing about it.

And was it all for nothing? After months of putting his Tower training above everything else, he was back to square one. Or worse, as now Sara seemed to have no faith or trust in him. But if he quit now, would Art drift away like they both had from Matt?

That thought destroyed the rest of his appetite and, after forcing down his last mouthful, he pushed the rest of his sandwich back into his lunchbox. It was then he heard sobbing from the stacks behind him.

Curiosity, and the need for a distraction, got the better of Zack. He stood up and peered around the side to find Charlie sitting on the ground between two rows of shelves. With a book on photography opened in front of her. She might have looked like she was reading if not for the wiping of tears with her sleeve.

Zack took a steadying breath and moved a step closer.

"I'd ask if you were okay…," he said.

"Oh, hey Zack," Charlie sniffled, "yeah, obviously not."

"Want some company?"

She patted the carpet next to her in reply. Zack crouched down on his knees, feeling awkward and aware, as always, of how close he was to her.

"Dave and I have been fighting. Since the Germany trip. I had like a hundred messages from him by the time we got out. He thinks I'm ignoring him. I guess he's kinda right. And he's so angry about it. I don't know if he's more upset that I might be breaking up with him or that I haven't," she dabbed at her face again before continuing. "One moment he's promising to be a better boyfriend, the next he's making demands like I have to message him back quickly. I don't know what to do."

"I think he's just scared of losing you, Charlie," Zack said.

"Yeah?" Charlie's tears made her blue eyes sparkle even more than usual.

Zack was lost in them when he heard himself say, "I would be." He slammed his mouth shut.

Charlie smiled at him. "That's kind, Zack." She was quiet for a moment before continuing. "Maybe I should break up with him. Let him go find a girlfriend who can be there for him. I don't know. Anyway, what are you doing in here?"

Happy to move the conversation on, Zack decided to be honest. "I needed somewhere to think. I lost one of my oldest friends today. Or I did a few weeks ago and didn't even notice."

He explained to Charlie what had happened that morning.

She reached out and squeezed his hand. "I don't think any of us really understood what the cost of the Tower would be when we started."

"I'm not sure if it's worth it. I don't think I'm cut out for this stuff," Zack said.

Charlie's grip tightened on his hand. "Go and ask that little boy's parents that question. You and Art stopped us from taking that creature back to them. The two of you got us through that weird kingdom. And you, you Zack, got that little boy home."

Zack's face burned and he looked away. "Yeah, but not with magic or anything. Mostly reading old stories and… stuff."

"… and dancing?" she suggested.

"Yeah."

"Well, it worked."

"I'd like to be able to do more magic, though, but I struggle to hold the focus with anything but the simplest of spells. How do you do it?"

"I concentrate on one thought. Usually, the thing I'm trying to do, or the why I need to do it. Either way, I hold that in my head while I work the magic."

Zack shook his head. "I can't seem to manage that. While I'm concentrating on one thought, a dozen others pop up and unless I'm doing something really simple, it all falls apart."

Charlie placed her fingers against his temple. "Busy in there, is it?"

Zack chuckled. "Noisy, at least." His heart thumped at the feel of her palm against his cheek.

"What the hell?" said an angry voice from above them.

Charlie snatched back her hand and Zack looked up to see Dave standing outside the shelves.

"Dave…" Charlie began.

"Nah, screw it," Dave turned to leave.

Charlie grabbed her bag and stood. "It's not…"

"…what it looks like?" he said over his shoulder. "Are you serious?"

Charlie stepped past Zack to follow her boyfriend. "It's just Zack. He's just a friend."

The librarian's shush, louder than the whispered argument that prompted it, quietened them and Dave left the library with Charlie in pursuit.

Zack stayed sitting in between the shelves until the bell rang, Charlie's words circling in his mind. Just Zack. Just a friend.

Zack kicked off his shoes next to the front door. His mother appeared from the study.

"You're home early. Is everything okay?"

"Yeah, but I've got an assignment to do," Zack said, which happened to be true.

"Are you sure everything is okay? I thought you were doing your assignments when you were staying back."

"I'm fine. I wanted to do it here today."

"Okay," she squinted at him, "last night's leftovers are in the fridge if you want something before dinner. If you want me to proofread anything, let me know. But don't stress too much about it. I'm sure you'll do well on it."

A guilt laden reminder, however innocent, was not what Zack needed.

"What if I don't?" He heard his voice raise to a shout. "What if I fail?"

She stepped towards him. "Zacky, I know Year Twelve can be stressful, but you've been putting in the work. You'll be fine."

"What if the effort isn't enough?" He stepped back away from her. "I could fail and all the work I've done will be for nothing. And telling me everything will be fine won't help."

"Zack."

"Leave me alone. I've got work to do," he stormed to his room and slammed the door behind him.

Sitting down at his desk, he already regretted how he'd spoken to her. He wanted to go out and apologise, but he was worried he'd make it worse. He'd been holding in these worries and fears for too long and now they were boiling over inside him.

He booted up his computer and opened the Ancient History assignment. A two thousand word essay on the relationship between Athens and Sparta. He'd written the barest of bones so far, but he'd found enough sources to piece together a decent argument. He pulled a few textbooks from his backpack and started typing. He hadn't written anything past the introduction before his eyes drifted over to the messenger icon on the screen. Was Art online? Matt? Charlie?

He pressed his palms against his temples. None of them were conversations he wanted right now. He returned to the essay, picking up from where he had left an unfinished sentence.

With the help of library books, his own notes and a liberal amount of googling, he spent the next few hours cobbling together an essay he hoped would scrape by. He heard his mother call out that dinner was ready, but between the assignment, his lack of appetite and his embarrassment, he ignored it and pushed on at the keyboard. The summer sun set before there was a tap at his door, pulling Zack from his edits.

"Come in," he said.

His father pushed the door open with a plate of stir-fried noodles, cutlery tucked underneath. "Hey mate, thought you might be hungry."

"Oh, thanks." Zack swivelled around on his seat and accepted the plate.

His father sat down on Zack's bed, facing him. "So?"

"I'm sorry, Dad. I had a rough day and…"

His father held up a hand. "I'm not the one you've got to apologise to. And, obviously, you're going to go do that in a bit. But do you want to talk about what's going on?"

Zack nodded. "I guess I've put a lot on my plate. I thought I could manage it. I've been pushing myself really hard and I thought it was paying off, but I don't think it's working anymore." He paused, trying to put his thoughts into words he could share with his father. "I've got this idea of what I want to be, but I'm not sure it's possible. And I'm scared I've gone through all this for nothing."

His father sat in silence while he spoke and for a few moments after.

"We're proud of you, Zack. We're proud of your results last year. We're proud of the effort you've been putting in. And we've given you a lot of freedom lately, because we can see how seriously you're taking your work."

His father was silent again, his mouth ajar as if he was trying to find the right words. "There's a lot of pressure in school to work out what you want to be. And then when you do work that out, there's the pressure of becoming what you want to be. That's fair enough, but you don't really need to know that yet. You're going to spend a lot of your life working out again and again what you are going to be.

"But the choices you're making now are deciding who you are going to be. That's much more important. And that's what I've been most proud of. You're thoughtful, smart, imaginative, mature and kind. And you're not the kind of young man who yells at his mother because he's had a rough day. So, don't let the 'what' you want to be change the 'who'." He slapped his hands on the top of his thighs as he stood up. "Now, eat something and then go apologise to your mother. I'm going to go water the garden, so you'll have some privacy."

"Thanks, Dad."

Zack's father left the room. With the plate balanced on his lap, he stabbed at a piece of beef. He chewed at it while thinking about what his father had said.

Zack leant against the side of the slide, stifling a yawn. Like the others, he'd woken to a group text from Art, asking everybody to meet up at Tatters Park before school. He hadn't been to the park since that morning almost a year ago, the day they first went to the Tower. Charlie sat on the swing, avoiding eye contact with Zack. Kimmy leant against the centre of the see-saw, her shoulder turned in a deliberate effort to place Tabitha out of her eyesight. Bast lingered away from the equipment, looking like he wanted to be anywhere else.

Art stood in the centre of the loose circle they'd formed, with Jackie right behind him. He scanned around at the others and took a breath.

"Okay, we need to get over whatever is going on here."

Kimmy glared at him. "Let me guess, because you like Tabitha's legs, you don't care that she screwed us over with the Tower."

Art returned the look, ignoring Tabitha's groan of frustration. "No, actually, I'm pretty annoyed. But that's not why I messaged everybody. Jackie had a dream."

"A dream? That's why I got up early?" Kimmy said.

"It's not just a dream. Jackie, you better explain it."

From the way Jackie peered around at the group, it appeared to Zack she would rather not.

"It's okay, Jackie," he said.

She stepped forward to stand next to Art. "My dream was a warning. At the start of the dream, I could hear the fairy queen's words and I knew they were true. Something is out there and it is very old, very hungry and it's coming. In the dream, I saw it was in Hades, but it wasn't from there. It was cold, and dark, and wet, like the bottom of the deepest well. And it's looking for a way to get here."

"That sounds awful, Jackie," Tabitha said, "but I'm sure it was just a nightmare. And no wonder, given everything we've been through lately. I've definitely had a few, myself."

"It wasn't," Jackie's voice was firm, "I could feel the danger, like it was a rock coming at my head. Something bad is trying to get into our world."

"If that was true, Jackie, wouldn't the Tower be all over it?" Bast asked. "I mean, there are really experienced Protection mages there. Why are you the one getting the warning?"

"I don't know," she said.

Art put a hand on her shoulder. "I believe her. It's her job to protect us and that's what she's doing."

"I'm not saying I don't believe her," Tabitha said, "but maybe she's confused. Or maybe it's something the fairy queen did to her."

"I trust her," Zack said, "but the mentors will say the same thing Tabitha said."

Kimmy snorted. "No surprise there."

"Well, we are supposed to be learning from them," Tabitha said.

Zack ignored the interruption. "What I'm saying is, while I trust Jackie got a warning in her dream, the mentors won't. Which means there isn't anything we can do about it except to be alert and be ready. I trust her, so I'll be looking out for whatever is coming. It's up to you guys if you do the same."

"Can you tell us anything about it?" Charlie asked. "Like, what does it look like?"

Jackie answered in a soft voice. "I never saw it. It was like it was always behind me. But this thing is smart. It's a hunter. And it's dangerous."

Zack wished he didn't believe her.

CHAPTER 25

ESCORT

Zack selected one of his preferred quarterstaffs from the racks in the training room and gave it a twirl.

Bast, already armed with the thin-bladed rapier, was quizzing Tabitha. "Did Junie say what we were going to be doing?"

"No. Like I said before, she told me to retrieve our weapons and head up to the gate room."

"Maybe this means we're off probation," Art's voice rang with hope.

"Maybe Tabitha's been putting in a good word for us," Kimmy said.

"Give it a rest, Kimmy," Tabitha said, "I don't have anything to do with this."

"Yeah, can we please put all this behind us?" Charlie asked.

"If we're back to doing real magic, and if Tabitha promises not to report on us again, then I'll let it go." Kimmy stood with her arms crossed, her long-handled axe in one hand.

"I promise," Tabitha said, "I won't talk about any of you to Junie."

"Good." Kimmy turned and walked out of the training room.

Zack was hopeful that would put an end to the tension, but he was worried today's task would turn out to be some kind of test that would set Kimmy off all over again. If his lessons with Sara over the past fortnight had been any indication, the probation had not lifted.

Medical textbooks and fundamentals still made up the majority of every lesson, as well as lectures on the dangers of magic and how magical creatures could not be trusted. Each lesson, Sara also tested his focus. He continued to fail. He tried clearing his mind, he tried Charlie's trick of holding a single thought, he even tried to use sheer determination and ignore all of his thoughts. Nothing worked. He tightened his grip on his quarterstaff and followed his friends up the stairs.

Junie was waiting for them in the gate room.

"Thank you for coming," she said. "Your task today is escort duty. You will accompany Demitri to another realm."

The teens looked over at a bearded man in jeans and a long sleeve t-shirt. He raised his hand in an awkward half-wave.

"The realm is a comparatively peaceful one, compared to your previous excursions. However, you must, as always, be alert to danger. You are to protect Demitri as he goes about his work. Any questions?"

Zack had a dozen questions, but keen to show his obedience in case Art was right, he kept silent. The other teens all shook their heads.

"Very good." Junie nodded to a third mage in the room, who incanted towards the central platform. Within moments, a grey, elliptical gate had opened up. Demitri stepped through, a well-worn rucksack over one shoulder, and the teens followed.

Zack's eyes took a moment to adjust. The dim torchlight of the Tower was replaced by the brilliant light of a midday sun. They had stepped out onto a tropical beach. The pure white sand underneath his feet led around twenty metres from the glistening blue water up to a dense rainforest.

"Wow, this is beautiful," Bast said.

"It is," Demitri said, "I like it here."

Zack closed his eyes and extended his senses. The Life here felt almost normal. Different from home, but then again, he'd never been to a tropical island, so it was difficult to know how different it was. There was, perhaps, a wildness here. Not the lurking hunger of Hades, or the chaotic whimsy of the fairy realm. Rather, an untamed feeling around the edges.

He opened his eyes to see Demitri ambling towards the trees.

"Um, Demitri, shouldn't we be going with you?"

The older mage turned around to reply. "No, that is not necessary. I'm just seeking a few samples. Keep watch here on the beach. I will not be long."

With that, he slipped into the foliage and disappeared from sight.

The teenagers looked around at each other.

"Well, that was a little strange," Bast said.

"It's totally a test," Art said.

"What do you mean?" Charlie knelt down beside Max.

"They want to see how we perform. Whether we follow instructions, if we can be trusted. That kind of thing." Art stabbed his sword down into the sand.

"So what do we do, then?" Zack asked.

"What we're told," Kimmy's tone invited no argument, "I am not staying on probation."

They all turned to face the tree line.

"Should we have insisted on going with him?" Tabitha asked.

"Not if it was a test in obedience," Art said.

"Yeah, that makes sense," Tabitha said.

"I'm already bored," Bast said.

"We could take it in turns to keep watch." Zack glanced around at his friends.

Jackie and Kimmy agreed to take the first turn and moved up a little closer to the trees. The others explored the narrow strip of beach closest to the gate. Art found a thin piece of driftwood, washed up on the sand.

"Hey Max," he said, "wanna play?"

The dog's tail wagged, although she didn't bark, and she bounded towards Art. He hurled the stick across the beach and Max darted after it, snatching it out of the air. Charlie applauded as her companion returned the stick to Art for another turn.

The game continued for another five or ten minutes before Jackie waved at them from where she stood watch.

"I think something's coming."

They ran up the strip to where she and Kimmy were peering into the trees.

"I'm not sure," Jackie said, "I'm getting a tingle of danger."

Zack listened. The forest was far from silent, but there was nothing that suggested something was coming closer. He extended his senses, but was overwhelmed by the amount of Life. He opened his eyes and shook his head.

Art also had his eyes closed, reaching out towards the trees. "I think there's something out there, but it's all too fragmented."

"Let me try," Charlie said. With Max standing beside her, she held out her hand towards the rainforest. After a short moment she opened her eyes and they were wide with alarm. "Back up, everybody. There's a bunch of creatures coming this way. Lizards, I think. They're scared and angry."

The teens followed her back towards the water, stopping about midway between the gate and the tree line. Reptilian heads emerged from the undergrowth. Their dark eyes scanned the area, while their long tongues tested the air. When they faced the group of humans, they slowed. One stepped out onto the beach. The lizard was massive, like a Komodo Dragon, but leaner. It crept forward across the sand on three pairs of legs.

"Can you get them to leave, Charlie?" Tabitha asked.

"I can try." Charlie locked eyes with the giant lizard and chanted. The lizard scuttled back, but then more lizards emerged onto the beach. The first one shook its head and hissed at the teens.

"There's too many of them," she said, "and I think they're responding to each other. It's a territorial thing. There's something here that doesn't belong and it's got them all riled up."

"Demitri?" Kimmy asked.

"I don't think so, but maybe?" Charlie readied her bow.

More than a dozen lizards had moved their way down onto the beach.

"What do we do?" Bast asked.

"We could run back into the gate, get help," Jackie said.

"No," Art said, "I reckon this is a test. Demitri has gone in, jacked them all up and pushed them towards us. We've got to show we've got what it takes to protect the Tower."

"Let's show them, then." Kimmy launched a ball of fire towards the closest lizard.

The flames crashed into the side of the reptile and it hissed in pain as it was knocked back and onto its side. It struggled to regain its footing while the other lizards skittered down the beach towards the teenagers.

"Kimmy!" Bast shouted.

"What? I thought it would scare them away."

"Nope," Charlie said, "all you've done is piss them off." She aimed down the length of an arrow and fired it at one of the oncoming creatures. The arrow lodged in the lizard's shoulder, but its thick hide prevented the arrowhead from penetrating too deep.

As their reptilian attackers surged forward, Kimmy threw more fire, striking another, while Charlie nocked and fired again. Jackie and Bast chanted their own spells and the others readied their weapons.

The lizards manoeuvred across the sandy beach with ease and the first of them reached the teens with a lunge, talons outstretched. Their speed took Tabitha and Kimmy off guard and both received deep cuts from the lizards' wicked claws. They turned at the last moment to protect their chests and the cuts fell on their forearms. Art and Bast were luckier, retreating back a step to avoid being harmed.

Kimmy slammed her axe deep into the shoulder of her attacker, while Tabitha's flail struck hers in its head. Bast thrust his rapier at the lizard in front of him, but the angle was off and the thin blade bent against the thick hide. Art, gripping his sword in two hands, swung at the extended leg of his own attacker, cutting it off. Charlie fired again, while Max bared her teeth, ready to defend her, and Jackie threw shields up, buffering the continued attacks of the lizards.

And Zack stood, watching. He knew it was his role, as a Life mage, to be ready to support his friends, but he felt useless. The assault continued and more lizards joined the fight. Jackie and Charlie crept forward to support the others. Despite this, Tabitha and Kimmy were each facing four enemies and could do little but defend themselves against the overwhelming numbers.

"Screw it," Zack said to himself and charged forward in between the young Air and Fire mages. He reached Tabitha's side in the nick of time and thrust his quarterstaff into the jaw of a lizard, preventing it from biting into her leg. He moved with his own momentum and spun, slamming the other end of the staff into the back of one of Kimmy's attackers. The blow knocked it flat onto the sand.

The two reptiles responded to his attacks by circling in on him. He lost sight of the rest of the battle and he parried a flurry of teeth and talons. To his right, he caught a glimpse of a spray of blood accompanied by a scream of triumph from Kimmy, but otherwise, this fight was his own. He slid his grip further down his quarterstaff and swung the full length of it at the front leg of one of the lizards. It landed with a satisfying crunch and the lizard fell back, supporting its weight on its other legs. The second lizard lashed out, trying to bite at Zack's leg, but he kicked at its jaw, pushing it away.

Zack focused on the lizard he'd already injured, doing his best to circle around it and keep the other one on the move. He swung again and again at its legs, and with each solid hit, the creature slowed. As he broke a fourth leg, the reptile slumped and seemed unwilling or unable to pursue him as it stepped back and away. He took a breath to prepare himself against the second lizard and glanced around.

Several of the creatures lay dead, but he and his friends were still outnumbered. On either side of him, Tabitha and Kimmy were each facing a single opponent. Both girls were covered in deep scratches and Tabitha was favouring her left leg. Art was being flanked by two of the creatures and was swinging his sword in a wide arc to keep them at bay. Jackie, too, had two lizards on either side of her. The small girl had fallen, her spear out of reach, and had resorted to throwing up a shield to hold them off. Bast was rushing towards her, sand flying up as he ran at an unnatural speed. Charlie and Max were also approaching but, with no clear shot, Charlie held her arrows.

Distracted by the sight of his friends in danger, Zack mis-stepped on the uneven beach and fell down. A lizard was on him in an instant, snapping at his face and neck with its gaping jaw. He gripped his staff sideways and pushed its centre forward into the lizard's mouth, holding it back from biting him. Already tired from the fight, his arms arched at the strain as the creature used all its feet to dig into the sand and leverage itself forward. Zack kicked at its legs but, on his back, he couldn't throw enough weight behind them and his blows bounced off.

Its mouth came closer to his face and its wet, acrid breath washed over his skin. His arms ached and weakened against the strength of the lizard's efforts when, all of a sudden, the lizard twitched in pain. A moment later, the lizard was knocked off him as the furry shape of Max slammed into its side. Zack's quarterstaff, still in the creature's mouth, was ripped out of his hands. He scrambled to his feet and saw the lizard had an arrow sticking out of its spine.

Charlie ran towards him, nocking another arrow.

"Thanks," he said, straining for breath.

"Thanks for holding it still for me," she grinned.

Any further discussion was broken off by Jackie's terrified scream. Zack looked towards her and found Bast and Tabitha engaged with her attackers. But Jackie wasn't screaming in fear for herself. She was looking over at her brother.

Art landed a swing on one of the lizards that had left him open and the other launched itself at him. The attack knocked him over and raked deep cuts across his abdomen with its talons. His blood splashed onto the sand as the lizard crawled over him, ready to bite at his neck.

"There's still too many, but I'll do what I can," Charlie began chanting. Her face strained with the effort. She screamed with exertion and collapsed to the ground. The effects were instantaneous and obvious. The remaining lizards hissed with fear, their eyes darting around. They broke off their attacks and fled up the beach and into the trees. Some, like the one Zack had injured, moved at a slower pace, but with no less urgency.

Zack ran to Art's side and knelt beside Jackie. She was staring at her brother's wound, eyes wide and face pale. Art held on to consciousness. He was not groaning so much as mewling. Zack inspected the wound and fought back panic of his own. The lizard's curved talons had dug in deep. The skin and muscle was shredded and, judging by the smell, some organs had also been cut.

"Oh crap," Zack whispered to himself.

Bast appeared over Zack's shoulder. "We need to get him back to the Tower."

Zack's mind raced. "No," he said, "moving him could kill him. And even if we got him there, Junie and that Movement mage can't help. It could be minutes before we got a healer to him. I don't think he has that long."

Jackie started crying.

"Then what do we do?" Bast said.

Zack took a deep breath. "I have to try."

CHAPTER 26
CONSEQUENCES

"Do you even know what you're doing?" Tabitha asked.

"I know the theory," Zack said, "and I think that's the only chance Art has."

"Please, do something." Tears collected on Jackie's cheeks and chin.

"Okay, everybody quiet. No distractions, no interruptions."

Zack closed his eyes and reached out with his mind towards Art's Life. Startled by how faint it already was, he almost lost his focus before he began. He located the injury, where Art's Life was working at repairing the damaged organs and blood vessels. It would be too little, too slow, but the Life endeavoured to do its work regardless of its hopelessness.

Not hopeless, thought Zack, because it gave him something at which to aim the flow of Life. He ran through Sara's instructions in the principles of casting spells. Source, Target, Intent. He gathered Life, taking a bit from himself to start and drew in the ambient Life that existed all around him. He directed that Life to where Art's own was doing its work, narrowing down the mist into a few concentrated streams. And the Intent: repair.

He focused on this and allowed the Life to flow through him and into Art. Sweat, far more than from even the exertion of the fight, streamed down his face and arms, but he focused. His body ached with fatigue, but it was working. Before his eyes the blood flow slowed as the veins and arteries repaired, the organs mended and Art's own Life grew inside his body.

Perhaps this would convince Sara he was ready for more complex magic. Or would she be angry with this attempt regardless of its success? Could she refuse to teach him and, if so, would that mean he could no longer train in the Tower? If he was excluded from the Tower, he wouldn't be there when his friends needed him. He could lose them as friends, the same way he'd lost Matt. And what would it mean for his grandmother? These thoughts lasted a mere instant, but it was enough.

Too late he realised his control over the streams of Life had wavered and the flow had gone astray. Art's bones thickened and grew, uninjured organs swelled, and nerves lengthened. Art was no longer whimpering, he was screaming.

"Oh no, I screwed up!"

"What in the heavens happened here?"

Zack looked up to see Demitri jogging towards him, a full rucksack on his back and a look of confusion on his face.

Kimmy shouted in response, "Giant lizards came out of…"

"We need to get Art back to the Tower. Now," Zack said.

Demitri nodded and, together with Zack, Bast and Kimmy, helped pick up Art and carry him to the gate. Charlie raced ahead with Max, disappearing through the grey light, while Tabitha followed behind, comforting the distraught Jackie. Art's screaming had quietened from his exhaustion, but he was writhing as they carried him, and Zack could see his enlarged bones pushing against his skin.

They strode through, entering the Tower. The mage who had opened it was alone and began her work to close the gate as soon as Tabitha and Jackie arrived.

The mage glanced over her shoulder as the gate shrank. "The girl and the dog have gone to let the healers know to expect you."

They hurried through the corridors and down a flight of stairs to find Sara waiting for them. She gestured for them to follow her into one of the practice rooms where they placed Art on a bed. Sara approached his side and the others stepped away. She took in the sight of Art with a gasp.

"What have you done?"

"He was dying," Zack said.

"He *is* dying," There was anger in her voice. "Everybody out. I will see to your injuries in a moment."

Zack went to follow the others but she placed her arm in front of him.

"Not you, Zack. Undoing what you have done will be painful. It may still kill him, regardless of what I do. You will stay and learn the consequences of your foolish actions."

She turned away from Art to face Zack. "But I cannot trust you with the knowledge of what I do. I cannot trust you with the little knowledge you have already. You will stand over there, facing the wall. If I see you turn, see you trying to catch the smallest glimpse of my magic, I will have you cast out of the Tower. Do you understand me?"

Zack managed a nod before shuffling away to stare at the stone bricks. He chewed on his bottom lip, trying to calm his frantic mind.

Behind him, Sara began her work.

"Art, can you hear me?" she spoke over the boy's groans. "I'm sorry, but this is going to hurt. Bite down on this piece of rubber and stay with me."

She chanted and the warm-cool swell of Life rippled through the room behind Zack. And then Art started screaming again. The piece of rubber Sara had placed in his mouth did little to muffle the sounds of his pain and Zack could do nothing but stand and listen, tears of guilt and shame running down his face. Zack didn't know how long it took, but it seemed an eternity. The rubber must have fallen from Art's mouth and his screams surged in volume. Sara did not cease her chanting, so there was nobody to comfort Art in his torment and Zack continued to hear what he had caused.

At some stage, perhaps an hour later, Art's cries of pain ceased, as did the flow of Life in the room. Zack couldn't help himself; he spun around in fear. Sara was standing beside Art, looking in Zack's direction.

"It's okay, Zack. He's resting."

Zack's stomach relaxed. "So, he'll be okay?"

"Yes. No thanks to you, however. Zack, what were you thinking?"

"He was dying! I was trying to save his life," Zack said.

Sara's face was red with anger. "By using magic you haven't been adequately trained in? He very nearly died in agony from your actions."

Zack's tears were hot on his cheeks. "Well, if you'd taught me more, it wouldn't have been untrained magic!"

"Taught you more? More?" Sara raised her voice. "If anything, it is clear I have taught you too much. I've foolishly given a child a chainsaw and have expected him not to lose any limbs."

"A child?" Zack's volume rose to meet hers.

"A child, Zachary. One who has not the maturity or discipline to be trusted with this magic."

"That's not true."

"Isn't it? Very well. Art could use a deeper, more soothing sleep. Perform the resting spell I showed you. Prove you have the discipline required for more complex magic."

Zack stared at her. She was serious. If he could do this, he could show her he was ready. This was his chance.

He moved to Art's side and took a deep breath in an attempt to calm himself. His body ached with fatigue and his mind raced, but he pushed it all to the side and focused on Art. He reached out with his senses and felt Art's Life. It was glowing calmly, recuperating, but echoes of the multiple traumas resided within. Zack pulled back and narrowed down his focus into Art's brain. He wondered if his friend would find it ironic, given his calling for Mind magic, but he pressed on, locating the regions responsible for regulating his sleep. This spell, in theory, only used a speck of energy, but it was complex and precise.

Zack gave a slow exhale and attempted to clear his mind as he called in Life towards him. However, thoughts of failure, of loss, of fear, rushed towards him and he dropped the spell before he started. He tried again, and again, but each time he was overwhelmed by distracting thoughts. No matter how hard he tried, he could not push them from his mind.

He dropped his head in defeat, and Sara moved opposite him and cast the spell instead. He followed her to the other side of the room, to let Art sleep.

"There is your proof, Zack. You are not ready. You lack discipline, and without it, you can do immense harm with your attempts. As we've seen," she gestured at Art, "and, as concerning, is your lack of common sense. Beyond making choices with your magic that are dangerous, is your refusal to listen to the more experienced members of the Tower about how magical creatures operate. You listen to that fairy creature as if she can be trusted. You try to persuade Junie something dangerous is coming. Magical creatures are drawn to our world, like gas into a vacuum, that is all. We have told you this, but you persist. Until you are ready to listen, to hear and to learn, there is nothing I can teach you. Nothing I will teach you."

Zack stood in silence, tears streaming down his face.

"Go. And think well on whether you have any future with the Tower." Sara turned back to care for Art.

Zack exited the room, wiping at the tears on his cheeks with the back of his wrist. He stepped through the door and his friends were there, looking at him. Two other Life mages were doing their best to appear focused on tending to the group's injuries, but it was obvious everybody had heard what had happened. Embarrassed, he slipped through them and fled down the stairs. He heard Tabitha calling out to him from above, but he didn't slow. Instead, he started skipping steps as he hurried towards the entrance chamber.

Once there, he plunged into the unnatural darkness of the exit and emerged into the twilight of an early autumn evening. He took a longer path towards a bus stop, hoping to avoid any of his friends and to allow him some time alone with his dark thoughts. His fears and worries raced around his mind, but by the time he reached the bus stop they had slowed and he climbed up the steps of the bus in a dull shock.

He slumped into the corner of the back bench and stared out of the window before remembering to turn his phone back on.

Alerts blared down the bus, notifying him of dozens of messages and missed calls. His mother, his father, his sister. He picked one at random, his heart in his throat.

Where are you? Babi is in the hospital.

CHAPTER 27

PRIORITIES

After everything the day had already thrown at him, Zack sat staring at his phone, struggling to comprehend the message. He took a moment before working his way through the rest.

Please call me back when you get this.

Are you on your way home?

Mum n Dad R worried. Where R U?

We're on our way to the hospital please call.

We're here now. Doctors say Babi has had a reaction to the medication. Deda called an ambulance. Please call back when you get this.

The information wormed its way into his reluctant mind. Zack's heart lurched at the unsaid implications of his whole family rushing to the hospital.

He listened to the voicemail messages. His mother raced through her sentences, pushing out the details before her emotions had a chance to derail the call. She ended by asking a dozen questions but they all equated to the same thing. Where are you? His father's voice was quiet and dry, trailing off as he struggled to find the right words. He didn't ask where Zack was, and instead that he hoped Zack would call them back as soon as he could.

Zack decided to start on his way to the hospital before calling them. He thumped the next-stop button and hurtled down the steps the moment the doors opened. It was a Saturday night in the Sydney CBD, and it took longer than he liked to flag down a taxi. When one finally pulled over, he bundled into the backseat and called his father.

"Zack," his father sounded tired, but relieved.

"I'm sorry, Dad. My phone was off and I only just got all the messages."

"That's okay. Are you home? We're all at the hospital."

"No, I'm on my way to you. Maybe fifteen or so minutes away? Is Babi okay?"

His father took a deep breath. "Okay? No, not really. The doctors say she's not in any immediate danger, but she could deteriorate. We're here for your Deda as much as anything. Ugh, speaking of which, he's hassling the nurses again. I'll explain more when you get here." His voice moved away from the phone. "Dad, come sit do…"

The call ended. Zack stared out the window of the taxi as it struggled through the Saturday evening traffic that routinely clogged Sydney's streets. Outside, people headed to venues, bars and clubs, living lives of blissful ignorance. If not for that night in the alley, almost a year ago, Zack might have been out there with them. In theory, anyway. On Saturday nights, he was more likely to be playing games online, but he might have been doing that in blissful ignorance. One choice to take a shortcut and his whole world had changed.

The taxi left the glut of traffic behind and started making decent time through North Sydney to the hospital. Once it pulled up outside, he paid the driver and bolted out of the car, through the doors and up three flights of stairs to the oncology ward. He spotted his grandfather first, pacing back and forth across one of the waiting areas. Zack slowed down as he reached him and gave him a hug.

His grandfather returned the hug, crushing Zack with a strength that shouldn't have belonged to somebody in his late eighties.

"Zacharias, you didn't need to come. You're young. You should be out having fun."

"Of course I came," he said, "do you know where Mum and Dad are?"

"Here, mate." His father appeared behind him, carrying four paper cups between his fingers. He offered one to Zack's grandfather.

"Coffee?" his grandfather asked, taking a cup.

"Tea," Zack's father scowled, "as if you need more coffee. You should be sitting down."

"I don't need to sit," the older man scowled back, his face a mirror of his son's.

"Should I go and check with the nurses where the cardiac ward is? That'll be fun for us all, running between your two beds. And how much use to her will you be if you collapse?"

"Don't manage me." But Zack's grandfather strode back to the waiting area and sat down, sipping his tea.

Zack and his father followed behind and Zack's mother flew from beside Ellen to give him a hug.

"Where have you been?" she asked without letting him go.

He decided to be vague, given he didn't know how many calls she'd made trying to track him down. "Sorry, my phone started to die, so I turned it off to save the charge, then I forgot all about it. I only turned it back on a little while ago."

"Well, you're here. That's what matters."

"So, what's going on?" Zack asked.

"You explain," she said to his father.

"Your Babi had a reaction to her medication. We're still not sure exactly what. She's on a lot of different things. They raced her over here to try to work out what the problem is. The issue is, they've had to take her off everything, including the painkillers."

"She's in a lot of pain?"

His father nodded. He glanced at Zack's mother.

"Tell him, Jon. It's okay," she said.

He steadied himself with a deep breath and when he spoke, he used a calm, quiet voice that seemed unlikely to reach where Zack's grandfather was sitting. "The doctor explained that the pain is a problem. It's stopping her from resting properly and she's exhausted. It's putting her body under a lot of stress and her condition is only going to deteriorate from there. But they can't risk putting her back on pain relief because that could react to everything that's already in her system."

"So, tonight could be goodbye?" The words stuck in his throat.

His father squeezed him on his shoulder. "Probably not. We're hoping not. But it's possible."

Zack and his parents sat down next to Ellen. His sister had her earbuds in, watching something on her phone. She had red rings and smudged makeup under her eyes. They sat in silence together, Zack staring at a TV screen without absorbing anything about the show.

An hour or so later, his mother left to stretch her legs and, a little while after that, his grandfather ventured off to find a doctor, with Zack's father trailing behind. Looking sideways, Zack noticed Ellen's eyes were closed. Unsure of whether she was listening to music or if she'd fallen asleep, he decided that now was as good an opportunity as any.

He slipped unnoticed into his grandmother's room, a private room opposite the waiting area, and stood against the wall, taking in the scene. Her bed was in the centre of the single room with a cadre of machines looming above it, beeping in a constant, soft chorus. She lay in the bed, twisting under the sheet, soft gasps of pain accompanying the beeps of the machines.

Zack's mind fought against the scene, refusing to accept it as truth. His grandmother looked so tiny and fragile, he wanted to believe it wasn't her. Once again, tears found his cheeks.

"I'm sorry, Babi. I wanted to help you, but I couldn't. I wasn't good enough."

Zack closed his eyes and reached out with his senses. He was worried about what he would find by doing so, but he did it anyway. His grandmother's Life was faint. Strained. The cancer's Life was there too, but the strain was something separate, something pervasive. Her Life still endeavoured, as it always did, but there was nothing left in reserve, no renewal.

He found himself drawn to the point in her brain Sara had shown him earlier that evening on Art. Not only could he not cure her cancer, remove her pain and give her back her life, he was too inept in magic to even give her a decent night's sleep.

He could try, he thought, but he'd fail. His mind would fill with distracting thoughts. His fears, his worries, his hopes. Here, with her, the one person he wanted to heal more than any other, he'd never be able to push away all the thoughts, and the spell would collapse. Without the Tower, he'd never learn enough magic to make a difference to her. Or to anyone. His friends would be sent on dangerous missions and he wouldn't be there to help them, to heal them if they were hurt. Or the Tower would assign them somebody else, another Lifer, and they'd move on without him. He'd lose the only friends he had left. He'd lose Art. He'd lose any chance he had with Charlie. He'd lose any chance of being special and making a difference to the world. And all because he couldn't focus enough to help this woman who had loved him all his life.

His mind was filled by these thoughts when his grandmother let out a loud groan of pain. He hadn't realised he had been holding onto the sense of her Life, when he found himself beginning to channel. His fingers wove in the air as he, nervous about the Life around him, chose himself as the Source. Still holding his sense of her Life, he found his Target with ease and his lips moved with arcane syllables and he breathed his Intent: Rest.

Life flowed from him and into his grandmother. He felt the touch, the familiar resonance that was her own Life and as the spell worked his Will, her body eased. She ceased her groans and gasps. Her body stopped squirming and relaxed, her chest rising and falling with deep, calm breaths.

Zack slumped against the wall, his muscles aching. The spell itself had not taken a lot of his own Life from him, but manipulating the delicate stream of it had tired him out.

A moment later, he heard his grandfather's voice outside the room. A beleaguered doctor, followed by Zack's father and grandfather, entered.

"I know it is frustrating," the doctor said, "but you must trust me when I say any intervention we take would put your wife at a greater risk. If she can hold on until her toxicity..."

His voice trailed off as all three men stared at the peaceful form of the woman asleep in the room. Zack took advantage of the distraction to slip out behind them and watched from the edge of the door.

The doctor swept the clipboard from the end of the bed and flicked through the first few pages. Her brow furrowed.

"Is everything okay?" Zack's father's voice was filled with worry.

"A moment please," the doctor replaced the clipboard before moving over to the IV stand to inspect the fluid bag.

"She seems like she's sleeping," Zack's father said, "isn't that a good thing?"

"Yes, absolutely. It's surprising, that's all. Please wait here. I need to check a few things. I'll be right back."

The doctor hurried from the room while the two men moved to the foot of the bed and watched Zack's grandmother sleep. Zack observed the doctor having a brief conversation with the nurse before she returned to the room.

"The nurse assures me no pain medication has been given. This was my primary concern given the change in her comfort. She's a very resilient woman. In the morning, we should be able to resume some mild pain relief and begin to reformulate her prescriptions. Now, if you'll excuse me, I have some other patients to see to."

"Thank you," Zack's father said as she left the room.

Zack's family loitered for another half an hour and his grandmother remained asleep. His grandfather relaxed enough that they were able to convince him to let them take him home, with the promise to return first thing in the morning.

While his father drove his grandfather home, Zack climbed into the back of his mother's car and settled in. It was then, as they drove away from the hospital, that Zack allowed himself to recognise what he had done. Somehow, he had managed a spell that had been beyond him two hours earlier. Something was different. It had *felt* different. As he started to analyse what he had done, he paused, realising one fact already.

He was not giving up.

CHAPTER 28

APOLOGIES

The euphoria of helping his grandmother had worn off by the time he got to bed and he laid awake, considering his options. He was still lost in them Monday morning in a double lesson of Biology. When it came down to it though, there was only the one option. He had to return to the Tower, apologise to Sara and do whatever it took to remain an initiate under her guidance.

The thought terrified him, an anchor against the buoying news that his grandmother was doing well, responding to her new medication regime and would be returning home in the next few days.

What would he do if Sara refused to take him back? She had said he needed to think about whether he had a future with the Tower, but what if she had already made up her mind?

And what if his friends didn't want him back? In all fairness, how could they? They had all watched as he mutated Art's body and heard the screams of pain as Sara healed the damage. How could they trust him not to do the same to them? He had dodged them that morning, avoiding any confirmation of his fears, but he couldn't any longer.

As if it was listening in on his thoughts, the bell rang, signalling morning break. He lingered in the classroom, his mind cluttered with vivid worries. He dragged his feet as he followed the other stragglers out into the quad.

Zack was most of the way to the bench when he noticed all six were already there. The group was talking quietly, but all of them were facing him. They shuffled their feet as he approached, looking like they were preparing to hold an intervention for him, he thought, as if they were about to start reading from sheets of paper and telling him they loved him. His nerves threatened to get the best of him and forced himself towards them and he couldn't trust himself to look Art in the eyes.

"Hey," Zack said.

They each waved or nodded to him.

"Hi, Zack," Tabitha said, "you had us all a bit worried. We haven't heard from you since…"

"Since I nearly killed Art?" Zack said.

"What?" Art's eyes went wide.

"I can understand if you want to ask Junie for a new Life mage for the group. Or if you already have."

"Zack…" Tabitha started.

"It's okay. How can you trust someone with your life like that when you've seen what I did? But can you at least come with me when I go back so that…?"

"Dude, stop!" Art grabbed him.

"I almost killed you, Art."

"You saved me, Zack," Art moved his hands to his friend's shoulders, steadying him in place, "I'm alive because of you."

"No, you don't know. You were out of it."

"They've all told me. Jackie's told me a hundred times. If you didn't do what you did, I'd have died on the beach."

"I screwed it up. I'm sorry." Zack's voice broke into a sob.

Art pulled him forward, holding him in a tight embrace. "Don't be sorry. We're all still learning this stuff. But you pulled it together and saved my life. Thank you, Zack."

Zack didn't respond. None of this had been a factor in all his wild thoughts. He put his arms around his friend and hugged back.

After a moment, they stepped away from each other. Zack remembered they had an audience and his cheeks were warm.

"I love it when straight guys cuddle," Bast said and Kimmy cackled in response.

The warmth in his cheeks burned hotter and hotter still when he saw Tabitha and Charlie beaming at him.

Zack shuffled in place. "So you guys don't seem to be done with me, but Sara still might be."

"Go and apologise," Tabitha said, "tell her you'll do whatever it takes. We want you with us."

"And we'll be right beside you, if you want us there," Charlie said.

"I do, thank you."

The sense of peace that speaking with his friends had given Zack evaporated as he stepped off the bus to go to the Tower. His mind provided dozens of potential conversations with Sara and none of them ended well. His mouth was so dry he struggled to swallow. Art gave him a sympathetic squeeze on the shoulder and Zack realised that, whether in conscious thought or otherwise, his friends had formed a protective circle around him as they walked. His determination surged; he couldn't let them down. He took a deep breath, stepped through the doors and into…

…chaos. Dozens of people, more than Zack had ever seen in the Tower in total, were in the entrance chamber. The room was abuzz with chatter and groups of people rushed around, most armed with a variety of weaponry.

The teens stood in the doorway, staring. One group bustled past them and out of the Tower, grim looks on their faces.

"Ah, I was hoping you'd arrive in time." Junie stepped out from behind a cluster of people and approached the teens.

"What's going on?" Tabitha asked.

"Our wards have detected a major incursion. Scores of breaches have opened up in western Africa. We've got to respond with overwhelming force to shut it down and to ensure the Silence after it's over."

"Does this happen often?" Bast asked, looking around as more armed mages exited the Tower.

"An event on this scale is quite rare. It might be there's been some ill-advised magic use in the area, or it might be random. We'll examine what caused it when the threat has been eliminated. But first we have to accomplish that, so we've sent out a call," Junie spoke while she monitored the room.

"But we didn't get any call," Kimmy said.

"No, you didn't."

"This is an all-hands-on-deck kind of thing though, right? We can come and help?" Kimmy asked.

"No. To put it bluntly, you've all been improving, but you're not ready for something like this. We're going to be spread thin and each unit needs to trust that each other unit is taking care of business. More bluntly, you'd be a liability."

Kimmy looked like she might choke.

"Do you need us to leave?" Tabitha edged herself in front of Kimmy in case she said something she'd regret. Or at least should regret.

Junie paused for a moment in thought. "No, stay here. It is good to leave somebody in the Tower. And we may be able to put you to use when we return. There will obviously not be any lessons, but if you wish to practice, perhaps weapons training will suffice for today?"

That seemed to be a clear enough direction to move out of everybody's way and the teens headed downstairs to the training room. A few more groups passed them along the way and Zack noted to himself that he was recognising maybe one in ten of them as people he'd previously seen around the Tower.

Once in the training room, they dropped their bags in a corner and sat on the benches, waiting for the already lessening stream of Tower mages to finish equipping themselves from the racks.

"There are a lot of people in the Tower," Art said.

"We knew that," Bast said.

"Yeah, but I don't think I really knew-knew it until now," Art said.

Kimmy tightened her arms across her chest. "This sucks. They still don't think we're up for it. Haven't we proved ourselves enough?"

Zack waited for Tabitha to reply, but it was Bast who spoke.

"Put yourself in their shoes, sis. You're about to head off to a massive battle. Would you want a group of less experienced teenagers guarding your back? C'mon, grab an axe, let's work off some stress."

"Maybe go easy, guys," Zack said, "I'm about to be the sum total of Lifers in the Tower."

Their eyes flicked to Art's chest and then back to him.

"Yeah, fair point," Bast said.

Zack joined them at the racks, picking a quarterstaff from the remaining selection. "There's more weapons left than I'd expected," he said.

Bast was testing the balance of the rapier. "A lot of them have their own. At least in the Movement school. I want to buy my own as soon as I can work out how to hide it from my brothers. Well, and as soon as I can afford it."

They took turns sparring against each other, practicing their routines without any real attempt to land a blow or harm each other. Zack's mind relaxed as he trained. The tension he'd been holding inside flowed out with each block and parry of his quarterstaff. He finished a round with Tabitha and was ready for another.

Before he could seek out another partner, Charlie beckoned him to follow her over to the side of the room. Her lips were pursed as he approached.

"Are you alright, Charlie?"

"Yeah, I just… uh… wanted to talk to you about what happened in the library."

Zack's heart crept up into his throat. "What do you mean?"

"Dave and I worked it out," she blurted, without making eye contact with him, "we're not breaking up."

"Okay," Zack swallowed, hard. "That's great. I'm glad it worked out."

"Yeah, I think it's best if…" A confused look crept onto her face and she looked away, out the doorway.

"Best if…?" Zack asked.

She held up her index finger without turning to face him.

Tabitha noticed the interaction. "What is it?"

"Sshhh!" Charlie responded, again without breaking her concentration.

The others took notice and moved to join them.

"We're supposed to be alone in the Tower, right?" Charlie asked. "Everybody else is off dealing with the breaches?"

"Way to rub it in, Charlie. Thanks," Kimmy said.

Tabitha ignored Kimmy. "Yeah, but why?"

"Because I'm sure I can hear somebody crying."

They all stood silently, straining to hear.

"I don't hear anything," Art said.

"Me either," Kimmy said.

Zack's ears picked up some kind of sound. "I think I can hear something."

Art raised an eyebrow at Zack.

"No, I can."

"Let's check it out," Bast said. "It's not like we're busy."

They followed Charlie up the stairs.

Kimmy grumbled. "Why exactly do we care if somebody else is here?"

"A crying somebody," Charlie said.

"Maybe somebody's already back, and they need help," Tabitha said.

They reached the entry room and stopped again.

"Okay, you're right, that's definitely somebody crying," Art said.

"Let's go find them," Bast said.

The group followed the gentle wailing up another flight of stairs in relative silence. The sound led them through the Tower. At each landing or corridor branch, they paused and listened, trying to determine the direction of the crying. The sound echoed off the stone floors and walls, making it difficult, but as it grew louder, it also grew clearer and they sped towards the source.

The group rounded yet another corner and slid to a halt. In the middle of the corridor stood a young girl. She was the obvious source of the crying and looked lost and confused, with her head down, staring at the floor. She rubbed at her face and didn't react to the teenagers' arrival.

"What's a little kid doing in the Tower?" Charlie asked.

"Somebody's kid?" Bast said.

"Have you ever seen a kid in the Tower before?" Tabitha asked.

"Jackie's the youngest I've seen and I get the feeling she's a special case," Art said.

"Well, either way, she's here. Maybe her mum or dad had to leave her here when they went off to deal with the breaches. We should see if she's okay," Tabitha said.

Zack glanced around at the weapons they'd taken with them in their hurry to investigate the sounds. "Um, we might scare her."

"Good point," Tabitha handed her flail to Zack before turning and approaching the girl. "Hey there, are you okay?"

The girl jolted at the sound of Tabitha's voice and her crying stopped. She took a step back down the corridor, away from them.

Tabitha followed. "It's okay, we're friends. What's your name? Are you lost? Maybe we can help you."

The girl swayed slightly, as if confused and didn't look up.

Beside Zack, Jackie whispered sharply, "No!"

Zack turned to Jackie. Her face strained, her eyes scanning the end of the corridor with a frantic urgency. The girl tottered another step back and to the side.

Jackie raised her voice. "Tabitha, no. Look at her shadow. It's not moving!"

CHAPTER 29

INTRUDER

The warning came too late. From right behind the girl, an inky dark green tendril lashed out at Tabitha, wrapping around her ankles. The girl, that was not a girl, rose from the ground, still limp, suspended by a writhing mass of green darkness.

A deep voice rasped from the centre of the girl's figure. "No, not lost. Found. I have tasted you once and I want more. I want to taste your world."

The teens looked on, stunned, but as it started to drag Tabitha towards it, she screamed, snapping her friends out of their shock. Bast and Kimmy ran forward. Bast traced with his fingers as he charged, picking up supernatural speed. He grabbed Tabitha under her arms, trying to pull her back from the creature.

Kimmy also incanted and moved her hands as she strode forward, stepping in front of her two friends.

"I've been wanting to try this one. Thanks for volunteering, bitch!" A thin line of white hot flame sprang from her hand, striking her target square in its centre.

The white dress caught on fire but, while the creature hissed, the flame did not slow it down. Another tendril struck out in response, but this time it crashed against an invisible shield, and Jackie grunted against the effort.

Art surged forward, past the struggling figures of Bast and Tabitha, and slashed down hard with his broadsword. His sharp steel carved deep into the ensnaring tendril and it recoiled, releasing its hold on Tabitha. She and Bast fell back hard onto the stone floor as Art pivoted, standing guard over them. A tendril whipped out and struck Max on her side. The dog crashed into the stone wall, falling to the ground with a yelp of pain.

Charlie called Max back to her side as she fired an arrow, striking the girl-shaped figure in its centre mass. The loyal dog bounded over to her with an awkward gait, placing less weight on her injured left paw. Undeterred, she turned to face the creature, teeth bared.

"Tabitha!" Zack slid her flail along the stone floor towards her.

"Thanks," Tabitha snatched the handle up as she regained her feet. She charged the creature with the head of the flail whirring above her head. "Keep your freakin' limbs off me!"

The mace head slammed into the hovering girl, and again the creature hissed. Another dark tendril lashed out, striking Tabitha in the chest and knocking her back. She was forced onto one knee to avoid falling and Kimmy stepped beside her, ready to attack.

"We don't seem to be making a dent," Art launched a wild swing in an effort to keep the creature's tendrils at bay. "We've burnt it, shot it, hit it. What do we do?"

Zack looked at the figure of the girl and an idea flickered in his mind. As yet more tendrils snapped out at his friends, he reached out with his senses. He found Life beyond his friends'. It was strange and alien and it left him feeling grimy from even observing it. It reminded him somehow of something toxic growing in a deep, dark cave. But more surprising was where that Life was, in the corridor.

"It's not the girl," he shouted to his friends.

"Yeah, no kidding Zack. I think we all worked out it's not a girl," Kimmy fended off an attack with her axe.

"No, I don't mean it's not a girl. I mean, it's not even that thing that looks like a girl. The real thing is behind her. It's like… like an angler fish."

"A what?" Bast asked, ducking under a tendril.

"You know, those ugly fish in the deep ocean. They have those lantern things in front of them that attract fish. The girl is the lantern."

"So, the actual thing is behind her?" Art asked, slashing his sword side to side.

"Yeah. Jackie got it right. Her shadow didn't move. Because…"

"Because her shadow *is* the thing," Kimmy said. "Well, that changes everything."

She shifted her axe into her left hand and then wove the fingers of her right in intricate shapes while whispering strange syllables. Another beam of hot, white fire soared out from her fingers. This time, it blazed past the girl-shaped lure and struck deep into the shadow behind her. The shadow didn't recede as it should have from the white light. Instead, the intense flames struck something. The creature screamed in pain and the teens couldn't help but try and shield their ears from the painful sound.

Five more tendrils erupted, clearly now not from the girl but from the shadowy mass behind her. Off guard from the auditory assault, and in the tight confines of the corridor, there was little they could do to protect themselves. Bast, with his heightened speed, managed to duck out of the way, but the others were not so lucky. Art and Tabitha were knocked off their feet as they were each struck in the chest.

Two tendrils flew at Kimmy. One wrapped itself around her ankle, while another hit her hard in the hip. The momentum from it sent her hard into the wall, but the first tendril's grip prevented her leg from turning with the blow. The combined result was a loud snapping noise as something in Kimmy's leg broke. She gasped in pain as she fell, her injured leg still in the grasp of the creature. Bast dove under two of the tendrils to reach Kimmy and slashed down hard with his blade, severing the tendril close to its tip. With a grunt of pain, Kimmy shuffled backwards, using her other leg and her elbows and Zack jumped forward to stand in front of her, his quarterstaff ready.

Art and Tabitha scrambled to their feet and, together with Bast, the three swung their weapons at the tendrils. The confines of the Tower's corridor were tight, though. Bast's shoulder bumped against Tabitha, while her flail tangled around Art's blade. Behind them, Charlie grunted in frustration, holding her arrow nocked in the absence of a clear shot.

"It's too crowded," Art said.

"I've got an idea." The fingers of Bast's left hand danced as he whispered and an orange glow flared under his feet. "I hope this works."

The young Movement mage bounded at the stone wall and kept running, his feet gripping to it as if he was on flat ground.

"Yes!" Bast ran down the corridor past the tendrils before the creature could react.

Charlie didn't hesitate. She let go and her arrow flew through the gap Bast had made, striking deep into the shadowy mass. In retaliation, a tendril lunged at her, wrapping itself around her waist. But Max was ready. She bit down hard, tearing into it with her sharp, canine teeth. The tendril released its hold on Charlie but, as it retreated, it coiled itself around Max. The dog struggled against its grip, but was unable to break free. Zack slammed his quarterstaff down on the tendril, but it had little effect against its rubbery exterior. It picked up Max and slammed her into the wall, letting her fall to the floor. Max lay still on the side of the corridor.

With an angry scream, Charlie charged forward, firing arrow after arrow in rapid succession. Meanwhile, Bast darted around behind the creature, slashing with his thin blade. While he seemed to be doing little damage, he was holding the creature's attention, and most of the tendrils chased him back and forth across the corridor. His speed and ability to walk on the walls gave him the edge he needed to keep out of their reach.

With Bast distracting it, Art ran forward towards the shadowy centre of the creature. He moved in alongside it and slashed at the dark mass with his sword, cutting deep into it. It shrieked again and recoiled from Bast. One tendril knocked Art's sword from his hand and three came slamming down at him to crush him into the hard stone floor.

Art screamed, but then stopped and looked up. The dark green limbs had stopped an inch above his head, blocked by a shimmering steel light. He turned to look at Jackie. His sister had her hand stretched out at him, her face strained in concentration and effort.

"Finally, you protected me!" he said.

"Really, Art?" Tabitha batted a tendril away.

"Oh, right," Art snatched up his broadsword from the floor. Gripping it in both hands, he thrust forward, using all of his strength and weight to plunge it into the centre of the shadowy creature.

It shrieked again, but this time, the sound was weaker and, within a moment, turned into an awful gurgling noise that made Zack's stomach turn. The tendrils thrashed one last time before collapsing to the floor.

They had won.

CHAPTER 30

FOCUS

They stood panting, looking over the oozing mass that the shadowy creature from their nightmares had become. Kimmy forced herself up on one leg and limped closer to the remains. Her face was a mask of pain and determination as she put her back to the wall closest to the dead creature. She took a moment to steady herself before incanting a spell and flame poured from her hands.

Zack held the back of his hand against his nose as the burning remains let out clouds of noxious fumes, but Kimmy didn't stop until there was nothing but a tar-like stain left on the Tower stones. Then she allowed herself to slide back down to the floor and rest.

"Oh, thank heavens," Charlie said, kneeling over Max. The injured dog lifted up her head and licked off the tears of relief that were dripping down Charlie's face.

Zack crouched beside Kimmy. "I'm not going to ask if you're okay."

"Good," her skin was pale and beaded with sweat, "I'm pretty sure that was my leg breaking back there."

"Sounded like it," he said, "but let me check if there's anything else."

Kimmy nodded and Zack examined her Life. He could sense the break, as well as minor bruises and strains, but nothing else that worried him. Importantly, her Life was strong, ready to repair the damage, however long that would take.

"I think it is just the break. When the others get back, they should be able to fix it, no problem."

She nodded. "Good. Hurts like a bastard."

Zack looked around at his friends. That thing, whatever it was, had been powerful, but they'd pulled together and defeated it. And they were right. Not only had it been tracking them through the realms, but it had been the very creature they'd encountered in the alley that night. Or so it claimed. And it had tracked them all the way to here. But how?

"Um, guys?" he said.

"Yeah, Z?" Art was lying exhausted on the floor.

"How did that thing get here?"

"Oh no," Tabitha said.

"Who cares?" Kimmy prodded at her leg and winced. "It's dead. More than dead."

Bast closed his eyes and reached one hand out down each end of the corridor. He spoke without opening them. "No, Zack's right. There's a breach open."

"Are you sure?" Art asked, his voice sounding hopeful.

"No. Breaches and gates are pretty advanced stuff. Maybe what I'm picking up is leftover energy. But do we want to take that chance?"

"What can we do if there is one?" Jackie squeaked.

"I should be able to close it. I helped the Grand Jerk close the fairy one. I think I can manage one solo. It's a lot simpler than opening one." Bast picked up his sword and stood.

"Okay, let's go check it out," Tabitha took charge. "Kimmy, we'll come back and get you after we…"

"The hell you're leaving me here," Kimmy pushed herself up against the wall with a wince. "I'm coming."

The look on her face ended any attempt to convince her to stay and Charlie approached and slipped her shoulders under Kimmy's arm to help her move.

"Max is staying. I don't want to risk her getting any more hurt," she said, helping her injured friend move as carefully as possible.

The group made slow progress through the corridors, following Bast's lead. After two turns, they followed him through an open door and into a room.

Tabitha started to speak, but they were all stunned to silence by what they saw. The otherwise darkened room was lit by a dim grey light from a breach in the wall opposite the door. Unlike the oval-shaped gates conjured by Tower mages, the breach's edges branched out inconsistently from its centre. A dark green liquid cloud, the same colour as the tendril creature, flowed out into the room. It bled into the air like drops of ink into wet paper, splitting out from itself one way, then another.

"Bast, you reckon you can close that?" Art asked, wide eyes transfixed on the breach.

"Uh, yeah. I'll try, I guess," Bast sounded neither convincing nor convinced as he reached out towards the breach. A moment later, he grunted, shaking his head. "No. Whatever that stuff is, it's holding it open."

"We need to get rid of it, then," Kimmy leant against the doorframe. "Time for some cleansing flames, I think."

"Were you in the Spanish Inquisition in a previous life, do you think?" Art asked.

"This is serious, Art," Tabitha said. "So, Kimmy, you burn it out and then Bast, you slam it shut. Everybody else, be ready for anything."

The others moved out of Kimmy's way to give her a clean shot. As with the previous creature, she summoned a white-hot bar of fire, which surged forward to strike the inky cloud.

The reaction was immediate. The substance burnt up in the intense heat, but no more than the point of impact. The rest of it responded with a violent frenzy, grasping out deeper into the room with heightened speed. It surged forward, reaching out for the teens and they countered, swinging their weapons at the approaching fluid mass. Art's and Bast's swords sliced through the substance like it was shaving cream and the severed portions fell lifeless to the floor.

Tabitha's flail, Zack's staff and Jackie's spear were almost as effective in cutting through the cloud, and even Charlie's bow was making a dent. Inert lumps of dark green ooze collected on the floor, which Kimmy burnt away while the others attacked.

They stopped most, but not all the grasping encroachment of the mass. Zack swung his staff through one portion, but another reached out from his flank. It touched him and the tip of it seemed to solidify into a sharp point. It tore at him, leaving a jagged cut as it raked across his skin. He slashed his staff through the cloud, separating the solid end from the mass, and saw other sharpened claws of cloud were tearing at his friends.

However, he also noticed something worse than that.

"It's coming through almost as fast as we can kill it!" Art shouted, panting, before Zack could voice the same thought.

"I can't close it unless we can push it back." Bast slashed away at the cloud.

"Push it," Tabitha said.

"What?" asked Zack.

"I have an idea. Cover me." She took a step back and dropped her flail.

Tabitha's fingers moved in rapid yet precise gestures while her lips mouthed unspoken words. She raised a finger and pointed it towards the gate. A jet of wind shot forward at the cloud and, where it struck, the fluid mass was blown back into the grey of the breach and Bast cheered.

But the jet was too narrow, and hitting too small an area of the mass. Every time Tabitha moved the jet across the cloud, pushing it through the breach, more leaked out of the grey light, flowing into the gaps she'd created. Art and Bast charged forward, hacking away at the edges of the mass, trying to make Tabitha's target smaller, but it was not enough. She screamed in frustration and the wind faltered and dropped.

"There's too much," she said, panting.

In the absence of the torrent of air, the mass surged forward, where it crashed against a wall of steely light. Jackie groaned as it pushed against her shield.

"Please hurry, I can't hold this for long," she said between clenched teeth.

"Hurry and do what?" Kimmy asked from the door. "Nothing has worked!"

Clutching at an open gash on his side, Zack had a moment of clarity.

"That's not exactly true," he said, his mind racing. "One thing did work, but we need more of it. Tabs, in theory, could you do that wind spell, but bigger?"

"Zack, I'm sorry, but I can't. I can't put enough into it. I'd pass out before I even got close to something that size. I'm not strong enough."

He smiled at her. "Alone, you're not. But you're not alone."

Bast had heard enough to catch on. "I thought I was pretty clear about never again!"

"If this doesn't work, it'll be easier to keep that promise, I guess. Get ready to close this thing up. Jackie, put everything you've got left into your shields. Everybody else, hold still."

"Wait, wait, wait. What are you trying to do?" Kimmy asked.

"I'm going to link us up, so Tabitha has more power for her spell," Zack said.

"Mate, are you sure?" Art asked. "You've never been able to do that. If you screw it up, we're going to be too tired to put up a fight."

"We're already too tired to put up a fight. Look." Zack pointed at Jackie. She was holding herself up against the wall, sweat beading down her too pale face as she held her shield in place. "We don't have a choice."

Art took one more look at his sister. "Do it."

Zack closed his eyes and inhaled. He found his quiet centre, away from the violence and the pain. He established, clear in his mind, the Source, the Target and the Intent, remembering the hours of time he'd spent with Sara attempting to create this shared channel. From here he didn't need his eyes to find his friends, he could feel their Life.

He reached out to them, forming the magical pipeline between them, and distracting thoughts rushed into his mind.

He'd never been able to do this before. He was putting his friends in danger. He was about to prove he had no place in the Tower. They were all going to die. He wouldn't live to heal his grandmother.

Even minor questions vied for his attention.

How could his friends trust him with this? Did he really belong in their league, with the powerful magic they had been casting? He was about to touch Charlie's life. Would it distract him again?

This time he didn't try and push them away or block them out. He accepted them. The same way he had with his grandmother in the hospital, he brought these thoughts inside his focus and answered each of them with the one simple answer.

This is why I have to do this right.

He'd never done it before, so do it right.

His friends were in danger, so do it right.

Prove you have a place in the Tower, save your friends, live to learn enough to heal your grandmother, earn your friends' trust, be in their league, impress Charlie.

So. Do. It. Right.

He reached out to Art's Life, the most familiar and opened a channel between them.

Next, he branched the channel out to Charlie. His stomach lurched as her Life flowed towards him like a caress, but it didn't distract him.

Again he branched out, this time towards Kimmy. There was a surge of frantic energy from her pain and fear as the connection was made, but her Life surged through towards him, immediate and ready.

He steadied himself, acknowledging the fear, the pain, the excitement, the hope and overall, the need. More important than anything else in this world, or, important for everything in this world, was the need for the channel, the need for a flow of Life's energy into one point.

"Get ready, Tab!"

Through gritted teeth, he reached out, connecting one last channel to Tabitha. The cocktail of Life churning within the network he held poured through him and into her as she completed her incantation. A wide torrent of air poured out of the young Air Initiate and towards the invader.

Tabitha cried out in euphoria. "This feels amazing!"

Jackie dropped her shield spell, letting the wind through and slumped exhausted to the floor. Tabitha's widened torrent struck the mass in force, jetting it back through the grey light of the breach.

She was doing it. Zack held the channel, allowing the Life to flow through him and into Tabitha.

"I need a little bit more," she said.

And she was right. The torrent was almost the size of the breach, but fell an inch or two short. He turned his senses to the channel, and there was nothing left to give. Art, Charlie and Kimmy were barely on their feet after all he'd taken from them.

There was only one thing he could do. He looked deep into his own Life, the Life that lived in his blood, in his bones, in his muscle and skin, and he threw it into the channel. It hurt. His nerves screamed in protest, threatening to drag his focus from the spell, but he held it, answering them with the same need.

Tabitha's spell widened and the entire dark green mass was forced from the Tower, back into the breach.

Zack's eyesight blurred, but he caught a glimpse of Bast charging towards it, tracing in the air with his fingertips as he ran. The breach shrank. A wave of dizziness came over Zack and he tasted something wet and metallic in the back of his mouth.

The grey light disappeared, and darkness claimed him.

CHAPTER 31
SANCTUARY

Zack awoke. The softness of a mattress and pillow lay beneath him and he wondered how he had made it home. When he opened his eyes, he found the shadowed stone of the Tower ceiling above him. Not home, then. He propped himself up to have a better look around.

"Hey there, pal. Easy does it," Tom strode over to him, "your body will still feel a wee misused. No sudden movements."

"Oh, okay," Zack scanned the room. He was in one of the mass recovery rooms in the Life quarters. Almost every bed was full, with many of the inhabitants unconscious.

Tom sat down on the end of Zack's bed. The Scottish Life mage looked haggard, his eyes dry and red, but he still managed a smile. "You get left out of the fun, so you go create some of your own, aye?"

Zack's memories pushed through his haze. He forced himself into a sitting position. "There was a breach."

"Relax, pal, we know. Your young man closed the breach. All your friends are well."

Zack let himself sink back into his bed, his vision beginning to swim.

"From the looks of it, you emptied your own tank. Takes a bit to recover from that. But you've had the worst of it mended. You're nae in danger."

"Thanks. Did you heal me?"

Tom chuckled. "You think she'd let anybody else patch you up but her?"

"Sara?"

"Aye. She'd be here now, but there are injuries far worse than those in this room. She and the other powerful Lifers are doing what they can. I've given all I can today, without ending up in a bed next to you."

"Africa went badly?"

Tom sighed. "Well enough, I suppose. But it was massive. Biggest incursion of breaches I've ever heard of. Waves of beasties. It got ugly, but the job got done. All of them closed. Then it was a simple matter of triaging the wounded and getting them back here. Of course, once we get back here, we find out you've thrown your own wee party."

"Where are my friends?"

"Debriefing with Junie."

Zack eased himself up, turning to stand up from the bed. "I'd better join them."

Tom stood with him. "You sure?"

"Yeah. I'll need to get home soon enough, anyway."

"They're down in the entry room." Tom walked him to the door before turning back to check on his other patients.

Zack padded his way down the Tower stairs until he found Junie and his friends sitting in an alcove near the exit.

"And you believe this is the same creature you encountered that night in Sydney all those months ago?" Junie asked the group as he approached.

"I do," Tabitha rubbed her leg where she had once been grabbed.

"That conclusion seems particularly sound, given the area of the Tower you encountered it in," Junie surmised.

Tabitha nodded. "Of course."

Her friends looked at her, confused.

Tabitha explained, "We were in the Air quarters. In fact, the room the breach was in is where I've had most of my lessons with Junie."

Junie nodded. "Yes. I think it's fair to say you were its target. Or at least, what it was tracking."

Zack sat down beside Art, his mind racing. "Then the breaches in Africa, they were all a ploy to empty out the Tower, while it hunted Tabitha."

Tabitha shuddered and Zack cursed his lack of tact.

"It's possible," Junie said, "but, unlikely. It would have been a far more sophisticated strategy than anything we've seen in a long time, but it is possible. More likely, it was merely opportunistic. The breaches weakened the barrier and perhaps this creature sensed its way through."

"What about the rest of that stuff that was coming through the breach?" Jackie asked.

"We're still looking at it," Junie said. "We're not sure, but it definitely seems to come from a remote realm. Remote and dangerous. You all did very well to survive it, let alone to defeat it."

They shared a round of tired smiles.

"As your liaison with the Tower, I am responsible for your assessment. It is for me to determine when your time as Initiates is to conclude. Over your time at the Tower, you have shown yourselves to be gifted, growing with your magic. But that is not sufficient. You must show a dedication of duty to the Tower and, through it, to our world. Your successful work with the changeling, including rescuing the true child, your defence of the gate against the lizards, and now, your defence of the Tower itself against truly eldritch forces. You have more than convinced me."

The teens looked at each other, eyes wide with excitement despite their fatigue.

Junie continued, "Your time as Initiates has come to an end. I welcome you all as full members of the Tower. Your mentors will be permitted to teach you more powerful magic. Your responsibilities and opportunities within the Tower will increase, and…" She gestured at them with a handful of envelopes she retrieved from her pocket. "… the rewards increase too."

She handed one to each of the newest full members of the Tower.

Zack watched as Art, with clear visible strain, forced himself to not look inside while Junie watched. Their liaison tapped Zack on the shoulder and beckoned him to follow her a few steps from the others.

She spoke to him in a hushed voice. "I am happy to see you up and about so soon, Zack."

"Thank you, Junie. To be honest, I'm desperate for more sleep, but I need to head home before my parents get worried."

She smiled at him. "It is sometimes the minor protections of the Silence that pose the most challenge. A time will come soon, once you progress with the Tower, and once you finish school, that we can facilitate a little more independence from your parents. That should make it a little easier to maintain the Silence."

Zack nodded, not quite sure what she meant.

"But that is for later. What I wished to say to you is that, while I can decide that you are full members, it remains your mentor's prerogative to determine the pace of your training. Sara has made her concerns to me abundantly clear in that regard."

Zack's face fell.

"I am sorry to say this, Zack. But without significant progress in your training, you will become a liability to your friends. They will need a Life mage as capable as they are."

Zack nodded again. "I think I've turned a corner. But I need to convince Sara of that."

Junie smiled. "Your friends painted quite the picture of what you were able to achieve, so I hope that is true. I suggest you make time before you go home tonight to speak with Sara."

"Thank you, Junie. I'll go do that now."

Zack pushed his fatigue aside and headed back up the stairs. Not sure of where Sara might be, he decided to start with her room and knocked on the door.

A weary voice responded, "Come in."

He entered and found Sara sprawled in her comfortable wooden armchair. "Ah, Zachary. I was hoping you'd come find me before you left."

He inched into the room. "Are you okay? I don't think I've ever seen you looking this tired." He stopped, realising how rude that must have sounded. "I'm sorry, I didn't mean…"

She waved him off. "No, that's a fair assessment. I haven't been this tired in years. There were many injuries. We lost some good people today. Not many, but too many all the same."

Zack was shocked. "I hadn't heard."

"I'm sure somebody is still compiling a report. All teams have checked in and anybody who can be helped, has been helped. There's nothing else we can do."

Zack nodded and finding he needed to sit, he did so.

"And you, my boy, are you feeling well?"

"A little tired too, I guess."

"No wonder, given how little Life there was left in your body when we found you. I need you to tell me what happened."

"I thought the others would have explained while I was unconscious," Zack said.

"Yes, they likely told Junie what happened with that creature and the breach. And I'll hear more about that in good time. Right now, I wish to know what you did. How did you burn your candle so low?"

Zack swallowed hard. He was worried this might be the final nail in the coffin for his training. But, he decided, there was no helping it.

"There was some kind of thing, like a dark cloud, flowing in through a breach. Bast thought he might be able to close the breach if we got rid of the cloud. We tried a few things, but the one thing that seemed to work was Tabitha's Air magic, blowing it back through. She couldn't put enough energy into it to push the whole cloud out at once. So… so I gave her some of mine and the others. I ended up giving her a lot of mine by the end of it. And she did it. She forced the thing out of the Tower and Bast closed the breach behind it. And that's about when I passed out."

Sara watched him through her dark, tired eyes and he sat, trying hard not to fidget as he waited for her to speak.

"So, at a time of crisis, you managed to hold together a working channel?"

"Yes," he said. "I've found my focus."

She nodded. "That is good to hear. But you could have died, giving so much of your Life up for that spell."

"I needed to. She couldn't have forced it out without it. I know it was dangerous…"

"It was dangerous," Sara said, "but dangerous does not mean it was wrong. Recklessness is wrong. But danger is what we accept in service to the Tower. I believe you when you say it was necessary, Zack. And that you accepted the risk to do what had to be done."

Zack's voice threatened to crack as he spoke. "Does that mean you will continue to teach me?"

"Yes. However, you must accept we will proceed at the pace I set. It seems you may have turned a corner with your concentration and that is good. But we will go slowly until I am assured of it."

He wanted to jump out of his chair and cheer, but he managed to maintain a modicum of dignity. "Yes, Sara. I'll do as you say."

"Good. Now go home. We both need to rest."

He walked back to the door.

"Oh, and Zack. Very well done, today."

He looked back over his shoulder and found her smiling at him. "Thank you, Sara."

Zack bounded down the stairs, his elation helping him to forget his fatigue. He found his friends loitering by the exit and Art shot him a hopeful, questioning glance. Zack's wide smile was all the answer his best friend required and he clapped him on the back.

"Thanks for waiting, guys."

"No problem, mate," Bast said, "can we get moving now? I want to be in my bed, but I'm still going to need to sit through dinner with the family."

"Sorry, yeah, I'm good to go," Zack said.

As they walked to the bus, Art whispered to him. "Did you look in your envelope yet?"

Zack patted his pocket, feeling the bulge of the envelope next to his keys. "No, almost forgot all about it." There was a glint in Art's eye. "Why? How much is in there?"

"Five grand," Art whispered. Then excitement took over and he shouted, "Five thousand dollars!"

Tabitha hushed him with a hiss. "Art, do you want to get us mugged?"

"Mugged?" Art laughed. "Who could mug us? Who could mug you? You'd blow them into the harbour from here. Anyway. I think I'm going to get a car."

The teens arrived at the bus stop and Kimmy turned to roll her eyes at Art.

"What kind of crappy car are you going to get for five grand?"

"Well, the salesman might find me to be a very persuasive customer." He wiggled his eyebrows for dramatic effect. "Plus, after Jackie chips in hers, it'll be ten grand."

Jackie was leaning against a telephone pole, her eyes closed. She snorted, "I'm not buying you a car."

"Buying 'us' a car, my dear sister."

The bus arrived and as they found their seats, the siblings began what Zack knew would be a long and hard fought negotiation. Zack dawdled towards his seat, taking a moment to look at his friends.

He knew these six were his closest friends now. All others were indeed 'others'. He still had a sense of guilt at that thought, but the guilt was muted by the knowledge that these six had placed their lives in his hands that evening and he had done the same with each of them. There was a bond connecting them that had nothing to do with the flow of Life between them, but with the knowledge they could rely on each other when it counted.

He turned back around to look out at the evening sky, the last rays of an autumn sunset touching the tips of the Sydney skyscrapers. The envelope in his pocket was filled with exciting potential, but it was nothing compared to Junie's other promise of 'more powerful magic.'

Lost in his thoughts, Zack didn't notice the man in the tattered trench coat watching the youths as the bus departed north to take them home.

ACKNOWLEDGEMENTS

Over the years, I've often daydreamed about publishing a novel. I've imagined what it would be about and whether it would be successful. I've wondered what the cover art would be like and whether it might end up on the shelves of local bookstores and libraries. And I've pondered the minutiae: chapter titles or no? Foreword? Prologue? And what I would say in the Acknowledgements.

The plan was always to be clever. Witty with a dash of irreverence. And almost certainly missing the brief.

But now that I have the privilege of writing one, I need to cast that plan aside because there are far too many people to whom I must offer my deep and genuine gratitude. It is a cliche to say that a creative work is not the product of the artist alone, and that nothing is crafted in a vacuum devoid of the impact and influence of others. And it is a cliche because it is true. More than just the support, encouragement and advice, without which I would not have reached the finish line, many can claim responsibility for threads of ideas that have been woven into characters, scenes and themes that have made the story what it is.

I first offer my thanks to Bradley and the rest of the team at the Shawline Publishing Group, who have helped me turn an unformatted lump of story into a book I could hold in my hands.

Thanks to the greatest of writing communities. All the Wabbers contribute to such a safe and encouraging space. Special thanks to the query support group, Kim, Haley, Sean, Janna, Rachel, Shelby and Trey, for the advice and shared ups and downs of the publishing adventure. And thanks too, to the beta read group, Lydia, Devis, Perla, Deeanna, Chrissie, Sharon, Allison, Karlynn and Kirsten who have been willing to read the fragments of early drafts as they've dribbled out, and whose feedback has made the world of difference.

And extra thanks to my generous critique readers. Danni, Sam, Becky, Connie and Lauren, I owe you all so much for working your way through early versions of questionable structure, poor descriptions and infestations of filter words.

Special callout to Heath, who stopped just short of physical bullying in his efforts to convince me to write something like this book. And to Taryn, who has been patient and generous in answering questions from outside my lived experience.

Thanks to Jamie, Luke, Adam, Siân, Brad, Damien, Matt, Maddie and Deanna, who played in the campaign that inspired this story, and who may recognise some key scenes such as burnt fingers and odorous gas clouds.

And thanks to my childhood friends. Brad, Michael, Luke, Mark and Nick put up with the kid who always wanted to live in a fantasy world, and were willing to visit him there as long as there were slurpees and doritos at the table next to the dice and the character sheets.

Not all my teachers left me with a heightened appreciation for creative writing, and I'll admit it was not always their fault, but some did. None more so than Mr Hancock who encouraged my embryonic talent for writing and, despite ensuring me that most people managed to 'grow out of fantasy and into proper literature,' did an amazing job of reinforcing my passion for it. Thanks too to Mark Tredennick, who taught me in one of his writing courses to 'write what you know,' before concluding that maybe most of what I knew was made up nonsense in my head and that I should write that.

And the deepest of thanks are reserved for my family.

Thank you to my grandparents, who were all storytellers. Especially Veronica, who could hold court with the simplest of recollections.

Thank you to my parents, Maureen and Andy, who passed on to me their love of reading and have always supported my own love of writing. And to Emma, who loves books more than I ever could, and prods me towards the ones she thinks I'll like. I hope you like this one.

And most of all, to Lisa, Ava and Nicholas, who fill my days and nights with so much chaos, nonsense and joy that my mind can't help but create fantastical stories just in an effort to make sense of the three of you. I love you.

Shawline Publishing Group Pty Ltd
www.shawlinepublishing.com.au

More great Shawline titles can be found here:

New titles also available through Books@Home Pty Ltd.
Subscribe today - www.booksathome.com.au